A Killing Among the Dead

Diana Wilder

BOOKS BY DIANA WILDER

Pharaoh's Son

The City of Refuge

The Safeguard

ISBN:1463673736
ISBN-13:978-1463673734

DEDICATION

To my sister, Judy - Thank you for your support, your excellent criticism, your insights into personalities, and your genuine interest in this story of a man fighting evil alone.

And your tolerance of someone tearing her hair out in despair.

I could not have written this or any other book without you.

CONTENTS

ACKNOWLEDGMENTS

Someone once told me that the best way to learn about a specific period of history is to read top quality fiction set in that time. I have read and enjoyed several excellent novels set in ancient Egypt - Eloise Jarvis McGraw's wonderful novel Pharaoh comes to mind. I hope that I may be adding to that group.

CHAPTER I

Wenatef opened his eyes to darkness and a silence so intense that it was stronger than any noise, stronger even than the pounding agony in his head. He drew a slow breath, the sobbing intake of air loud in the stillness. Another breath, whimpering with pain and the sudden fear that he was blind. But that fear faded. The darkness was outside him, not within his eyes.

He lifted his head from the floor and then lay back again. He was bound hand and foot; the cords were well tied and thick. A rope was cinched about his upper arms and chest, as well. They were taking no further chances with him.

…Where was he?

It was colder than a house would be, the silence so intense he could almost feel it. He was in the hills, probably in a tomb. The air was heavy with myrrh; he was in a burial chamber.

He struggled to a sitting position, shivering. The effort made him dizzy, and he doubled against his knees, gasping with the sudden, tearing pain that lanced through his left side, bringing the taste of blood to his lips. A wave of weakness washed over him and ebbed.

Merciful Amun! he thought. *I am dying!*

His time was short. He refused to die like this, tied like a steer for slaughter. At least he could meet his end with his back to a wall.

He pushed his way across the floor, knocking jars aside, the clatter of their fall muffled by the tomb's silence. His shoulder struck something square and sharp. The base of a

1

statue, probably a king's. Well, then. He would die at the feet of a king.

It took every ounce of his fading strength to haul himself up on the plinth. He groped behind him with his bound hands and located the statue's feet. They were side by side - a seated statue. He could feel the block that served as the statue's seat. He collapsed against the carved legs and stared into the darkness that seemed to be closing about him, remembering the days and weeks that had brought him to this place, wondering who had betrayed him and brought him to this death...

CHAPTER II

The scream had risen among the cliffs, vibrating between the rocks before it broke. Wenatef, sitting in the shadowed area near King Seti I's tomb, sprang to his feet, his head cocked, a hand on his dagger. That one scream had ended abruptly, and the sound was distorted by the circling hills and valleys so that he could not tell where the cry had come from. He had sent one of his men east...

Wenatef adjusted his short, military kilt, listening, his hand clenched about the lion-headed gold pendant that hung at his neck, then stepped into the sun with a regretful grimace. It had to be Merihor. He was skittish - people said it was in the blood. He came from a line of Seers of Amun that had fallen on bad times and left the great temple at Karnak. The 'sight' still cropped up in his family from time to time. Everyone laughed at Merihor and no one took him seriously among the Guard of the King's Tomb, except Wenatef, its commander. Merihor irritated him, but his sensitivity, though it could sometimes be morbid, made him a sharp-eyed sentinel.

He heard feet scrabbling on gravel and turned to see Merihor running toward him, past the zone of the tomb of Ramesses I, the stones scattering as he rounded the turn, almost losing his footing. His breath was coming in groans through a slack mouth. He saw Wenatef and stopped for one trembling moment before he dropped to his knees, spent.

Wenatef's vexed smile faded to a frown as Merihor raised a ravaged, tear-streaked face. His flights of fancy had never

3

before brought him to this state.

Wenatef hurried to his side. "What's wrong, Merihor? " he exclaimed.

Merihor's eyes were wide in a pinched, white face. He drew a deep breath that shuddered in his throat. "Thutmose the Great," he gasped.

Wenatef frowned. The great conqueror, Thutmose III, was buried in that valley. "What did you find?" he demanded.

Merihor looked up into Wenatef's eyes. "Have you ever dreamed of your own death?" he asked. "I have, and it's always the same. It's as if -"

Wenatef gripped his shoulder and shook it. "What about Thutmose the Great?"

Merihor continued as though Wenatef had not spoken. "Slashing at me... Again and again until I can't fight any more, seeing death coming at me and I'm powerless to stop it.... And in that tomb - in that tomb..." He shuddered and spoke through convulsive sobs, "In that tomb, by the light of that smoking wick, before Thutmose himself, I saw the death and felt it again."

Wenatef's grip tightened. "What *about* that tomb?" he demanded. "Were you *in* it?"

Merihor drew a shaking breath just as voices sounded along the path.

Wenatef lifted his head. They were coming from the west, as though they were following Merihor... Something felt wrong. There was no time to leave, and he needed to think.

His mouth tightened as he took the flask of beer, part of his lunch, from the sack at his waist, opened it, and poured some over Merihor's chest and then made him drink some of it before re-stoppering it. Then he released Merihor and scrambled to his feet, his voice rasping.

"Look at you!" he snapped. "Drunken, stinking, blubbering like a lovesick youth-!" He cocked an eye at the path and continued as Merihor gaped up at him.

"I'm not drunk!" Merihor began. His eyes dilated as he looked back toward the hills behind Wenatef.

Wenatef turned. Two men were approaching, a strongly-built man accompanied by a younger man with a smooth, cynical face. The younger man's blue clay badge, in the form of a reclining jackal over nine bound prisoners, marked him as a member of the Necropolis Police.

Wenatef ignored them. "Not drunk!" he repeated. "You reek like a brewery!" He looked up and pretended to see the newcomers for the first time. Merihor shrank back against the ground, groping for the amulet about his neck as the younger man started toward him.

"What happened?" he demanded.

Wenatef had an impression of a predator swooping down upon its prey. He could feel Merihor trembling. "Drunk," he answered.

"I have seen my death," Merihor said, covering his face with his hands. He suddenly reared upward, his hand jabbing toward the younger man. "Your sacrilege will unleash a terrible vengeance!" he cried. "The gods themselves will pursue you and you'll die in the places you have defiled!"

The young man's brows drove together.

The other man looked at Wenatef, who shrugged and said, "He is drunk."

"He speaks oddly for a drunkard," the younger man said in a soft, dangerous voice that made Merihor shudder. "He needs to explain himself." His gaze narrowed on Merihor. "Come along."

Wenatef was still smiling. "I told you he's drunk," he said, "You aren't likely to get coherent answers until he's had a chance to sleep the beer off. Don't waste your time with him."

"I'm not drunk!" Merihor objected.

The older man folded his arms and looked Wenatef up and down in a pensive manner. His gaze lingered on the gold pendant about Wenatef's neck before lifting to his face again.

The younger man was scowling. "He is coming with me for questioning."

Wenatef's smile faded. "The man is under my command," he said. "I see you're with the Necropolis Police: get on with your patrol."

The young man's smooth face was suddenly somehow ugly. "You take a lot upon yourself," he said. "Who are you?"

Wenatef's smile was back and very cold. "I am Wenatef, son of Hapuseneb of Thebes," he said. "I am Commander of One Thousand in the Army of Lower Egypt, and Second-in-Command of His Majesty's personal bodyguard. The Lord of the Two Lands has chosen to post me to the necropolis as Commander of the Guard of the tomb he is constructing here."

The younger man's expression was odd, as though he had just received word from a land that he had once lived in and remembered with regret. "Hapuseneb." he said. His voice almost seemed to quiver.

"That's right," Wenatef said. His eyes narrowed and he continued more softly, "But as for you: your insignia identifies you as an officer of the Necropolis Police. Your manners mark you as a very junior one." He let the rebuke sink in and then added, "It is late and you must finish your patrol. Good day to you both."

The silence stretched out. The younger man seemed shaken; his eyes were fixed on Wenatef, as wide and staring as Merihor's.

The older man spoke for the first time after another moment of silence. "I greet Commander Wenatef of the Guard of His Majesty's Tomb," he said. He looked at the younger man and added softly, "We misunderstood the problem, didn't we, Unas?. We'll trouble you no more, Commander - and we thank you for your patience."

But the other made no reply, and the man finally led him

away. As they went on, the young man dragged to a halt and looked over his shoulder at Wenatef one last time.

Wenatef waited until they were out of sight and then pulled Merihor to his feet, tucked the flask of beer under his belt, and started back toward Deir el Medineh, the town of the necropolis workers.

"I'm not drunk," Merihor said again.

"I know it," Wenatef said. "The less people who hear what you just said the better, until we thrash out this whole matter. You won't be killed if -"

"But I have seen my death," Merihor said, his voice like that of a sleep-walker. "And I have seen you before Anubis at the Weighing of the Heart - and you weren't ready."

"The gods forbid that," Wenatef said with the humorous indulgence of a man who has faced his own death and won.

CHAPTER III

Wenatef took the workmen's footpath back to the Valley of the Kings. He walked slowly past the cliffs and sun-bleached rocks with his eyes fixed on a skein of butterflies that hovered before him, imprisoned in a capricious twist of wind. He usually rode this way in a chariot, as befitted an officer and veteran of the Nubian wars, but his was tethered at Pharaoh's tomb. He was returning to speak with Duwah, the architect who was directing its construction.

The sentries sighted him; the blare of a trumpet split the afternoon stillness, followed by the shrill neighing of Wenatef's horses, hitched to his chariot and tethered in a patch of shade by the tomb.

Wenatef raised his hand to wave at the guard and ascended the slope to the tomb entrance. Several of the workmen who had heard the trumpet came to stand at the opening to watch him come. Duwah was standing among them, smiling a greeting and looking more like a fat, comfortable grocer than a famous architect.

He came forward and took Wenatef's arm. "It figures you'd be in time for lunch," he said with a grin. "You can share mine! His Majesty has remembered his servants, and the supplies have finally arrived - just in time for the festival. No more hunger for a time, at least."

Wenatef nodded and sat with his back against a relatively smooth section of wall. He looked around at the sketched-in preliminary decorations while he stretched his kilt across his knees to make a sort of platform.

Duwah handed him a triangular loaf of bread and opened

a small jug of wine while Wenatef ate. "The bread's from that Syrian baker in Thebes," he said through a lump of half-chewed dough. "You know the man: the one with the pretty daughter."

Wenatef laughed and sipped wine. "Every Syrian in Thebes has a pretty daughter," he said. "'A moon of beauty with arms as warm and soft as a spring breeze, lips as sweet as persimmons, hair that lies over her back like a shadow- and for a small consideration, she is yours for the night!'"

Duwah spat on the ground and wiped his mouth. "You know the girl," he said. . "I don't think you ever pass a pretty girl without stopping to flirt with her."

"Not often," Wenatef admitted, handing the jug back to Duwah. "I've never had to pay for one's company, either."

They ate in silence for a moment before he said, swallowing a mouthful of bread and pulling off a chunk from the roast goose, "I have to go to the Necropolis Police after we finish."

Duwah looked at him over his crust of bread. They had been classmates together under the meanest scribe-priest ever seen in Thebes. "Tell me," he said.

Wenatef shook his head. "Merihor was coming past Thutmose III's tomb and he saw something that frightened him. I wonder..."

Duwah's eyebrows rose. "What does that have to do with us?" he asked.

Wenatef took up a persimmon and bit into it. "Nothing at first glance," he admitted. "Merihor jumps at the slightest thing - which is why I like to post him as lookout - but he spoke as though he had actually been inside the tomb. He wouldn't say what he'd seen, but he was upset, and he spoke of curses. What do you think? Tomb robbers?"

The architect shrugged. "Maybe. There always human jackals hovering around a burial, hoping to find something worthwhile. I remember hearing of a scandal during Ramesses VI's reign. Some of the village leaders were implicated. It ended badly."

His gaze was distant for a moment. It shortened and shifted back to Wenatef. "But nothing came of it," he concluded. "And if this does involve tomb robberies, that's no business of yours. Leave it alone!"

Wenatef shrugged. "I've no wish to step on the toes of the Necropolis Police. But Merihor was almost mad with horror this time, and I can't help wondering - "

"Enough of Merihor," Duwah said.

Wenatef frowned at Duwah. There was something dire beneath the architect's almost flippant attitude, as though he was trying to hide something that concerned and frightened many people.

He pushed to his feet and brushed the crumbs from his kilt. "That was a good lunch," he said. "I'll provide the next, since I go to my farms in two days and I'll be able to bring back some fresh fruits."

He went to the entryway to gaze out at the western horizon while Duwah spoke to the workers who were carrying baskets of rubble from the interior of the tomb and dumping them down the hillside. He decided to make a report to the Necropolis Police. Its commander, Si-Iset, had become a friend, and his calm good sense would be equal to any problems.

He smiled when Duwah returned and pulled his leather driving gloves on.

"Where are you going?" Duwah asked.

Wenatef slapped the hippo whip against his palm. "I have some business to see to about the valley and by the river. I'll be back before sundown.

CHAPTER IV

The westering sun blazed before Wenatef like a shield of molten brass as he approached the temple-fortress of Medinet Habu, the headquarters of the Necropolis Police. He reined his horses in for a moment and shaded his eyes with his hand to see the square-shouldered pylons looming before him out of the glare. He was approaching the main gate; mud-colored hovels and high white townhouses clustered about the temple walls, the town of priests, police and temple workers that had grown up around the complex. Gold-tipped pennon staffs flashed in the sun, and the crisply carved and brightly colored scenes of the battles of Ramesses III seemed almost alive in the glare of sunset that glinted from the inlaid eyes of the colossal statues standing like great sentries to either side of the gateway. A river of people passed beneath them, leading cattle fattened for the temple sacrifices, carrying geese and ducks and offerings of vegetables and fruits.

The gate guards stood easily in the shade cast by the pylon. The badges hanging about their necks, marked them as part of the police garrison headquartered there.

Wenatef reined his horses to a halt and waited as one of the guard came to him.

The man, a Squad Leader, recognized him; he bowed and clasped his forearm in salute. "Life and health!" he cried with a welcoming smile that was mirrored by the men behind him.

"And to you and all your men, good Khentiy," Wenatef

replied with an inclination of his head. "Where's Captain Si Iset? I need to speak with him right away."

"Didn't you hear?" said Khentiy, straightening. "He was called away to Tanis five days ago. Personal business. His message said that he was sending word to you from Karnak."

Wenatef frowned and stepped down from the chariot as Khentiy went to his horses' heads. This was not good news. "When is he returning?" he asked.

"We don't know," Khentiy said. He eyed Wenatef's frown and added with a little less animation than before, "The Platoon Commander Roy answers for him now."

Roy? Wenatef had never heard of him. "Who is he?" he asked.

Khentiy raised his hands in a gesture eloquent of puzzlement and resignation. "He comes from Karnak, Commander," he said. "His posting was announced at the same time Si Iset wrote to tell us he was leaving. In fact, Si-Iset was summoned to Karnak, and the next thing we knew, he had sent us the note and Roy was in command."

Wenatef was frowning. "That's odd," he said. "He didn't come back here to tell everyone in person, and introduce his successor?"

"We were told there was no time," Khentiy said. He added after a moment, "Roy was in the personal guard of Lord Nuteruhotep."

Wenatef eyed the man's face, which was as carefully expressionless as his own. Roy's credentials were not reassuring; Wenatef's family had had some dealings with Lord Nuteruhotep, Amun's steward in the great temple at Karnak.

But there was no help for it. He handed his reins to one of the guard. "If he's in command, he's in command," he said. "Where is he? It's urgent."

One of the other guards spoke up. "I saw him before the North Wall, Commander," he said. "He's there with Captain Seneb."

"Then I'll go to him there," Wenatef said. "Lead me to him, Tjah."

* * *

"This disturbance was in the area of Thutmose III's tomb, you say?" asked Roy. He was standing with the carved expanse of the north wall behind him. When Wenatef arrived he had been speaking with the young man Wenatef had seen near Thutmose III's tomb - his name was Unas.

The conversation had seemed private and very urgent, but he had dismissed Unas and listened to Wenatef's account with surprising calmness.

Wenatef's gaze strayed from Roy and Seneb to the depiction of Ramesses III's naval battles against the Sea Peoples, carved on the wall of the temple behind them. The carvings seemed, for a moment, more real than the people standing before them. He could almost hear the creak of oars in the oarlocks, the plash of water...

Wenatef blinked and focused his attention again on the two officers.

"This is a serious matter," said Roy, whose wide collar of multicolored stones and heavy, perfumed wig marked him as a man of wealth. "I shall look into it personally, with your permission."

As a high ranking officer and an acknowledged hero of Egypt's armies, Wenatef had encountered a certain amount of deference from other men, but Roy's obsequiousness, when he was serving as the acting Commander of the Theban Necropolis Police, rang false, and it puzzled him.

"You're in command here," he said with a shrug. "Do as you see fit. There's no need for me to step in."

He stole another glance at the naval battle. He could almost hear the cries of the drowning men. He tore his attention away with an effort. As he looked back to Roy and Seneb, he caught a glimpse of the young man, Unas, half-hidden in a doorway, staring at him with narrow eyes.

He met the young man's gaze and watched him shrink

back before he turned back to Seneb and Roy. "I'm sure you'll detail some men to investigate things," he said. "I didn't have time, myself, to look around. I was lucky to have someone with me, or I would never have been able to pinpoint the location."

This last sentence seemed to surprise Seneb. "Then you didn't see anything yourself?" he asked.

Wenatef smiled at the man. "Be reasonable," he said. "It's an area of high cliffs and rocks. Things didn't feel right."

There, Wenatef reflected. *That should do just fine.* He did not know what Merihor had seen or done, but he intended to find out. In the meantime, what he told the Necropolis Police would suffice. "I leave the matter in your hands," he said.

Roy and Seneb traded glances again. "I accept it," Roy said after a moment. "But how do you know it was near Thutmose III's tomb? Did Merihor tell you?"

"Every foot of ground in that valley is sacred to one king or another," Wenatef said, removing his driving gloves and slapping them against his palm. "The workers at Deir el Medineh know where one tomb ends and another begins, no matter how well hidden they might have been by their architects and carvers! If it wasn't his tomb, then it was another's. Merihor's family has worked in the necropolis for generations! He may be too fond of the beer and the wine, but he knows his land, and when he told me what I saw was in the area of Thutmose III's tomb, I believed him. What do you say?"

Roy looked across at Seneb and Wenatef had a fleeting impression of something unpleasant in that glance, but it was gone the next moment. "I'll look into it personally," he said. "Will Merihor bear out what you have said?"

Merihor again. Wenatef had not been the first to mention him. He shook his head. "Merihor saw nothing that I saw," he said. "He only told me the area I had come from. That's all. You'll find him of very little assistance, I'm afraid."

Roy frowned. "But Unas said -"

"Unas wasn't there. When Unas came along with his friend-"

Seneb interrupted. "A friend?" he repeated. "Did he -"

Roy silenced him with a sharp glance and said, "Pray continue, Commander."

Wenatef eyed the two of them, aware of undercurrents to the entire conversation. He was beginning to regret reporting to the Necropolis Police, but the thing had been done and must be followed.

He said, "When Unas came along, Merihor was drunk. I'm not sure how he managed to smuggle it in under my nose, but I plan to find out. But you said you'll go to the area and make sure it's secure and everything is in order."

Roy nodded. "We will," he said. "At once."

"Then I'm content," Wenatef said. He nodded to both officers and then, looking at his gloves as he pulled them on, added, "And have you received any word from Si Iset?"

"Si Iset?" Roy repeated.

Seneb spoke over him. "His family is well, Commander," he replied.

Interesting, thought Wenatef as he nodded. "That's good to know. And now, if you will forgive me…"

The two officers left. Wenatef paused before the naval battle, smoothing his gloves. He frowned at the ships, at the wounded falling into the water, the Egyptian sailors swinging their oars, pushing the Sea People beneath the ocean. Two ships were about to collide - Wenatef heard the crash, saw the splintering timbers -

My imagination is getting as vivid as Merihor's, he thought. He looked once more at the sea battle, but this time he saw only a carved stone wall and heard the cries of kites and hawks far above the desert.

He reclaimed his chariot and clucked to his horses. The mortuary temple of Amenhotep III lay to the west. He could just glimpse the shoulders of the two colossal seated statues of the king. The waters of the inundation came almost to their bases; there was no sign of the river turning.

CHAPTER V

Wenatef returned to Deir el Medineh some time later, tired and disturbed. He had been a fool to tell his concerns to the Necropolis Police once he had learned that Si-Iset was away, but he'd had no choice. He couldn't escape the feeling that it had been unwise and possibly dangerous.

He let his eyes rest on the distant ribbon of green and blue that was the Nile, flowing north toward his home in distant Per-Ramesse, and then frowned at the cemeteries stretching to his left. The tomb-covered hills rose about him, bare and brown, channeling his gaze northward toward the bend of the Nile. After ten generations, the tombs of the Deir el Medineh workmen took up more acreage than the town itself. The town was situated in a valley, the tombs, terraced and topped with small pyramids, climbed the hillside. He stepped down from the light leather and wicker chariot and went to his horses' heads.

Wenatef's hand, half-raised in a salute to the dead, lowered as he remembered the loaf of bread, intended for his lunch, lying uneaten in the sack at his belt. He had some water as well and a date sweet. He did not need them, since he would soon be eating his supper. He tethered his horses to an outcropping of stone and walked among the tombs until he found one that was usually neglected. The family had died out and there were no more offerings now, except what kindly disposed visitors left there.

Wenatef knelt at the niche of the tomb and set the food upon the offering slab. "'A thousand of bread and of beer,"

17

he said quietly, a thousand of geese and oxen, of linen and alabaster, of sweets and of all good and pure things, for the venerated Hapy and all his family'."

A wind rose, stirring his hair. It was drawing toward evening; time to go home. He sat back on his heels and looked up at the clusters of small tombs, monuments of generations of artisans, so peaceful and content in their littleness.

One of the horses snorted as Wenatef heard a scrape and clatter behind him. He turned and looked up as a shadow fell across his shoulder.

"A tomb-offering, Son of Hapuseneb?" Unas asked. The words were lightly spoken, but the tone of voice was ironic.

Wenatef stiffened at the implied mockery. "'As you see," he said. "Blessings come to those who remember the dead."

"Indeed?" said Unas. "Blessings from whom? The carrion lying in the tombs?"

Wenatef gathered himself to rise.

Unas' hand descended to Wenatef's shoulder and held him down. "No," he said with a smile, "I didn't mean to interrupt your...devotions. I wanted to ask if your man - what was his name?" He paused, but when Wenatef did not supply it, he said it himself, " - Merihor. I wanted to ask if he was all right."

Wenatef stared at the man's hand until Unas withdrew it. "He's fine now," he said.

"That's good," Unas said. "His distress was -"

"He was drunk," Wenatef said. "The good thing about being drunk is that you ultimately sober up. He'll be fine." He got to his feet. "Is there something that you need from me, Guardsman?"

Unas shrugged. "My patrol took me nearby," he said. "I saw you and thought to speak with you about this afternoon. That's all. What did Merihor see?"

"He saw a flask of beer and drank it," Wenatef said. "I

made a full report to your superiors at Medinet Habu; talk to them. As for your patrol: this is my territory. I have assigned some of my men to come here regularly; you need not come here again."

Unas' expression was ugly for a moment. It eased. "I understand," he said. He looked down at the offering slab, lifted an eyebrow at the food set there, then bent down, took the date sweet, and bit into it. "Good night," he said as he turned away and went down the hillside.

Wenatef watched Unas depart. Something in the way he walked caught Wenatef's attention. He moved like a priest. Unas... A priest...

The thought touched a buried chord of memory. Wenatef's father, Hapuseneb, had been high in the priesthood of Amun. Wenatef remembered that his father had once spoken of a young man named Unas. Something mentioned in passing and only half-heeded. He strained his mind and then gave up the effort as the spark of memory faded.

His horses watched him come. Brightfoot was whinnying and tossing his dark head while Swift stood stolidly, her ears flicking back and forth as Wenatef stepped into the chariot and gathered the reins.

** ** **

They were abreast of the walls of the town five minutes later. Wenatef could see the townsfolk moving busily in the coolness of late afternoon. People saw him and shouted greetings.

"Commander Wenatef! Pharaoh sent the food! Will you eat with us at the festival?" This from Duammerset, the bright-eyed daughter of the village Foreman, Khons.

Wenatef laughed at her and shook his head. "You'd better ask your mother and father first!" he called back.

Bakenmut, Khons' young son, who would one day be Foreman himself, shouted, "But they told us to ask you! Will you come?"

19

"If they're asking, then of course," Wenatef called back. He watched them run off and then continued along the wall, answering greetings from the other townsfolk, and pausing to bow to Thutiy, the village's embalmer, who was a particular friend.

"I see there's been good news, Master Thutiy," Wenatef said, reining in his team for a moment.

Thutiy smiled. "Good news that has been long in coming," he said. "But delay makes things sweeter, sometimes. Will I see you at the festival tomorrow?"

"Of course!" Wenatef said. "We can take a cup of wine together!" Brightfoot shook his head just then.

"That fine fellow if yours is getting impatient," Thutiy said with a chuckle."

"You're right," Wenatef said. "Best get him to his dinner!" He shook the reins and headed along the wall reaching the village's well. The womenfolk chattered and laughed together as they lowered their jars into the water and brought them out filled and dripping, while the young children ran about underfoot.

Commander Wenatef!

The cry went out like a signal trumpet; Wenatef was surrounded by a host of laughing, chattering children, all of them reaching for his hands, pleading for a ride in his chariot, making extravagant promises of future assistance in the care of his horses, and comparing him with 'Nakht', a prominent figure in village folklore, miraculously strong and cunning, who took from those who had too much and gave to those who had nothing. The comparisons, not favorable to Nakht, were voiced to the accompaniment of brightly speculative glances.

Wenatef scooped up a wriggling armful of children. ""You're a plague of flattering locusts!" he laughed. "It's a wonder my horses haven't trampled you! Neferabu! Webkhet! Get away from their tails! Now! Make yourselves useful, you! Fetch me a drink of water and some for the horses, and then we'll see about rides."

He watched the children run off to obey him and then turned to exchange greetings with Dhutmose, the Scribe of the Tomb and his son, Butehamun. They had just returned from Karnak; they wore long, formal robes with wide collars of fragrant flowers about their shoulders.

Wenatef grinned and gave Dhutmose the military salute, right fist to left shoulder, and the Scribe returned the gesture. Dhutmose had been something of a hero since the time a year before when the supplies from His Majesty had been late in coming, something increasingly common in recent years. He had assembled six strapping young men of the town and traveled south as far as Kom Ombo to collect food from local temples and farmers. Some of the payers had been irate; Dhutmose sported a scar on his cheek that was just beginning to fade.

He fingered the scar with a smile. "You seem to be suffering a plague of ankle-biters," he observed, watching the children returning with bowls of water.

"I like them," Wenatef answered as he knelt before one toddler. "They think I'm greater than your mysterious 'Nakht', and you know how susceptible a soldier is to flattery."

He turned to the little girl. "Thank you, Aahmose," he said. He smiled at Dhutmose, lifted the bowl of water to his lips and drained it. He lowered it and faced another ten very full bowls. He looked up at Dhutmose.

"I'll have some of that water, if I may," the scribe said, accepting a bowl from another child. This was agreeable to the children; Dhutmose was almost as great a favorite as Wenatef.

Dhutmose handed the bowl back after drinking his fill. "And now," he said, "suppose some of you water the horses as well? They're thirsty, too."

Wenatef watched with a rueful smile as the children obeyed. "It's pretty obvious who the seasoned father is," he said.

Dhutmose ignored Butehamun's unfilial snort and took a packet from the sash that belted his trim waist. He handed it to Wenatef. "Captain Taharka asked me to deliver this to you," he said.

Wenatef nodded and looked at the packet of papyrus. His name and direction were written in an elegant, flowing hand on the front. He opened the letter and read:

> *Taharka greets Commander Wenatef in life, prosperity and health, the Guard Captain Taharka of Karnak to the Commander of One Thousand, Wenatef of Thebes:*
>
> *May you be in the favor of Amun-Re, King of the gods, of Ptah of Memphis, of Montu, bringer of war, and of all the gods and goddesses in Karnak, may they give you favor, love and cleverness, wherever you are. Further, how are you? Are you doing well? Behold, I am doing well! My wish is especially to see you!*
>
> *Taharka says further to the Commander Wenatef, behold: word has come to me of the presence of Khaemwase in the area under the control of the Commander of One Thousand. Beware, for he's dangerous!*
>
> *Seldom do the wise need more than one warning.*
>
> *I have given commands to those that serve beneath me that you be given what help you may wish from the Guard of the God.*
>
> *This letter is written by the hand of Thutnefer, Scribe of the Archives. May*

*you be in life, health and prosperity all
your days!*

Wenatef set the note aside with a frown.   "Who is
Khaemwase?" He asked.

Dhutmose and Butehamun exchanged surprised looks.
"Khaemwase is a criminal, known in the north," Dhutmose
said.   "If his territory has expanded to include Thebes, then
Thebes is in trouble."

Wenatef handed him Taharka's note.

Dhutmose read the message. He drew a shaking breath
as he handed it back, but said with a fair imitation of
calmness, "I have delivered the letter. I'm sorry that it's bad
news... I would like to speak with you later this evening,
when you have returned from taking the horses to their
pastures."

Wenatef nodded and put the question of criminals out of
his mind, bending his attention instead to the logistics of
giving twelve children rides in a chariot pulled by two horses
without exhausting either the horses or himself.   This
occupied him for well over an hour, and by the time he had
taken the chariot to the stable near his house and then walked
the horses to the meadows by the river, it was almost time
for the evening meal, and the setting sun was casting long
shadows from the shoulders of the Libyan mountains.

CHAPTER VI

Wenatef thought he heard a faint murmur of sound through the closed door of his house. The sound stopped as he entered to find Duwah and Dhutmose inside.

Duwah rubbed his shaven head and looked away. "Tired?" he asked.

"Very," Wenatef replied, puzzled at their unease. He sat down on a low stool and pushed his hair back with one hand, and then scowled at the dust on his fingers. "Well. You said you wished to speak with me. Business or pleasure?"

Dhutmose looked down at his long-fingered, strong hands and then over at Wenatef. "I've heard something disturbing," he said. "Merihor."

Wenatef raised his eyebrows and then shrugged. "Merihor has fits whenever they suit him. Sometimes I think he fakes them to avoid his duties for a day. I only put up with him because he's an excellent lookout and not a bad archer, either. As for today, he - "

"Merihor is my cousin, Commander," Dhutmose said, leaning forward with a faint smile. "You don't have to protect him from me. I have some questions I hope you can answer."

Wenatef frowned. "Can it wait until I've washed? My hands are dirty and my face too." There. That would give him time to think.

Dhutmose inclined his head. "Take your time," he said. "I know you went to the Necropolis Police about this."

Wenatef inclined his head as graciously as Dhutmose and went into the other room. His misgivings about the Police had returned. He finished his washing and went back to find that Duwah had taken a jar of wine from his store, found three cups, and was pouring. He handed a cup to Wenatef..

"All right," Wenatef said, darting a vexed glance at the wine. "Merihor was upset by something he thought he saw. He never told me what it was. He spoke of sacrilege and the vengeance of the gods shortly afterward." He frowned for a moment. "But how could he know if the tomb had been violated?" he said almost to himself.

Dhutmose interrupted him. "Were you the only one to hear?" he asked.

Wenatef paused. "No," he said after a moment. "He told two people who came upon us right afterward."

"What!" cried Duwah. "You never told me this!"

"You never asked," Wenatef retorted.

Dhutmose sat back frowning at his cup. "Who were they?"

"A junior officer with the Necropolis Police. His name was Unas. I'd never seen him before today. Another man was with him," Wenatef paused to sip at his wine, "I never learned his name."

"From the Necropolis Police?" asked Dhutmose.

"No," Wenatef replied. "In fact, he spoke with a northern accent."

Dhutmose's frown deepened a little but he said nothing.

After a moment Wenatef added. "Things had happened quickly; I needed time to think. I made it look as though Merihor was drunk. After they left I took him back to his home. For all I know he's there now. I returned to the Tomb and spoke to Duwah-"

"-Who suggested that you let the matter drop," Duwah said.

"I couldn't do that," Wenatef said flatly. "Merihor saw something. It is my duty to report such matters to the Necropolis Police."

"To whom of the Necropolis Police?" asked Dhutmose.

"Si-Iset?"

"Si-Iset's is gone," Wenatef said. "They said he was called away to Tanis," He nodded at Dhutmose's expression. "It surprised me, too. Squad Leader Khentiy told me that Si-Iset sent a message to me from Karnak. I haven't received it."

"Who *did* you speak with?" asked Dhutmose.

"I spoke with Roy, Si-Iset's replacement. Seneb was the other officer."

"Was Unas there?" asked Dhutmose, his voice expressionless.

"He was when I arrived," Wenatef answered. "He left shortly after, though I did see him later this afternoon."

"Where?" Dhutmose rapped out.

Wenatef did not like the feeling of being interrogated like a felon, but he replied evenly. "I met him among the village tombs," he said. "I think he had been waiting for me. He questioned me about Merihor."

"What!" said Duwah.

Wenatef's smile was grim. "I sent him away with a flea in his ear," he said. "I played down Merihor's part in the discovery at Medinet Habu, if that's what's worrying you, but I had to report this. I claimed that I was the one who had found something. That's as far as it goes, for my part, for now. Now tell me, why is everyone so concerned with Unas? Who is he?"

"He has high connections," said Duwah. "He's the nephew of the Steward at Karnak."

Nuteruhotep again. The prick of memory returned. "So?" said Wenatef.

"Be careful of him," said Dhutmose. "Young men can be dangerous and dishonest. Sometimes more so than older men. He's one to watch."

"I ordered him to keep away from the village," Wenatef said. "I plan to enforce that command. Do you think I have done ill, then?"

Dhutmose shook his head. "No," he said. "You're an honest man and a brave one, Wenatef. You did as you thought best. For the rest, we'll see what happens. But please, have no further dealings with those three men in particular. How you came to speak with them, of all the good men in the Guard..."

Wenatef drew himself up. "I don't understand," he said.

"There's nothing to understand at this moment and there may be nothing to fear," Dhutmose said. "But let us handle matters."

"Merihor saw *something*," Wenatef repeated.

"Forget it," Duwah said.

Wenatef looked from one to the other shaking his head. He had a right to know what was happening and a duty to investigate anything that might endanger his men. He did not like being held at arms length and treated as an outsider. He drew breath to speak his thoughts, but a loud rapping at his door interrupted him.

"Come in!" he called, and watched without surprise as the two Foremen of the town entered.

Khons bowed to Wenatef, lifted an ironic eyebrow at Dhutmose and Duwah, and said, "We heard."

"Heard what?" Dhutmose demanded. His voice was sharp.

The co-foreman, Harmose, blinked at him. "Heard about Merihor," he said, sitting against the wall.

"There's something you haven't heard," Dhutmose said with unaccustomed grimness.

"Oh?"

"Khaemwase is here."

Khons drew a slow breath. Harmose raised his head.

Khons looked down, saw the wine, and helped himself. "The question," he said, "Is what to do."

"The question," Wenatef grated, "Is what are you all talking about?"

Khons looked at Harmose and then at Duwah and

27

Dhutmose. "He doesn't know?" he asked. "Didn't you tell him?"

"It's too much of a risk," Dhutmose said.

Wenatef touched his palm to his forehead in an exaggeratedly servile bow. "Your humble servant can't thank you enough for such an expression of your esteem," he said.

"Don't be a fool," Duwah snapped. "It's nothing! We-"

"Nothing?" Wenatef interrupted with narrowed eyes. "One of Merihor's flights of fancy is treated as a grave matter by all of you, but when I say that I have gone to the Necropolis Police to make a report and suggest an investigation into matters that are their proper concern, I'm suddenly beset with people asking pointed questions as though I am suspected of some crime. I am commanded to avoid the police without being given any reason, When it becomes clear that there may be a dangerous situation here that directly affects my men, I'm told insultingly enough that it's" nothing" or that it's too great a risk to tell me. Has it occurred to you that if you hadn't descended on me this evening, I might have continued as usual?"

Dhutmose looked away, and Khons shook his head. Harmose, an old man with the muscular shoulders of a stonemason, said gently, "You have to understand. This concerns the honor of the community, and the less people who know of it the better. Do you think we're discussing a matter that's familiar to everyone at Deir el Medineh?"

"As a matter of fact, I do," Wenatef said, folding his arms across his chest.

Harmose drew himself up, glaring. After a moment's silence he said "No and no. You are a soldier and under orders. Here are our orders to you: leave this alone! There are a great many who could be hurt. With the favor of the gods and a little discretion, no one will be. That's all. Do you think that you are Nakht, that you can wade into such deep waters without risk?"

Wenatef nodded. His mouth was very straight, and his

eyes were narrowed. "You've made yourselves clear," he said. "Now let me do the same: I am not under your orders: I hold a royal commission. You requested an experienced officer to command your guards when Captain Seti was killed, and His Majesty ordered me to perform those duties. He made me responsible for the safety of those who work on the tomb, whether they're actually at the Tomb or not. I rank as a Commander of One Thousand, and I'm a man of property and some influence in Thebes. I have heard no complaints about the performance of my duties from Pharaoh and I have never avoided danger."

"Wenatef," Dhutmose began.

Wenatef silenced him with a gesture. "Let me finish," he said. "Now, in a matter that certainly concerns the performance of those duties, I'm told that I may not take a hand. I need to know from where this danger may be coming, not just for your sakes but because I took Merihor's discovery upon myself when I spoke to the Necropolis Police. Well? Duwah? Dhutmose?"

Duwah's eyes were full of trouble. "We can't say," he said, "We can't say. The honor of our village – " he almost stammered, "It may be nothing - "

"Your reaction this evening has shown how ridiculous that statement is!" Wenatef snapped.

Harmose looked down. Khons frowned and Dhutmose met Wenatef's gaze squarely.

"Well?" Wenatef said.

Harmose sighed. "We are sorry," he said.

Wenatef moved his shoulders and then sat back. "I see," he said.

"We in the village love you," Dhutmose began.

Wenatef's smile was ironic. "I can see how much you all love me," he said. "Very well. If you feel I can't perform my duties properly, I bow to your judgment. I have completed His Majesty's assignment and I'm not obliged remain here any longer. You must have another Commander chosen by the time the inundation has reached its peak. That gives you two months at the most. Until that time I'll continue as usual unless you would prefer to name one of my subordinates fill the position?"

"We don't want you to leave us because of this, Wenatef," Khons began as the others murmured among themselves.

Wenatef looked straight at him. "You should have thought of that sooner," he said. "By the turn of the Nile I will be back in the delta with His Majesty." He inclined his head to the village captains. "That is all," he said. "It's late and I'm hungry and tired. There was much to occupy me this day. Tomorrow is a festival day."

Wenatef and turned to Khons. "Given the state of things, I will understand if you wish to withdraw your invitation," he said. "If not, then I'll be dining with you. Good night. I'm sure you can find the door by yourselves."

Dhutmose and Khons lingered by the door after the others left.

"I'm sorry it must come to this," Dhutmose said. "We can't change our position. Whether you stay or go, you're welcome in this town, and my own regard for you hasn't changed."

The words disarmed Wenatef. He bowed, and Khons said, "You'll still dine with my family tomorrow at the festival, won't you?"

"Of course," Wenatef said.

Nevertheless, after the others had departed, while he munched on a cold supper, Wenatef decided to speak with Merihor the next day.

CHAPTER VII

The feast of Pharaoh Amenhotep I was Deir el Medineh's chief festival. It lasted for four days, and people came to the town from north and south to enjoy the food and festivities and hawk their wares and produce.

The town was filled with music, feasting and dancing. Games were announced,, prizes won, people lingered along the streets to chatter and catch up on gossip. Some of Wenatef's men held a contest of archery for the Vizier, Prince Sekhemkhet, who was honoring the town with a visit. Several of the officers of the Necropolis Police and some of the Guard of the Temple of Amun came to compete.

Wenatef watched the shooting from the Vizier's shaded booth. His arms were folded across his chest and he was smiling as one of his best archers, a lad of about twenty with the royal name of Ramses, eliminated most of the competition before being defeated by a veteran of the Necropolis Police.

Wenatef finally strung his bow and entered the contest at Sekhemket's insistence. He won easily and then earned the respect and liking of all the onlookers by ordering that the prize, three large jars of the finest wine available in Thebes, be opened and shared among the spectators.

Through all the contests and all the festivities, though he smiled and spoke to the townsfolk and the Necropolis Police officers and laughed with the children, Wenatef kept alert for a chance to speak with Merihor, to question him now that he was a little calmer, and find out what it was that he had seen, and who might have seen him.

Unas was at the village as well, with Roy and several of the other Necropolis Police officers. Wenatef did not like the way he was watching Merihor, but Merihor was always with one or the other of the foremen, or else with Dhutmose. Wenatef saw him talking furtively with Thutiy, once. Thutiy's expression had seemed somehow bleak, but it had eased when Merihor, seeing Wenatef watching him, had flinched and then touched Thutiy's arm. Everything was blandly innocent, and that left Wenatef seething behind his equally bland smile.

Merihor kept darting frightened looks at Unas, almost clung to Dhutmose, and cast several despairing glances at Wenatef before finally joining the serious drinkers and passing from the company of men capable of knowing their own names, much less remembering what they had seen the day before.

** ** **

"Everything going well?" Duwah asked later that afternoon as Wenatef was sitting on the western wall of the town, frowning at the distant outline of the mountains beyond the bend of the Nile. The sound of festivities had faded; there would be feasting that night, but now everyone was taking a siesta in the heat of the day. Wenatef had thought himself the only one astir.

"Never better," he replied, not looking down even when Duwah grabbed his ankle and pretended to pull. It was an old sort of horseplay that dated from their times as children together in Thebes.

Duwah released the ankle and leaned against the wall, his head level with Wenatef's knee. He placed a couple of honey cakes on the wall. "Help yourself," he said.

Wenatef did, saying nothing.

Duwah also ate in silence until, wiping his hand across his mouth, he looked up at Wenatef. "I'm sorry about all this," he said.

32

Wenatef's mouth tugged into an unwilling smile. "Oh forget it, Duwah," he said. "It can't be helped."

"Can't it?" Duwah asked, looking up with sudden intentness. "I'm not sure you realize what's at stake."

Wenatef looked down at Duwah and said, "Never mind. Matters are settled to my satisfaction. I've been fretting for travel, and now's my chance. You all have matters under control, or you think you do. This town is your home now, but it never was mine. I came in part for your sake, you know. His Majesty commanded me to set up a guard force after Captain Seti died, and I have, so my duty here has been discharged. You have plenty of time to replace me, and from the archery I've seen this afternoon, I won't be missed."

He eyed Duwah's suddenly forlorn expression and said, "Ramses, for example. It's fitting that he should step into his father's place."

Duwah was frowning ahead of him. "Very fitting," he agreed, but with a distracted air. "Royal blood will tell."

"What do you mean?"

"Oh, an old story," Duwah said, summoning a smile. "Pharaoh Seti was grieved by the death of his oldest son, Nakhtamun, who should have succeeded him. He came to the Valley of the Kings to mourn. He met a maiden of the town, and she...eased his grief, shall I say? She married a village man soon after, though she and the king had had a summer together, and within six months of that marriage she had borne a fine, strong son who bore a striking resemblance to the son Seti had lost. Ramses is a direct descendant of that baby. He's a good lad, and to hell with him. Wenatef, why can't you stay with us?"

"I'd only fret if I did," Wenatef answered. "Ever since the fighting in Nubia, the mountains seem to be calling to me. It's as though this world - this valley, the tombs, all of Egypt - are doorways into something larger and deeper. Don't be sad, Duwah. You've always known I was a wanderer at heart."

"Since you were a boy," Duwah agreed. "I remember when we were reading the story of Sinuhe, you were so eager to learn of strange lands. Old Akhtihotep thought you were mad, and maybe you were. You haven't changed, and I guess I don't want you to. But I can't help thinking that when you leave this time, I'll never see you again."

"Maybe not," Wenatef said, his eyes lifted toward the sunset. "Probably not." He shook his head and looked down at his friend. "Maybe what I've been pining for is my tomb."

Duwah's eyes, darkened with kohl and powdered malachite, widened in shock as his hand groped for the amulet he wore around his neck. "Your tomb -" he breathed.

The words and the slumberous peace of the afternoon were torn in shreds by a series of screams.

Wenatef was off the wall in one smooth motion and pelting along the twisting expanse of the town wall with his drawn dagger in his hand as the screams continued in increasing volume and frequency. He rounded the corner of the southern end of the village and came to a halt.

Merihor was doubled against the ground, his hands clenched against his heart as though to ward off the stroke of a knife. His face was against the dust, which tangled in the threads of spittle that flecked his cheeks and hung from the corners of his mouth.

Unas was standing over him, his expression an odd mixture of fury and chagrin. He tried to fumble his knife back into its sheath. Wenatef heard him hiss "Stop it, you sniveling fool!"

It was enough. Wenatef took three quick steps forward, slammed his hand down on Unas' shoulder, gripped, and sent him sprawling in the sand and stone-chips with a shove from an arm made strong by years of drawing powerful bows.

"You!" he snapped. "Out!"

Unas started to pick himself up from the dust. His eyes were blazing as they flickered from Wenatef to the crowd of townsfolk that had converged on the scene.

34

Wenatef turned to look at Merihor. He had half-raised himself and was staring at and through Wenatef with an expression of bewildered fright, as though he were seeing something other and more terrifying than the man who stood before him.

"This is an outrage!" Unas sputtered. His kilt had come unfastened. He tried to rearrange it with shaking hands.

Wenatef bent to take Unas' knife from the ground. "Sheath your knife!" he snapped. "This town's off limits to you from now on, and I'll make it hard for you if I find you within half a league of here! Now get out!"

Merihor was still staring up at him with wide eyes. "Death facing vengeance," he said. "I see death facing vengeance -"

"Stop it!" Wenatef snapped. He lifted his eyes to the jostling crowd that had gathered. "Take him home," he directed. "Dhutmose, I want a word with you. Immediately."

The Scribe of the Tomb nodded, as though he had been expecting something like this all along, and followed Wenatef a short distance along the wall while the crowd dispersed.

Wenatef waited until they were alone before speaking. "Merihor is one of my men, and this incident concerns me as much as you," he said. "If he continues as terrified as he is now, he'll be useless to me and a danger to the rest of my men. Let me talk to him. You don't want me to know about this mysterious thing that Merihor saw and that has you so worked up? I won't ask about it: you have my word. But I must speak with the man. Now."

Dhutmose drummed his long fingers against the wall and then nodded. "Very well," he said. "I'll speak to Merihor, and then you can, too."

"When will that be?" Wenatef asked.

CHAPTER VIII

It was that evening. The festival ended that evening and the village was quiet. Wenatef was sitting in the courtyard of one of the tombs high along the hillside overlooking the town. The sky was still tinged with pink, but the stars glimmered overhead, cool and serene after the noise and upset of the day.

He sat quietly, his shoulders propped against a wall, his face tilted toward the stars. Could he stretch out his hands and touch them if he stood on the highest mountain on earth? Or were they really, as the old legends said, flecks on the dark hide of a heavenly cow? The swath of flickering stars that wandered across the night sky was said to be the ripples of the passing of a great crocodile.

He smiled at the stars and looked down toward the village.

A slow-moving figure was making its way among the tombs to where he sat. Merihor of course, but why was he walking like that?

Wenatef leaned forward with a frown. The last time he had seen any man walking with such a wealth of despair was when he had been in Nubia, holding a beleaguered fortress garrisoned with wounded and dying men who had despaired of rescue.

Wenatef said his name softly, and Merihor looked up, saw him, and paused to stare up at him for a long moment. He finally lowered his head and threaded his way among the pathways to Wenatef.

"You came, finally," Wenatef said.

"Yes, sir," Merihor said.

Wenatef could see that the man was trembling. "Are you afraid of me?" he asked.

Merihor did not answer. Wenatef looked at the man's white, drawn face and swore silently. "Look at me, Merihor!" he said. "I haven't put you in any danger! I took the danger upon myself! I want to help you now -"

Merihor lowered his head. "I know," he said. "You're always kind to me..."

"Then pay attention," Wenatef said. "I don't know what you saw and I don't want to know. But you're one of my men and I'm responsible for your safety. Do you think you're in any danger?"

Merihor's eyes filled with tears; they glistened in the starlight before he drew his knees up and lowered his head to his folded arms. "I have seen my death," he said. "I saw it and it was terrible."

"So have I seen my death, time after time," Wenatef said. "From the arrows of the Nubians, or in the dark, struck down by my own men. I have seen myself beset by Libyans or drowned in the Nile or wasted by fever until there was little of me left to embalm. But each time, through the favor of the gods, I was able to avoid the death. Surely you, too -"

"This time I saw my death," Merihor repeated. The words had the sound something said over and over until they are burned into the brain without sense or reason.

"Stop it!" Wenatef exclaimed. "Why are you acting like this?"

"I - I don't know..." Merihor began to cry. "It's everything," he said between anguished, gulping sobs. "People coming to me. What did you see?, they say. What did you see? Tell me! Tell no one! Forget it! Remember everything! Trust no one! Mingle with the crowds so they know nothing's wrong! And then I ask if they'll want to kill me - the - the evil ones - and I'm told to forget it. They'll take care of it. I'll be safe. But how can that be when I saw my death?"

Wenatef frowned. "Do you truly think you're in any danger?" he asked again.

Merihor wiped his eyes, bit his trembling lower lip, and nodded.

"Then listen to me. I own land north of here along the river. Take your family and go there in secret. You can be escorted by Dhutmose if you don't trust me. Stay there until this has been resolved. You'll be safe and so will your family. You'll be out of harm's way. Those you fear won't know where to look for you. I'll write a letter for you, or Dhutmose can. What do you say?"

The look of befuddled panic was gone from Merihor's eyes for a moment. "Why are you doing this for me?" he asked.

"Because I'm your commander and you're one of my men," Wenatef answered with equal quietness. "I am responsible for the safety of all my men, and I'll guard it with my life if I must."

Merihor sat quietly, chewing his underlip, frowning at the horizon. Finally he shook his head. "No," he said. "I have seen how it'll be. You say you can protect me, but it's no use. I'll be slain alone and undefended and far from my home. There's no escape!"

"Merihor - "

"No! I won't! There is no escape for me or for you! We have been marked and we can't fight the fate that is laid upon us by the gods!"

Wenatef rose to his feet and looked down at Merihor, wearied by his illogic, angry with his hysteria. "No one will force you into anything," he said. "But I'll tell you something else: you won't be coming to the tomb tomorrow. I won't have you with my men until you master this tendency to hysteria. It makes me sick and it isn't helping anyone else. Go home and get some rest. I won't speak to you any more, so you can relax. And tell your father's cousin that I won't be interfering for good or for ill any more. Now get out of my sight! Don't come back to the Tomb until you're capable of behaving like a man and not a hysterical child!"

Merihor left, then, still sobbing. Wenatef watched him go and then sank back down against the wall. His eyes were stinging, and he shook his head. Fear and hysteria were Merihor's constant companions. He had been a fool to let him join the troop of guards. He could understand why his ancestors had been driven out of Karnak all those years ago.

A wind had arisen; Wenatef turned his face into it, caught in the grip of weariness beyond anything he had ever felt. So much had changed and so much for the worse. Gone were the days of the old virtues, gone were the great kings and with them the might of Egypt. Gone were the honest, fearless men and women who had made the land great. Egypt was peopled by crawling, fearful insects of men, temple-trained and content to rest within the bounty of the temples and spend their lives bent over papyrus, copying ancient texts so that there would be more scrolls to gather dust in the archives of the great temples

Egypt was scorned by those very peoples who had brought tribute in bygone days when King Seti or Thutmose III wore the double crown. Who paid tribute to her now? Who, indeed, when Nubia had arisen in rebellion, when Byblos and Tjekker laughed openly at the crumbling might of Egypt, when the Sherden and the Sheklesh wrested land from Egyptian citizens and claimed it for their own, and no one tried to stop them?

The wind was stronger now, pushing Wenatef's hair back from his forehead. He leaned his head back against the wall of the tomb and raised his eyes to the stars glowing above him, clean and bright and remote. They had seen the great days; they would see other great times - but not for Egypt. Egypt was dying, falling to ruin along the great silver river.

CHAPTER IX

Distractions in the form of Libyan raiders occupied Wenatef for the next several days. They had been sighted by children playing above the Deir el Medineh necropolis, a thin line of black heading toward them, half obscured by clouds of dust. The children ran to their mothers and the word spread until Wenatef, patrolling with two of his men, received the report.

He reined his horses in and looked down at the winded runner before him. "Did anyone notice how many there were?" he asked. "A small group or a large one? How armed?"

"They were seen at a distance, Commander," the runner answered. "By children. But it sounds as though the group wasn't large."

Wenatef looked over his shoulder at the Peak. "Hm," he said. "I wonder if I can see them from the heights." He turned back to the runner. "Are you done in, Mekiwetef?" he asked, "Or can you carry another message?"

The runner lowered his head, but one of the men with Wenatef spoke up. "I can deliver the message, Commander."

"Good, Sennedjem," Wenatef said. "Go to the Necropolis Police and tell them that a group of Tjehenu has been sighted, and that I'll be going forward to engage them. I'll need back-up troops. Archers if possible, good spearmen if not. Tell them it's urgent - and thank you."

He slapped the man's shoulder and watched him go, then handed the reins to the runner. "Hold them while I try to see the raiders," he said.

Wenatef walked back to his chariot twenty minutes later, shaking his head. "Fifty of them, maybe more, and moving slowly. I wonder if they mean to attack us. Possibly they're looking for food. I heard of a plague among their herd beasts..."

He got into his chariot, gathered the reins, and looked back toward Deir el Medineh. "I hope they've hidden themselves," he said, and then looked down at the runner. "Get in," he said. "We've a ways to go."

** ** **

There were about a hundred Libyans in the force approaching the necropolis, and they were routed by Wenatef's twenty men and a contingent from the Necropolis Police led by the Platoon Commander Roy. Unas was there as well, but Wenatef, needing every archer he could find, raised no objection. The composite bows of the Egyptians were strong and accurate, and the Libyans were never able to close in and fight hand to hand.

The survivors of the skirmish fled into the desert, pursued by Wenatef and his men, who lent wings to their retreat with volley after volley of arrows, and then returned past the wounded and dying Libyans. Wenatef directed that they retrieve their spent arrows, and then turned his attention to the captured raiders.

There were several of them, fair-haired and pale-eyed, with skin burnt a darker brown than Wenatef's. His men had given the mercy-stroke to the more seriously injured ones, and now stood awaiting his decision on the fate of the rest. He paused before them, eyed them and called to his men.

"Those," he said, pointing. "Him - him - he with the brown cloak - and the young one. Bind their wrists and take them to Dhutmose. Their wounds aren't serious. We can bring them to Karnak as soon as possible, a gift to His Holiness."

One of the wounded men raised himself and clutched at

Diana Wilder

Wenatef's knees to gabble a plea for mercy in a heavily accented traders' patois, sobbing out a story of a starving family and a pregnant wife.

Wenatef eyed the man. He had a gaping tear in his flank where an arrow had caught him glancingly as it sped past him. Another arrow was embedded in his thigh. Wenatef knew that the man would have had no hesitation about cutting his throat if their situations were reversed. The carved and painted reliefs of Thutmose III at Karnak had showed him grasping such a man by the topknot and rearing back with mace raised to dash his brains out. He bent over to look down into the pale eyes of the wounded man who was now weeping quietly against the ground.

"It would be best to kill him," said a voice beside Wenatef. The speaker was Unas, who was staring down at the prisoner with an odd glint in his eye. "What's the point of letting him live?"

The prisoner understood him. He flattened himself, gabbling a near- hysterical string of pleas for mercy.

Wenatef forestalled him. "Don't be afraid," he said, reflecting that he was not Thutmose III. "No one will kill you. Why did you come against us?"

The man drew a gulping breath. "Gold..." he said. "We heard of gold buried in the hills..."

Wenatef stepped quickly back. "There's none here," he said. "They lied who said there is." He looked over his shoulder at the other Libyans who now stood in a ragged line, their arms pinioned behind them, waiting to be led back to the village. He nodded. "Be at peace, Tjehenu," he said again, using the Egyptian name for the Libyans. "Your life is spared."

"He should be killed," Unas said again.

Wenatef frowned at him. "You seem anxious to do the honors," he said. "In this case it is unnecessary. His life is spared."

"That is folly!" Unas said.

42

Wenatef drew himself up. "Are you arguing with me, soldier?" he demanded.

Unas raised his head and met Wenatef's gaze for a moment. His eyes dropped. "No, Commander," he said. "I am not."

"That is good," Wenatef said with slow deliberation. "It would have been unwise." He turned away and found himself facing the archer, Ramses. The young man was gazing intently at the wounded man, an odd twist marring the elegant line of his mouth. It was probably his first glimpse of the folk whom his great-great grandsire, the great Seti I, had fought two hundred years before.

Wenatef decided that the moment was too poignant to interrupt. Besides, he needed someone to take the prisoners to the village while he finished his patrol with the rest of the men.

"Pick three others, Ramses," he said. "And then bring the captives to Deir el Medineh. Send someone ahead to warn Dhutmose. We'll bring them to Karnak as a gift to His Holiness."

Ramses' eyes, fixed on Wenatef with the proper degree of pride and deference, suddenly widened and dilated.

Wenatef whirled around in time to see Unas take a quick step backward, his hand beside his body, near the mace that hung at his belt.

"I said his life is spared!" Wenatef said. "I'll take no more insubordination from you." He looked from Unas to Roy, who was standing behind him. "I do not want this man to be part of any of your patrols that deal with me and mine. Am I understood?"

"You are understood, Commander," Roy replied with a narrow look at Unas.

"Then go," said Wenatef. He looked at Unas. "And you, Unas: I have warned you before. I have a long memory."

** ** **

They returned to a hero's welcome at Deir el Medineh.

Collars of flowers were set about their necks and they were greeted with cheers and applause and jars of beer.

"Good fighting!" Duwah said, slapping Wenatef's shoulder and sitting down beside him. He offered a jar of new-brewed beer. Wenatef took the jar, sipped, and handed it back with a word of thanks.

"Not bad," he conceded. "Though I wish I'd had a contingent of Nubian bowmen and another of chariots. But there'll be time to gather them. The Tjehenu will be back." He smiled grimly at Duwah's horror-stricken expression and nodded. "Oh they'll be back, Duwah. Don't doubt it. Not this week or next - not that I can say. But they'll return in greater numbers.

"They're hungry and homeless and Thebes is rich - hundred-gated Thebes, the flower of golden Egypt. That's how they view her and us, and they saw how few men withstood them this time. You would do well to approach the authorities and ask that the necropolis and Deir el Medineh be given a garrison again to protect them."

"A necropolis and a city of workmen?" Duwah asked, incredulous.

"A necropolis and a city of workmen," Wenatef repeated. "I spoke to one of the captives. I asked him why he came against us, what he sought from us. Do you know what he answered?"

He raised the jar of beer to his lips and drank, watching Duwah.

Duwah inserted his fingers beneath his wig and scratched. "Land," he answered.

"No," Wenatef said. "They would go to the delta for that. The land is richer there. No, Duwah, he answered 'gold'. He said that we have tons of it. Rich treasure buried beneath our feet, enough to feed millions of millions..."

Duwah frowned. "Enough to feed half of Egypt, hidden underground... And we are plagued with droughts and food that's not delivered... The temptation's so great for some. So great for many, and there's so little we can do against the many. So little..."

And then he handed Wenatef the jar of beer again with an attempt at a laugh. "I shouldn't be such a prophet of doom!" he said.

"Don't doubt it," Wenatef countered. "Look, Duwah, if you'd use the brains that are supposed to fill your skull, you'd see without having to think too hard. You are the first settlement they'll come across if they approach from the desert. And what's buried in the necropolis? All the jewels and beautiful implements, rich beds and clothing that the dead will need in the afterlife. Were we greedy men, Duwah, we would be tormented with the urge to dig."

He looked over and saw Duwah's expression and decided to let the matter drop. He continued, " - and don't doubt that the Bedouin would be perfectly capable of digging here!" He nodded at Duwah and drank more beer. "Do as I say: request the garrison. Storm the authorities with words, if you must, but don't stop until you have that garrison!"

"I'll talk to Dhutmose," Duwah said. "He has direct access to Herihor."

Wenatef sighed and rubbed an aching shoulder. "So long as you talk to someone, Duwah," he said, but he was not reassured by his friend's expression.

** ** **

Wenatef gave some intense thought to the question of marauding Tjehenu over the next few hours and as a result of those hours of thought he spent a long time questioning the Tjehenu prisoners. Afterward, he went to Dhutmose with the request that the Scribe send a message to Prince Sekhemkhet, requesting an audience.

Dhutmose, who had been engaged in copying from one page to another with his flowing, elegant script, set his brushes aside and folded his hands before him. He frowned down at them before looking up at Wenatef. "The raiders?" he asked.

45

Wenatef nodded. "They're camped to the west in great numbers. They'll be coming again and we simply don't have enough men to withstand them."

"But your troop did well yesterday, and you have all the men of the village."

"It isn't enough," Wenatef said. "Most of you more or less know how to handle a bow, but you don't do it well enough to hold off a large, determined force. We need a garrison. I spoke to Duwah about it. We need trained archers. We were only able to do as well as we did yesterday because we could pour arrows into that group before they came within reach. That's the only way we can fight them, and twenty men just isn't enough against a large force."

"I see your point," Dhutmose said. "I'll send the message today. It may be several days before you get a reply."

"A few days won't matter," Wenatef said. "I want to be here for the rest of the week at any rate. This specific group got a mauling from us; they'll be regrouping. That'll also give us a little time to heal our prisoners. I want to bring them to Karnak as a gift. But tell Prince Sekhemkhet that while there is no need to move immediately, the arrangements should still be made quickly." He added, "I'm sure you can phrase it diplomatically."

Dhutmose nodded again. "I heard what Unas tried to do," he said

"It's all of a piece with what's gone before," said Wenatef.

"Before?" Dhutmose repeated.

Wenatef folded his arms and frowned down at his feet, sandaled in plaited papyrus. "There's something about him that I should remember, something my father told me," he said. "I can't put my finger on it. But I know he was at Karnak as an acolyte."

Dhutmose looked thoughtful, but he said nothing.

Wenatef shook his head. "It's the business of the priesthood. It's not for me to comment. What's past is past, after all. But there was shame that time, and he's made me remember. I'll be watching him."

"Don't watch too closely or obviously," Dhutmose said. He nodded at Wenatef's surprised expression. "It could be very dangerous." He drew a deep breath and then said in a different tone. "I'll write to Sekhemkhet about that garrison now."

CHAPTER X

Wenatef stood in the great courtyard of the Vizier's palace at Thebes. The prisoners were behind him, roped together and standing with heads lowered beneath the hot sun. Ramses stood behind them, his bow strung and ready, his eyes flashing with interest. He had never been to Thebes in his life, and he had observed their passage through the tumultuous streets of the city with wide, excited eyes.

Wenatef brought his right fist to his left shoulder and bowed to the Vizier, smiling at the promise of a fair-sized troop of men for the town. Farewells were spoken and Wenatef stepped up into his chariot, unknotted the reins from the rail, and chirruped to his horses. They started forward, the prisoners followed him, and Ramses brought up the rear, as regally grim as one of the reliefs of Seti I.

Wenatef turned and caught Prince Sekhemkhet gazing after them with an odd expression of longing and fear on his face, like a man who has caught a glimpse of a distant past and wishes that he could leave the present and step into it. He bowed to Wenatef and Ramses and turned back toward his home, moving slowly, his head lowered.

The street that they followed paralleled the river; it was filled with throngs of brightly clad merchants crying their wares under striped cloths. Men of Byblos with fine wood for carving, goldsmiths and the makers of necklaces of carnelian and jasper and precious blue lapis. Buyers crowded around them, men and women both with kohl-ringed eyes, clad in linen garments of all colors, striped, patterned, or flashing white, their heads covered with to keep the sun at bay.

They were in the midst of the city's noise, the cry of vendors, the jingle of jewelry and, once, the sound of a flute shrilling the notes of a dancing song while the dancer whirled in the dust, her henna- tinted hands and feet sparkling in the brilliant light. The noise died as Wenatef's group approached. Bargains were halted, hands raised to gesture fluttered and sank to stillness, and kohl-dark eyes widened.

"They are so silent," Ramses said to Wenatef.

"It's been a long time since Thebes has seen foreign prisoners," Wenatef said. "What was ordinary once is now a cause for wonder. In Thutmose III's time prisoners from the Keftiu, from the Tjehenu, from Cush - they would have been something commonplace. But these men are not, and their presence here is cause enough for someone to say, 'In the fifteenth year of His Majesty's reign, when - "

He did not finish his sentence. One of the merchants leaned over and spat noisily. "'His Majesty's a broken reed! Unfit to bear the name of Ramesses, and as for 'Lord of the Two Lands'- !"

"Whether or not The Lord of the Two Lands is fit to bear the names," Wenatef said levelly, "He does bear them."

The merchant eyed Wenatef. His gaze lingered on the fine bow he held, and then moved to the line of prisoners behind him, stopping finally at Ramses, who was glaring at him with princely affront. The man's eyes swung toward the great first pylon of the Temple, now clearly visible above the noise and the throngs, and narrowed, concentrating on the features of the colossi of Ramesses II. His eyes widened slightly: he bowed and turned away without further comment.

They passed through a wide avenue of silent, staring people, which closed behind them to form a larger and larger procession. Wenatef was as fond of pageantry as any Egyptian of his time, but there was something almost funereal about this procession, as though he and the people who followed him were carrying the corpse of Egypt's greatness to its tomb.

They had entered the avenue of ram-headed sphinxes; the pylon towered before them, topped by eight bright pennons fluttering in the wind that swept along the river. The tall, gold-sheathed doors swung open as he approached and a line of white-clad priests came toward him.

Wenatef stepped down from his chariot and bowed, then straightened. "His Majesty Ramesses XI presents to this gift of slaves to Imperial Amun," he said.

The lead priest inclined his head. "The gift and its bearers are welcome," he said, and motioned them to follow him within the temple.

The crowds behind them remained where they were, watching in a silence that was broken at the end by a cheer as the tall doors closed behind Wenatef's group.

** ** **

Sunset found Wenatef seated high atop the hillside overlooking Deir el Medineh, his eyes turned northward toward the distant bend of the Nile, now pink in the approaching twilight.

The village below him sparkled in the darkness of its valley, lit by hundreds of lamps. Wenatef could hear music, softened by distance. One of the sculptors was holding a feast to celebrate the marriage of his son. The younger girls would be dancing before their elders, he knew, and there had been plans of wrestling contests and trials of archery.

High, clear laughter pealed out from the street, and a girl's voice cried something merry and faintly mocking. A boy's voice replied, the words blurred to Wenatef's hearing, and the voices mingled in laughter that softened and faded.

Wenatef sat back, feeling the earth beneath and behind him, bracing his shoulders. It was still warm from the afternoon sun, as unchanging as the sun's rising and setting. He needed to feel things that did not change, to know that he could anchor his spirit to them and not fear their betrayal. There was so much that changed, so much that became twisted.

He drew a deep breath and watched the sun's final flare of scarlet fire as it plunged into the realm of the night. Stars glittered above the horizon as though sparked by its vanished fire. The thought came to Wenatef that the stars were always there in the sky, and it was only the absence of the sun that enabled them to shine by night. As the sun died in the west they blazed into life in the east.

He lay back against the ground and gazed up at the stars above him, at the Bull's Head and the Brothers, and thought of Karnak.

He, Ramses and the prisoners had been escorted into the great temple's courtyard, where the captives had been taken from them. The senior priest had spoken words of praise and directed that they be taken to one of the pavilions in the inner courtyards and refreshed with wine and fruits before their departure. And then he had left them.

Wenatef had watched him go, turned to accept a cup of wine from the acolyte before him - and had frozen in shocked anger as he gazed over the man's shoulder. The wall behind him had recently been sheathed with new sandstone, and was carved to show a man offering to the gods, worshiping, fulfilling all the duties of His Majesty. The name, enclosed in a royal cartouche, or frame, was Herihor.

Never in all the history of Egypt had a man dared to usurp the functions of royalty and then openly admit it, as though it were a praiseworthy act and not treason. In the time of mighty kings like Thutmose III, Seti I, Ramesses II or Ramesses III, such presumption would have been punished by the man's execution and the obliteration of his name from every monument he had ever touched. But there was Herihor, usurping the attributes of royalty before an officer of His Majesty, with never a hint of furtiveness. And the shaming thing was that Wenatef, an officer high in the service of His Majesty, had been unable to do more than level a sharp gaze at that wall and those carvings, coolly thank the priests, gather Ramses and the rest of his men, and leave the temple without touching the wine.

He drew another deep breath and looked at the stars glinting above him like the points of leveled spears. They would not be so bright if the sun were in the sky. Herihor would have been nothing if the Lord of the Two Lands were still truly lord. But His Majesty was only a name and the shadow of greatness. Egypt had passed its time of glory.

Others would attempt to recall Egypt to her lost glory. Such an attempt would be like propping up a decaying corpse and pretending that it was alive again. Egypt was dead, and what would come in later years would be only a dream, a shadow, an echo.

He lay back and watched the stars and turned his thoughts to other, fairer lands.

CHAPTER XI

Merihor returned to duty just as the Libyans came in force and kept Wenatef's attention well away from the question of Egypt's decay.

Wenatef had been the first to sight them. He had climbed to the crest of the Peak with several of his men and frowned westward. He could see them the distance, like a river of living smoke.

"They are coming in numbers this time," said a voice beside him. "I can see their long hair streaming behind them, their spears clutched in their hands burnt red by the bite of the sun..."

Wenatef turned and saw Merihor standing beside him, gazing at the horizon, his eyes wide and unfocussed. "Their pale eyes are narrowed on the vista of Thebes and the wealth in tombs of the Great Ones. See them racing toward us... Racing..." His words trailed off into silence and he lowered his head.

Wenatef turned away from him and frowned at Ramses, who stood behind him. The young man had been formally named as his second in command after he had announced that he would leave Deir el Medineh, and now he dealt with Ramses as though he were an apprentice.

"An army," he said. "Coming in force this time."

Ramses cast a glance at the horizon and then followed Wenatef down the slope of the Peak toward the rest of the patrol waiting below.

The men were standing at ease, some on one foot, leaning

on their spears, their heads lowered in the sun. One was seated on the ground, drawing aimless designs in the dirt with a fingertip. They rose as Wenatef and Ramses approached.

"A large group of raiders are coming from the west," Wenatef said. "We don't have much time. Pennut, you and Merneptah will go straight to the village and tell everyone to run for Medinet Habu. Tell them not to bother with their belongings. Better to lose a few trinkets than your life. Pinehas, you're a swift runner. Go before them to Medinet Habu. Tell them to make all ready. Tell them that I, Wenatef, Commander of One Thousand and Commander of the Guard of His Majesty's Tomb, order that they send their troops to me. Go now. There's no time to lose."

"And the rest of us?" said Ramses. "There are nineteen in this troop, all told."

"There'll be more," said Wenatef. "We'll take the guards from the mortuary temples." He turned to one of his men. "Paynedjem, you will come with me in the chariot. I'll need a charioteer to drive while I shoot, and you know how to handle my horses."

Merihor watched as Paynedjem climbed into the chariot. He touched Wenatef on the bronze bracer that circled his wrist. "Commander," he said.

Wenatef, preoccupied with the coming of the Tjehenu, spoke shortly. "What is it, Merihor?"

"It's coming quickly now," Merihor said. "Too quickly to stop. I can't escape my own fate, and you must be prepared for yours. You can't hope to fight them as you are now. You'd have to go to the Land of the West and return with an army. We must speak very soon."

His words made Wenatef frown, but time was pressing. Wenatef nodded and stepped into his chariot beside Paynedjem. "We'll speak soon," he said. But his mind was occupied with troops and weapons.

** ** **

A Killing Among the Dead

Paynedjem reined Wenatef's horses before the great
pylon of the mortuary temple of Ramesses II. The huge
stone gateway reared above the noise and bustle of the town
that had grown up around it. People thronged the courtyard
before the pylon, leading cattle fattened for the temple
sacrifices. Motion ceased as they turned to stare.

Wenatef's voice cut through the commotion like the blare
of a trumpet. "Bring the guard!" he cried. "Danger from the
west - follow me!"

Women screamed and cattle bellowed. Men stopped
where they stood and stared at Wenatef while the guardsmen
reached for their swords. "There's no time to waste!"
Wenatef shouted above the surrounding din, "Follow me
now! I'll give an accounting !"

He gripped the rail as Paynedjem wheeled the chariot,
and looked once over his shoulder. Armed men and chariots
were pouring through the pylon. He motioned for them to
follow and sped back toward the gates of the temple
complex.

** ** **

The road between Deir el Medineh and Medinet Habu
was choked with fleeing villagers laden with their
belongings. The raiders had just been sighted, and people
were milling about, screaming prayers and pleas to the
village captains for protection. Wenatef drove his chariot
into their midst and stopped, raising his arms for silence.

The village folk were too terrified to halt. Wenatef drew
a deep breath. "Stop!" he roared above the din. "Stop and
listen to me!"

The people grew quiet. A tiny child close by him began
to sob. Aahmose. Wenatef bent quickly and lifted her. She
clung to him, shivering.

"Drop the trash you carry," he directed. "The hills will
protect you: climb them and leave us to fight. The gods are
with us." He gave Aahmose to her mother and watched as
the villagers were herded up the hillsides, to take shelter

among the rocks. And then he turned his troops to meet the wave of attackers pouring down the roadway.

** ** **

The Tjehenu moved as swiftly as a desert whirlwind, in greater numbers than Wenatef had seen before. This time they had archers with them, shooting short bows that lacked the range and accuracy of the Egyptians' but were deadly enough at close quarters. The roadway was choked with the dead and the wounded as the fighting raged back and forth during the afternoon that passed before the Tjehenu were driven away.

Wenatef returned from the fighting and drove directly to Thebes, to seek an audience with the Vizier and urge that the villagers be moved to safety before more lives were lost.

Prince Sekhemkhet listened and finally agreed to have the people of Deir el Medineh placed within the walls of the great fortress-temple of Medinet Habu. A council was convened to consider the suggestion, and a decree was sent within the week from His Majesty himself, commanding the relocation of Deir el Medineh before the next inundation.

Dhutmose received the news with surprise and directed an odd look at Wenatef, but said nothing.

** ** **

Merihor's wife, Tamit, came to Wenatef two days later saying that her husband had been missing. She was twisting her hands in the cheap linen of her skirt and staring at him with anxious, shadowed eyes. "It was the day after the last attack, Commander," she said. "He slept ill that night, murmuring of fate and blood." She shivered and her hands were stilled for a moment. "The next morning he went out toward the necropolis, and he was alone, though you had said that everyone should take an escort, or go armed..."

Wenatef nodded and smiled at Merihor's youngest son, Wahankh, who peeped at him from behind his mother's skirt and pulled his Horus-lock.

"He - he said that he was being called - I haven't seen

him since. I wish he had gone to your farms, as you suggested. I'm so afraid -" She bit her lip and looked down at her son.

** ** **

They found him after half a day's searching, in the desert beyond Thutmose III's tomb, a tattered mass of bones and flesh, drying in the sun.

Unas had come to him saying they had found something that might interest him. Unas' expression had seemed odd, but he had been appropriately deferent, even apologizing for being so close to the town after Wenatef had commanded his virtual exile. Wenatef had nodded, taken several of his men and went with him, resolving to do some serious thinking about Unas very shortly.

The corpse had almost blended with the sand. Ramses had been the first to see it. Wenatef had stared for a moment and then knelt beside the body, touching the deep gouges across the chest. The guardsmen stood in a half-circle, some of them sucking the knobs of their sticks, their eyes shifting sideways in the presence of death.

A hawk, soaring overhead, screamed suddenly and swooped down to flutter above them. Wenatef could feel the faint wind from her wings as he raised his head and met her eyes.

A slashing death, Merihor had said... Wenatef looked up at the silent motion of the hawk in the brilliant sky, then lowered his eyes to the half-circle of faces around him, registering different degrees of shock and disgust. And then he fixed his gaze on Unas' face, remembering the past weeks.

CHAPTER XII

Unas' voice was calm and pitying when he spoke. "The Libyans must have found him after that last battle and done this," he said.

Wenatef set his memories aside and turned to Unas. "Do you think so?" he said. "Why?"

Unas folded his arms and frowned at Wenatef. "But Commander," he said. "Isn't it obvious? We defeated them, and they found one of our men and killed him."

"Whether they went back to the desert is more than I can say," Wenatef said, his eyes narrowing. "But I do know that this area, specifically, has been patrolled night and day by my men, by the Karnak Temple Guard, and by a troop from the Army of Upper Egypt. There were no Libyans."

"There can be no other explanation for this," Unas said in a curiously restrained voice, his gaze as direct as Wenatef's.

"It's obvious, then, that you have never fought the Tjehenu," Wenatef said with amused contempt. "They don't do this - " he touched the slashes with a scornful fingertip, " - to their foes. They slice off the ears and nose and privates to deprive the enemy of any joy in the Land of the West. They don't waste their time with this sort of nonsense. A Tjehenu warrior would scorn this, and no one knows that better than me."

He got to his feet and frowned down at Merihor's body. "Well. We have a murder. I am alerting the Theban Guards."

"Oh no, sir!" Ramses spoke beside Wenatef. He was respectful but firm.

"What?" Wenatef said.

Ramses would one day be a stately man. Even now, as a young man newly admitted to adulthood, he had the same elegance that marked the carved reliefs of his great ancestor at Abydos and Gurna. He blushed now and said, "Please, sir. Look again. A lion did that. You can see the marks of the claws and where he tore Merihor's throat - " He paled and swallowed for a moment. "I - and my father, may the Gods rest him! - we have seen many lion kills. This is obviously one. There were no Libyans to kill him, they were driven into the desert, and our patrols were very tight. We would have found a murderer. This was done by a lion."

"I have seen men mauled by lions," Wenatef reminded Ramses with a gentleness that might have alarmed his subordinates back in Per-Ramesse. "I was even attacked by one, myself. If you mean me to think that this botched business was the work of a lion -"

"Please, sir," Ramses said. "Our patrols were very thorough. Look again. See the claw marks? See the throat? This is the work of a lion, one that I'm familiar with. You must agree on that!"

Wenatef looked down at Merihor's wounds, his eyes narrowing again. That 'must' had been oddly emphasized, hinting not that Wenatef would be convinced by the sheer weight of the evidence, but that it was necessary for Wenatef to agree that the killer had been a lion because it was the safest thing to do.

He frowned and moved Merihor's arms and then leaned on the thigh bones. None of the major bones were broken, as they would have been in a lion mauling, and none of the thick muscles or entrails had been devoured.

He looked up at Ramses, scanned the semicircle of faces surrounding him, and then looked across at Unas, standing alone and almost defiant, looking down at the corpse with the face of a man approving his own handiwork. Wenatef had not been meant to see that expression; he shifted his gaze as Unas looked up.

"You may be right, Ramses," he said. "We'd best get him back to the village. Hekanakhte and Huy, take the body to Thutiy the embalmer. Tell him that I'll be by to arrange matters with him after I speak with the widow. Dhutmose will be paying for the funeral in behalf of His Majesty. My chariot will bear you, but go carefully. Three men are a little heavy for it."

He rose, looked down at Merihor's corpse one last time, and then nodded to his men, who slung it over the railing of the chariot and then climbed in, gathering the reins. The body was stiff, like dried meat, jerking and swaying to the motion of the chariot.

Wenatef turned back to his men. "Mentuhotep, Pennut, you two go to the Theban Guards. Tell them there's been a killing. Bekenkhons, Hesunebed, you two go along to the Tomb and warn the workers there, then go home. We've all earned a rest. Ramses, string your bow and then come with me. You and I will take a turn or two around here to see if we can spot any tracks or lions."

He looked at Unas again, a long, considering stare that continued through the silence that seemed to shroud them both. "And as for you, Unas," he said at last, "I will remember your assistance in this matter."

Unas turned on his heel and left. The other Necropolis Police followed him. Some of them directed puzzled looks at Wenatef. The rest of the men scattered, except for Ramses, who waited with his bow ready Wenatef took one last look at the spot where Merihor's body had been found.

He looked up at Ramses and his eyes narrowed. "We'll scout the area for lion tracks," he said. His voice was level. "They would probably pick their way through the larger rocks. Do you see any blood?"

Ramses seemed surprised, but he answered calmly enough. "No. I did look, but there's none here."

"As though he were killed somewhere else and brought

here to be found," Wenatef said.

Ramses lowered his head.

Wenatef glanced at the men of his group, who were now well out of earshot. "Now," he said, "Tell me why you were so anxious to get me to admit that that murder was the work of a lion, despite all the evidence.

Ramses looked down and tried to hide the flush that colored his face. "Sir, it was obvious-"

"The only obvious thing about Merihor's body was that no lion killed that man. Why were you so insistent?"

"It's dangerous to think otherwise," Ramses said. "Didn't you know? My father was killed by just such a lion. You're showing interest in the same matters that interested him."

"Merihor interrupted the robbery of a tomb," Wenatef said with sudden conviction, the first time he had actually voiced that thought. "That's why the village leaders are so frightened." He frowned across at Ramses. "They're frightened because your father - may he live and prosper in the fields of Yaru! - looked into a similar matter and met this fate."

Ramses looked down. "I can only say that it's dangerous," he said. He lifted his head with a flash of wrath. "And I'll tell you that I will avenge his death in whatever way I can! Please don't ask any more. It isn't safe."

They walked a while in silence as Wenatef considered what Ramses had said. He had known little of his father, Seti, except that he had been a splendid archer and had met an untimely death.

Tomb Robbery. That was all it could possibly be. He could stake his life on it and, he knew that he probably would be doing just that if he pursued the matter any further. The thought did not trouble him; he had been prepared to sell his life dearly many times before, against the rebellious Nubians, against mutinying soldiers at Semna and, most recently, against the Tjehenu in the desert. If they tried to send him to The Land of the West, he would take a few of them along as an escort.

Wenatef smiled at the younger man. "Say no more, Ramses," he said. "You're a good lad. I don't go looking for trouble, I promise you that, and I thank you for the warning."

But, he thought to himself as they began to climb the path leading to the backbone of the hills, he would not run away from trouble if he found himself facing it, either.

CHAPTER XIII

Wenatef was making his way down the main street of Deir el Medineh. Tamit and her children were wailing and tearing their clothes in the house behind him. It had been very difficult, and he felt an urgent need for something to steady him. A good long drink of wine, maybe, and then he would go to Master Thutiy to inspect Merihor's corpse. The wine shop stood in the middle of a grove of persea trees, watered out of the town's precious store and cherished because of their welcome shade.

The ground beneath them was bare and clean, perfect for resting on the low stools provided or just squatting. He purchased some palm cakes and a small jug of sweet wine from the shopkeeper, and he ate and drank and chatted with the man, who was more than happy to share the wine - it was a good vintage - and add to it from his own stock.

"I don't give this to just anyone!" he said, squatting down beside Wenatef. "Nectar like this comes rarely into my hands. Herihor himself snatches up all he can find! Aye, more than His Majesty! But when the sun sets, the moon rises."

Wenatef lifted his eyebrows. "And what's that supposed to mean?" he asked.

"How do you describe a king who can't get supplies to his servants in time? We aren't in the middle of a famine! And he can't protect his lands from rabble from the desert! His Majesty's loosening his hold on Egypt."

"Plain speaking," Wenatef said through a mouthful of

cake.

"It's nothing that hasn't been said before," said the man.

"No," said Wenatef. "Nothing that hasn't been said by everyone. I saw the carvings."

The man's eyes sharpened. "At Karnak, eh?" he said. "I've heard of them. Well, who's to say it's not for the best?" He opened his own flask of wine and topped Wenatef's cup. "Drink," he said.

Wenatef did, paused to stare at the wine, and then drank more deeply. "This *is* good," he said.

"Nectar suitable for the gods!" said the shopkeeper. "And you deserve it."

Wenatef looked up.

"I heard," said the man. "After fighting off the Tjehenu - a feat that even Nakht couldn't match! - you arrange to save our lives for us. And then one of your men dies."

Wenatef nodded.

"A lion, they say," the man persisted.

Wenatef did not like the line of talk. He merely shrugged and said, "So we think."

"Was Unas there?" asked the man.

"Yes," Wenatef answered. "With the Necropolis Police."

The shopkeeper scratched the stubble on the back of his head with his fingertips and nodded. "So I thought," he said.

"What do you know of Unas?" Wenatef asked.

"A vicious young man," said the shopkeeper. "He was dismissed from the Temple by his own uncle for a number of reasons..."

"What were they?" Wenatef asked. He felt the touch of memory again. *A pity*, Hapuseneb had said. *A terrible pity that it should have happened.* But what?

The man filled his cup again. "Hard to say," he said. "No one liked to talk about it, but I think he's off-balance."

"That may be," said Wenatef. He drained his cup and set it aside.

** ** **

A Killing Among the Dead

"He was brought in this noon," said Wenatef, looking across at the young man before him. "We think he was mauled by a lion. I would like to see him."

The young man's dark eyes were speculative and fixed, but he nodded once. "Follow me, Commander," he said.

They found Thutiy in one of the inner rooms, bent over a table with a knife in his hand. He looked up as Wenatef entered, and set down the knife.

"Commander Wenatef," said the young man. "He's come to look at Merihor's body, Grandfather. He says he was killed by a lion." The last sentence was said in a curiously flat voice.

Thutiy turned his dark eyes on Wenatef. Killed by a lion?" he repeated, and stepped aside from the table. "Here he is."

Merihor was on the table, partially eviscerated. The lungs, liver, stomach and intestines were set to one side. Wenatef turned aside, gasping for air. He had overcome his battle nerves because it had been necessary, and the sight of a corpse did not trouble him, no matter how badly hacked or pecked by scavengers. But not the sight of a human being laid upon a slab for butchering. Merihor's entrails seemed exactly like the innards of a slaughtered steer, and the incongruity, the wrongness of it, smote him in the stomach like a fist.

A hand slipped beneath his elbow and guided him toward an area that seemed somehow brighter and cooler, as a voice spoke kindly to him. The words were lost in the roaring in his ears, but a cool wind was suddenly brushing his face and his sight cleared after a moment.

He looked up. Thutiy was standing before him, watching his expression. As Wenatef lifted his eyes, he smiled and said to the young man, "Go to the storerooms, Nebo, and mark the linen I set aside from that brought by Merihor's friends. I'll also need tubs filled with natron - two of them - and some damp cloths to wipe my hands on."

65

He watched his grandson leave and then came closer to Wenatef. "Will you be all right, Commander? I should have prepared you. Forgive me: I forget that the first experience with this- " he motioned toward Merihor's corpse, " - tends to be unnerving."

Wenatef was far from feeling well again, but he looked up, caught Thutiy's expression, and began to laugh. "I'm ashamed," he said. "I'm acting as squeamish as a boy at his own circumcision."

Thutiy's mouth moved in what might pass for a smile, but he still scanned Wenatef's face. "There," he said. "I think you're better. You're a good man, Commander. It speaks well that the sight of one killed like that would unsettle you. I was unsettled, myself, when he was brought here."

Thutiy's eyes were veiled for a moment and his mouth grim, but he continued calmly enough, "Do you want to view the wounds? I've covered his face and the rest, so you won't be troubled again. Would you like me to leave?"

Wenatef frowned at Merihor's corpse. "No," he said. "I have some questions for you."

Thutiy said nothing as Wenatef bent over Merihor's body and examined the wounds. The flesh had been cut rather than torn, the wounds too clean to have been inflicted by a predator's claws. The injuries to the neck were nothing like the massive crushing wounds inflicted by a lion, which seizes its prey by its neck and breaks it between its jaws. Wenatef had never seen a big cat's kill with a slit jugular vein. And, too, Merihor's skull was fractured. The only broken bone, apparently, in the body.

He straightened and looked at Thutiy. "Killed by a lion," he said, the third time someone had uttered that sentence in that room. "Do you agree?"

Thutiy seemed surprised. "Is that what they told you?" he asked,

"Let's say that I had the feeling that I would find it safer accept that explanation," Wenatef said.

66

Thutiy's frown deepened. "What were the other explanations?" he asked.

"The Tjehenu that we have been fighting recently - or else murder connected with a crime."

Thutiy turned away abruptly. Wenatef had the impression that he was afraid but he was perfectly composed he turned back with a small linen towel in his hand. "Why not the Tjehenu?" he asked.

"The mutilation's not in their style, for one thing," Wenatef answered. "For another this area - the area in which Merihor was found - has been heavily patrolled by my men, the Temple Guard, and by the Army, because of its closeness to the royal tombs. There were no Tjehenu."

"Could they have killed him somewhere else and left the body where you found it?"

"Why travel to a more dangerous area just to drop off a piece of carrion?" he asked. "They would have left him where they killed him. I know. I have fought them time and again, defending..."

"...what you love." Thutiy finished for him, almost as though he were talking to himself. "Defending the life you love and the folk you love and the king you love, without thought of reward. You're like me, doing now what I have always done..." He met Wenatef's gaze and then looked down.

The strangeness of the moment faded. "Well," Thutiy said. "It's either lions, then, or murderers. Is that what you think?"

"It is," Wenatef said. "You know, better than many, the sort of wounds inflicted by a big cat on a man. Do these match, in your opinion?"

Thutiy's lively eyes lowered. "The wounds in the chest - maybe. Though it would have to be a lion with very sharp claws. The neck puzzles me. I have yet to hear of a lion that kills its prey with a crushing blow to the skull and then takes the time to tear at the chest and throat without bothering to go after the softer parts."

Wenatef's mind filled with a vision of Merihor, surrounded by faceless men, staring at the drawn, glittering knives that shone yellow in the torchlight - screaming, screaming - and then crumpling to the ground, the scream cut off in his throat, to lie twitching and trembling with a crushed and bloody skull. The vision was small and dim, as though Wenatef were viewing it from a great distance through a haze of smoke.

"He was murdered," "he said.

"We all come to death," Thutiy said. "Some slowly, some swiftly. This death was one of the swift ones. The mutilation was caused after this man was killed by the blow to the skull. There's much blood in the body still, even though the slashes are deep. His heart wasn't beating, and he was dead before he fell to the ground. He felt nothing, for all that he doesn't make a pretty corpse."

He seemed about to say something further, but Nebo returned just then with the towels. Thutiy wiped his hands and told Nebo to wash the organs thoroughly and cover them with natron. "I'll remove the brain tonight," he said. "The body will be laid out to dry in natron tomorrow morning. I'll stitch up the wounds," he said with an eye on Wenatef's face, "And make him fit for the Fields of the West." He lifted an eyebrow at Nebo. "This death was a very great pity. I hope there will be no others."

It was a strange day, Wenatef reflected. Thutiy had spoken as though this was a matter over which he had some control. But then the old man turned back to Wenatef and they both plunged into the business of funeral arrangements.

Wenatef haggled over the price using all his skill, but well aware that he was going to be manipulated into paying the price that Thutiy wanted. Afterward, Thutiy poured Wenatef a cup of wine and sat with him on the roof of his workshop, which also served as a terrace. The night air was cool and soothing after the heat of the day, and the constellations blazed above them, seeming no farther away than the points of Thutiy's small oil lamps.

The embalmer drank his wine and said, "Earth and heaven are so close sometimes. It's hard to tell where one begins and the other ends."

"Sometimes they run into each other. I wonder…" Wenatef said, remembering the reliefs at Medinet Habu. "I wonder if there is a door somewhere..."

Thutiy's eyes seemed to shine in the reflected lamplight. "There is a door," he said, his eyes lifted to the stars. "There is a door... It is called death, and it's not a door that you should open yourself."

Wenatef thought of Merihor passing through the door. As in the inner room, Wenatef could suddenly see Merihor. This time he stood before dark doors that seemed to be made of wood. He was weeping and trembling, but he raised his hand to knock.

The doors swung inward. Slow, silent motion, and beyond it a brilliant light that banished all shadows.

Merihor was walking through the doors, still trembling -

Don't be afraid, Merihor! Wenatef thought with an urgency he could not understand.

Merihor squared his shoulders and strode across the threshold and into the light, and the doors closed behind him. Wenatef could see the outlines limned with brightness, like liquid fire, and then all was dark and he was suddenly back on a rooftop in Deir el Medineh, sipping wine and gazing at the stars.

"Murder's a serious matter," Thutiy said without looking at Wenatef. "Will you be looking into it?"

"As much as I can," Wenatef answered. "I don't think I'll find anything, but I must try."

"I would expect no less," Thutiy said, the lines of his face deepening in a smile. "You're as straight and uncompromising as a spear, and you don't tolerate evil."

He stopped and looked down with a slight cough. "I beg

your pardon," he said after a moment.   "That was impertinent. I didn't mean to presume upon our friendship. After the way you led the fight against those Libyans, and anyone could see   how far above your men you are in ability."   He stopped, coughed discreetly again, and said, "How beautiful the stars are tonight."

Wenatef looked at the sky again, the wanderlust within his heart waking to full awareness, and for a moment, with the points of light around him and throughout the village, he seemed to be walking among the stars along a roadway of wind.   And then he blinked and was upon the earth once more with an old man looking into his eyes and wondering if he had been offended.

CHAPTER XIV

The number of lion sightings more than tripled in the week following the discovery of Merihor's body. There were four sightings by Wenatef's company alone: the shadow of a hawk circling above the Valley of the Kings, a cat sunning itself among the rocks, a large boulder casting an elongated shadow in the afternoon sun, and the movement of another of Wenatef's men among the rocks. In each case the 'lion' was located and investigated before being dismissed as a mistake, though in the case of the cat the 'lion' left when they first appeared, more frightened than Wenatef's men.

Wenatef shared the joke with Thutiy one afternoon while they were riding in his chariot. The old man often spoke of the time he had served as an officer's charioteer at the garrison of Beth Shan in Palestine. Wenatef suggested the outing.

They tooled along the path from the village to the temple of Medinet Habu as the wind cooled their faces and whirled the dust of the Valley behind them. They returned through the Valley of the Kings after eating a lunch in the shade of the Temple wall.

Thutiy held the reins on the way back, his long kilt whipping behind them like the tail of a comet, and though he gathered his light shawl more closely about his shoulders, he was laughing aloud in the wind. They paused beneath the shadow of the Peak and gazed about them at the silent valley slowly turning golden in the afternoon light.

Thutiy looked around and drew a deep, satisfied breath

that puffed out his withered chest for a moment. He expelled it with a slight wheeze, frowned at the sky, and said, "This spot is so beautiful - and yet so lifeless, like a landscape beaten of gold. Wasn't it here that Merihor was found?"

"Close by," said Wenatef. "Just over there."

Thutiy nodded. "He wasn't a pretty sight," he said.

"No," Wenatef said. "I think he surprised a tomb robbery."

Thutiy's expression was odd and he spoke carefully. "Your mind is alive with suspicion," he said. "You see a tomb robber in every villager, and you don't know who is innocent."

"I can't seem to stop myself," Wenatef said.

Thutiy nodded and drew the team in. "Let's sit down for a moment here, in the shade," he said.

Nothing more was said while Wenatef helped Thutiy descend from the chariot, and then hobbled the two horses.

Thutiy spoke when they were both settled comfortably in the shade. "There is much to corrupt here - " his hand moved in a half circle. "So much, and so little to stop the greedy ones from seeking it. They think, 'Where is the justice that allows wealth to be buried far from the living, who sweat and starve? Aren't the kings our source of life? Then why waste this treasure? Wouldn't the Great Ones want us to use their wealth to nourish the land?'"

"I've heard those arguments," Wenatef said. "While I can't say what the Great Ones would think about it, I do know that what is buried there does not belong to me."

"The situation is a little more complicated than that," Thutiy said. "We can argue it back and forth and end up no closer to a resolution than we were at the start." He paused, eyeing Wenatef, and then added, "But you may be sure of this: the villagers are not involved with this."

He raised his hand to forestall Wenatef's words. "Oh, I wouldn't be surprised if some of the people at Deir el

Medineh have ancestors who dug at night during the terrible times and tried to fend off starvation with the gold of the kings, but is that so wrong? What do the actions of our ancestors have to do with us?"

"It is sacrilege and robbery, no matter when it was done," Wenatef said.

"There are reasons and reasons for robbery," Thutiy said. "Some are worse than others. But this is not what troubles you, is it?"

Wenatef did not answer.

"No," Thutiy said. "What troubles you is that you suspect your friends of having a part in this scandal. Is that it?"

Wenatef stretched his legs out before him and sat back.

Thutiy waited for him to speak, but then continued. "You went to the Necropolis Police, didn't you?" he asked. "You have done what was necessary and the matter is out of your hands. You have your duty to protect the men who work on the Tomb. That is enough to keep you occupied until you depart after the turn of the Nile. You know nothing, really, of what is happening. After all, all that you do know is that Merihor - who always was a tiresome one - had a fit and is now dead -"

"Murdered," Wenatef pointed out.. "It's hard to remain inactive when there is something afoot that is so foul that I can almost smell it - and there is no one - no one at all! - to care about stopping it - "

"What sort of talk is this?" Thutiy demanded. "Do you think you stand alone against this evil? You're younger than I had thought! Don't you know that even in the most corrupt of times God is never without His witnesses? You aren't fighting alone! Others are looking into it – others who have much at stake!"

When Wenatef did not speak Thutiy continued. "You are the guardian of the tomb that is being carved. Is there anything that you should have done that you haven't? No? Then unless you actually find them at work, leave them alone!" His voice quieted. "Be at peace," he said. "You're safe and so is the village. I promise that on my soul and on my honor."

CHAPTER XV

Wenatef dined with Thutiy the next evening. During the meal the old man brought up the subject of the week preceding Merihor's death. He said that the embalming was going well, and that he was planning to return some of Tamit's linen to her, since he didn't think he would need it all for the wrapping. And then he had looked up at Wenatef and said, "For a man who died such a terrible death, his expression is very peaceful. There'll be some time before I must wrap him - perhaps I should bring Tamit here to look on her husband's face one last time. He seems so peaceful...it would ease her, I think."

Wenatef had no particular opinion one way or another on the therapeutic benefits of viewing corpses, but he murmured something suitable and then found himself, almost against his will, assigned to bring Tamit to the shop the next day.

"Yes, the expression is calm, almost sweet," Ipy said. "And yet he was like a man going about in fear for his life the weeks before he died. I wonder what could have made him so afraid."

Ipy was looking straight at Wenatef, who shrugged. "We were under attack," he said. "Merihor was a good archer, but he loved his life as much as anyone else. The thought of losing it to a pack of wretched Libyans would upset anyone."

"No," said Nebo, breaking into the conversation for the first time. "It dated to the time before the attacks. I had heard something about...about possible tomb robbery."

Thutiy sighed and reached for the bowl of mixed fruits

sweetened with honey. He took a sticky handful, chewed noisily, and then washed his hands. Blue lotus blossoms had been set before each of the diners; Thutiy raised his own bloom to his nose and sniffed at it. From that moment he left the conversation in the hands of his son and grandson.

"This is a necropolis," Wenatef said. "There are always rumors of tomb robbery."

"You didn't judge it a rumor in this case," Nebo said.

Wenatef frowned at him. He didn't like this young man, and he couldn't quite say why, since Nebo was always scrupulously polite to him. But there it was. "What do you mean?" he asked.

"Our friends in the Necropolis Police say that you saw something near the tomb of Thutmose III," Ipy said, sitting forward. Nebo, too, was leaning toward Wenatef, and his expression was hard to read.

"You made a report to two of my friends on the force, Roy and Seneb," Ipy said. "Seneb told me that it was you who made the report and you who claimed to have noticed something amiss. And yet it seemed that Merihor was terribly upset about something. Very odd: I watched you on the evening of that day. You were letting the village children ride in your chariot. You were at ease, laughing at their chatter."

Wenatef did not like the intentness of Ipy's gaze. He dipped his fingers in the bowl of water beside him, wiped them, and lifted his eyebrows at the man. "What is your point?" he asked.

"This: which of you saw the disturbance at the tomb?"

"Why do you want to know?" Wenatef asked. His gaze was very level. "Have you joined the ranks of the Necropolis Police now?"

Ipy sat back with a frown.

Thutiy raised the lotus again. "It's just idle interest," he said, meeting Wenatef's gaze directly. "Nothing more. Rumors get started. That is all."

Wenatef considered. He had tried to protect Merihor. Now that Merihor was dead, there was no reason to continue his pretense. He did not like Ipy or Nebo, and he certainly didn't like this line of questioning, but he knew nothing of matters, and it wouldn't hurt to say so.

"I lied," he said. "I don't know what caused it. I have some influential connections, so I took upon myself the responsibility for reporting the disturbance. I was relaxing nearby and Merihor's commotion awakened me. You can decide for yourself just how much I actually saw. Merihor was always an odd one. They say he had the 'sight'."

He shrugged. "What else could I do?" he asked. "It was my duty to report it. The Necropolis Police took my report and found nothing, so for all I know, Merihor stumbled over a scorpion and took fright."

Thutiy smiled at Wenatef and directed an oddly intent stare at Nebo and Ipy. He seemed almost triumphant. "There," he said. "That's that. Enough about Merihor and tomb robbers. We can sit on the terrace and enjoy the night air..."

Diana Wilder

CHAPTER XVI

"You've come to see how we're doing, eh?" Duwah asked, wiping his forehead with the back of his hand, "Then we're out of danger from the Libyans?"

"For the most part," Wenatef said. "I've arranged for lookouts on the heights, and it seems we'll have a breathing space. I hope so. I'm tired."

Duwah shook his head. "Come inside," he said, "Come inside. You're just in time to take the late meal - and I think you planned it that way!" He took up a torch, which had been thrust into the ground, and led Wenatef into the tomb.

Wenatef looked around at the antechambers, tallying the changes. "You have the drawings well underway," he said.

Duwah cast a skeptical eye back at him. "Don't fool yourself," he said. "This is only the beginning of the Tomb. There is room after room here that has to be completed, and some that have yet to be excavated. It'll take years - if we're allowed to complete it. I'm not sure we will be."

"What do you mean?" Wenatef asked.

"When the king dies he is buried, no matter what state his tomb is in. His Majesty isn't a young man now, and I don't know how much longer we'll have to complete this tomb. We may have to abandon it. We'll be abandoning it for a time while we move, at any rate."

"You'll be better there," Wenatef said. "Medinet Habu is a good, strong fortress. It was built on the site of Seti I's old garrison, wasn't it? There's plenty of room to house you, the Necropolis Police is based there, the walls are and thick – it's withstood attack before."

"What has?" asked Dhutmose as he came up behind them. It was an ordinary work day; he wore a short, workman's kilt, and his only adornment was a string of flowers given him by his youngest daughter. He carried a roll of papyrus, but he smiled and put the roll aside when he saw Wenatef.

"Medinet Habu," Duwah said.

Dhutmose nodded and looked around the tomb. "I had suggested that once, myself, to the Vizier and to Herihor. Prince Sekhemkhet was inclined to treat the idea as a joke, but Herihor looked thoughtful and said he'd consider it. Your actions made all that unnecessary." he smiled at Wenatef and added, "The word of a military man always prevails with a general."

Wenatef bowed with an ironic smile. "I'm still leaving after the Nile turns," he said.

Dhutmose and Duwah traded helpless looks, and finally Duwah said, "It's time to eat. Let's sit down somewhere out of earshot of the others and talk things over."

Wenatef shrugged. "That's fine," he said. "I have some figs and some meat left over from last night's supper."

They pooled their provisions, located a shady spot among the rocks along the hillside, and sat down to eat. They were silent for a time as they took the edge from their appetites.

Dhutmose finally sat back, wiped his mouth with the back of his hand, and said, "Have you spoken with Tamit since the day Merihor was found?"

Wenatef nodded. "I gave her the news that first day, and stayed with her for a time, until her family came. Since then we've had words as well - but only to say hello and ask how she was doing."

"Poor woman," Duwah said. "To lose a baby and a husband within three months. Poor woman."

"I believe it is universally agreed that Tamit is unfortunate," Wenatef said.

"And you're still making inquiries into of Merihor's

death," Dhutmose said.

"No," Wenatef said.

"What? But you've spoken to Thutiy since then."

"Thutiy happens to be a friend."

Duwah spoke with an odd intentness. "It was a singular lion that killed Merihor, but I've seen several such." He was not smiling. He drank from their skin of wine and then said, "Wenatef, let me speak plainly - "

Wenatef slapped his thigh in exaggerated astonishment. "Ye gods of Egypt!" he cried. "A miracle! Duwah - the architect Duwah, mind you, not the goatherd who lies half the day in a drunken stupor - is about to speak plainly!" He folded his arms and flashed an ironic smile at Duwah. "Speak, then - speak plainly and astonish us all!"

Dhutmose's mouth was showing signs of a quiver. He forestalled it by biting into an onion and chewing loudly.

Duwah shot Wenatef a look of annoyance, but tried to continue. "You've asked some questions that have disturbed some people. Wenatef, there are evil folk in the world."

"You're treating me like an idiot!" Wenatef complained. "We've already discussed this. I'm doing nothing further."

Duwah nodded after a moment, then his face cleared. "Promise me one thing, Weni," he said, getting to his feet. "Promise me that you'll be careful. There is hidden danger to - to many, as Dhutmose has said."

"Of course," Wenatef said with a smile. He started to make a comment about the progress of the carvings when he was interrupted by a shriek of fear and pain, the thud of something heavy striking the ground and then the clatter of loose stones and sand.

Dhutmose and Duwah exchanged surprised looks and ran to the entrance with Wenatef right behind them.

A man lay at the base of the cliff half-covered with scree and dust. His leg was twisted and bloody and he was moaning and thrashing from side to side. The dust darkened to mud where it clung to his damp flesh.

"Merciful Amun!" gasped Duwah, falling to his knees beside the man. "What happened?"

Harmose came forward. "He was loafing," he said. "Runs in his family, as Dhutmose knows. He heard me coming, woke from a sound sleep up there among the rocks above the doorway, where he thought I couldn't see him, the jackass! - lost his balance, and fell." He spoke with a mixture of concern and affectionate annoyance. "Anpu, can you hear me? Does it hurt?"

The injured man groaned and opened his eyes and announced to everyone that he was dying.

"Don't be a fool!" snapped Dhutmose, bending over him. "Wiggle your toes."

Anpu obeyed.

"There," said Dhutmose. "You aren't hurt badly at all, though I think your leg - "

Anpu screamed as Dhutmose touched his ankle. "You're killing me!"

"Shut up, you son of an ass!" snapped the foreman. "Hold still! You only have yourself to blame!"

Wenatef squelched a smile. From what he could see, Anpu had a badly sprained leg with a few cuts. He was milking his pain for all it was worth, but he would be unable to walk back to Deir el Medineh in his present state. He shook his head and went back to his chariot.

The horses nickered as he approached, and Brightfoot, who was a special pet, lipped at his shoulder. He patted the glossy, curved neck and led the team back toward Anpu and all the would-be helpers. Anpu could ride the chariot, but he'd need someone to steady him and another to guide the horses.

The workmen were still clustered around him, laughing and offering advice. Wenatef looked up at the sky. Stars were beginning to appear, and the moon was rising on the eastern horizon, three-quarters full and red as the seeds of a pomegranate. Everything was beautifully serene, in sharp contrast to the shouting and wailing behind him.

Wenatef took a deep breath and led his horses back to the throng. "Take Anpu back with you to the town?" he said. "It's close to quitting time now, anyhow. You can explain to his wife, then, and you can take him directly to Master Imhotep."

They decided that Duwah would drive and go with the foreman. All further work on the Tomb was called off for that evening, and the men went home with Dhutmose at their head.

The Scribe held back to speak to Wenatef for a moment. "You'll be coming with us, won't you?" he asked anxiously, looking around at the quiet valley.

Wenatef smiled. "Of course not," he said. "I want to watch the sunset, and I'll get a good view from the hills. I was planning to do it, you know, whether or not I was driving back to the village. I've done it before. Don't worry. I'll be safe."

"You'll be careful, won't you?"

Wenatef laughed at him. "I don't plan to go nosing about tombs at nightfall, Dhutmose!" he said. "Don't worry. I'm not looking for trouble. It's been some time since I watched the sun set from the hills. Go home. I'll be fine."

Dhutmose still looked doubtful. "I don't want you facing the tribunal of gods before your time," he said, half under his breath. Then he shook his head and smiled. "I don't know why I said that," he said. "Be careful in this valley after dark. That is all."

He joined his men, and they headed off down the path to the village, laughing and chattering. A couple of workmen turned back to call farewells to Wenatef, and Dhutmose cupped his hands about his mouth and called, "Be careful!"

Wenatef waved and turned away, and the sounds ceased as though they had been cut off and he was entering the realms of silence, and everything was lost in the radiance of the sky.

A Killing Among the Dead

** ** **

The sun fell away toward the horizon, dipped lower and was slowly swallowed, and the sky darkened from pink to rose to purple with flecks of brilliance scattered through it like jewels flung by a lavish hand.

Wenatef watched from the heights, sitting motionless, his arms about his knees, heedless of the passing time. It was as though he was sitting on the borders of the Land of the West, and he only needed to step down to enter it.

The words of an ancient song came to him:

I have heard the old songs inscribed in the tombs,
How they praise life on this earth
And mock the region of the dead.
But why do they say this
About the land of Eternity,
So just and fair,
Where fear is not?
There is no more strife there,
Nor does any there take arms against his fellow.
That far, fair land so free of enemies!
All our kinsmen from the earliest days of time rest there.
The uncounted millions come there, every one.
For none may linger in the land of Egypt;
There is none who does not pass there.
The span of our earthly deeds is as fleeting as a dream;
But fair will be the welcome that awaits him
Who reaches the hills of the west.

CHAPTER XVII

Wenatef closed his eyes and opened them again. The sky was completely dark. How long had he been sitting there? He looked up at the path of stars glittering across the zenith of the sky, at the Bull's Head, which had risen. Near midnight, then.

He pushed to his feet, cursing under his breath. He had been caught in a daydream, and now the Valley was growing cold, and the long walk to Deir el Medineh lay ahead of him. But then he smiled. The night was bright and peaceful. He would not mind the walk. He cast about for the path to the town, then shrugged. It would be pleasant to follow the line of the hills edging the Valley and rest a few minutes more in the serene silence.

He began to walk, looking up at the stars and the moon and then down at the stones that clustered about his feet, outlined in silver with the touch of a master scribe. He spared an amused thought for his horses, snug in their stable by now, and then he thought with more urgency about supper. His stomach, clearly, was not a citizen of the Silent Lands, where want did not exist.

He caught a sudden faint glow of torchlight in the dark hills beyond a cluster of rocks. He moved closer to the light, peering at the group of men standing in the light of one torch and speaking agitatedly. A search party? He could see other torches in the distance, but surely no one would stray this far across the Nile and into the desert!

He frowned and looked more closely. Many men, and he

could hear the sound of implements against stone. Tomb robbers!

He hesitated as he tried to decide what to do. His bow and arrows were with his chariot - the more fool he for leaving them there! - and while the spare bowstrings in the pouch at his belt could serve as garrotes in a pinch, they weren't much good for anything else. He did not even have a knife. Best to get away with his skin in one piece, but then woe to those robbers! He had encountered the evil now, and he would fight it as long as he could!

He took a step backward. Rough hands seized and pinioned him. One clamped hard over his mouth.

Someone called to a man named Ipuky while another informed Wenatef that he would be food for crocodiles if he moved.

A man with a torch came up to them and looked Wenatef over. He was past middle age, with a grim face that reminded Wenatef of the old scribe-priest he had once studied under with Duwah, one who had enjoyed beating those children he had been assigned to teach.

"We found him spying on us, Ipuky," said one of the men, twisting Wenatef's arms more tightly behind him. The man named Ipuky hooked a finger about the thong circling Wenatef's neck and pulled the Gold of Honor up. "Hm," he said. "I think I know who he is, but we can have that confirmed later." He let the golden pendant fall.

"Are you going to take that?" one of the men asked.

"No. Leave it on him for now. There's someone who'll want to see it."

"Don't we kill him, then?" asked the man whose none-too-clean hand was clenched over Wenatef's mouth. "They'll be after us for certain then, especially after that last killing."

Wenatef closed his eyes. Merihor.

"He's seen too much," the leader, Ipuky, said, "But there may be others with him. Let him go a moment, Khai. I want to question him. The rest of you, tie him securely - what's that at his belt? Bowstrings? An archer! I do know who you are, my lad. Use those bowstrings to tie him, and make sure you do it right."

This was done as Ipuky watched, his hand on a knife.

"Let him go now," he said, and watched as they released Wenatef. "Now, archer. Who is with you?"

Wenatef shook his head. If he told them he was alone, they would not believe him. And even if they did, then they would kill him out of hand. But if they thought they could get some information from him, then he might have a chance to escape later.

Ipuky brought the knife to Wenatef's throat and pushed. "I'll ask again," he said. "Who in the Tomb Guard is aware of this? Or the Necropolis Police? Or the Theban Guard?"

"I will tell you nothing, robber," Wenatef said.

The men holding him gripped more tightly and the knife dug deeper into his flesh.

"You'll find it much more pleasant to tell me," Ipuky said.

Wenatef shook his head. "I'm not telling you anything, robber," he said, "except that if you release me now and turn yourself in to the courts of the Mayor of Thebes, I'll do what I can to help you. Ignore what I say and your lives will be short and your hereafter as well. Can you face the Devourer of Souls? I thi-"

Ipuky's hand cracked across Wenatef's mouth, knocking him sideways to his knees and making the night reel around him. He blinked to clear his vision after a moment. The other men were pale and wide-eyed; Wenatef had touched them on a raw spot. But by the narrow blaze of Ipuky's stare, Wenatef judged it time to waver if he wanted to live.

Just then two men appeared, shouting with excitement. "We've almost broken through!" one of them cried.

A Killing Among the Dead

Ipuky looked at the man and then at Wenatef. "Right," he said. "This one can wait. We're running out of time, and the people from Bubastis -"

He didn't finish the sentence, but it was enough to alarm Wenatef. Ipuky continued, "Tie his feet and gag him. I'll question him later. Someone can stay with him. Keep an eye on him. As for you - " He turned to Wenatef, "I'll finish with you later." He watched as Wenatef was gagged with a strip of linen and then thrown down on the ground and his feet tied as well. Then he left.

Wenatef waited until the man had gone and then half raised himself to look around. A leather-shod foot slammed into his shoulder and pushed him back against the ground. He looked up past the sandal, along a foreshortened leg, and up to a face that was terribly familiar.

"Why, it's Hapuseneb's son, the hero of the armies," said Unas, leaning all his weight upon his foot. "You ordered me out of your territory: but now you're in mine. Maybe they'll let me have you when they're finished with you."

He watched Wenatef's expression and then reached for his knife and drew it with almost sensual slowness. "You wanted to know what Merihor saw," he said. "They say curiosity killed the cat. In my world it is the cat that kills the curious... But you'll see."

He set the point of the knife at Wenatef's collarbone, lightly, so that he could feel the sharpness of the blade, and then slowly drew the point down along Wenatef's breastbone to his waist. "A little more pressure," he said, suiting actions to words, "And you would be laid open from neck to navel."

The slight movement of the knife had drawn blood. Unas watched it for a moment with a smile, his eyes heavy-lidded in the torchlight, before he bent forward, touched the thread of blood with a fingertip, and then raised his finger to his mouth and slowly licked the blood off. "Sweet," he said.

"Like the taste of revenge."

Wenatef made a convulsive movement, which he tried to still.

"Did I frighten you, son of Hapuseneb?" Unas purred. "Heroes are never afraid - are they?"

"We've broken through!" shouted a man behind them. He was carrying a small bronze statuette, mounted with gold. He came to a halt and furtively licked his lips when he saw that he was speaking to Unas.

Unas rose to his feet. "Right," he said, his voice changed from the low, almost throbbing purr it had been. "Get the gold off that - " he nodded to the figurine, " - and keep an eye on him, Khai. As for you -" he turned back to Wenatef. "- I'll finish with you later."

He wiped his knife on Wenatef's kilt and then hurried off toward the rest of the gang.

** ** **

Wenatef watched for some hours as the thieves brought their plunder from the tomb. They stripped the gold away from the base parts and tossed it into a heap. They seemed to take special pleasure in mutilating the figures.

Khai, his guard, noticed his intent gaze. The man rose to his feet, sauntered over to Wenatef, bent casually over him, and struck him back-handed across the face, drawing blood. He laughed, struck again, and then sat squarely before Wenatef, his back blocking out all view of the thieves.

Wenatef was lost in pain and dizziness for some minutes. Khai's back was still blocking his view when he finally came to himself and lifted his head., but that blocked their view of him as well.

He had noticed, when they tied him, that they had knotted a strip of cloth about his ankles instead of his bowstrings. The knot was within reach of his fingers, and he thought that if he could only get his feet free and make his way into the desert, even with bound hands, he had a chance of getting back to Dhutmose, stopping the thieves and saving his own life.

He stretched his hands down to his ankles, praying that his position would not be too contorted and attract any of the thieves' attention, and that his guard, who seemed more engrossed in eyeing the growing pile of gold than in guarding him, would not notice.

His prayers were answered, and after what felt like hours but was probably closer to twenty minutes, his ankles were free. Now to get away...

That took longer, because Khai kept glancing his way and smiling ominously. Wenatef lay quietly and finally closed his eyes, as though the blows to his head had made him lose consciousness.

It worked. Khai grunted, got to his feet, and went to the shaft lancing into the tomb. Some coarse conversation ensued and he finally descended into the tomb.

Wenatef sat up, slowly rolled to his feet, and made his way into the hills. His shoulders ached, his hands and wrists were numb and the gag was choking him and cutting the corner of his mouth, but those were minor worries compared to the problem of getting as far away from the thieves as he possibly could.

CHAPTER XVIII

The Valley of the Kings is set within high cliffs, with the tombs dug into the hillsides. Since the thieves were working just behind the crest of a ridge to avoid being seen by anyone below, Wenatef decided to go into the valley itself. He had to head north in order to catch the main path to Deir el Medineh, though he knew that he could cut southwest across the hills and join the path that way. It would save time, but there was the chance that he might run across more thieves. He chose the longer way.

It was nearly impossible to pick his way down the steep sides with his hands lashed tightly behind him, half-choked by the gag. He stopped, staggering, and looked behind him. No sign that they had missed him yet, but he knew it was a matter of time.

He took a step, skidded, and tumbled in a mad scrabbling of loose rocks and sand. He landed on his side, bruised and winded, but otherwise unhurt. The fall had been a blessing in a way, he decided, climbing to his feet and trying to catch his breath. Breathing through the gag was difficult, though, and he had to stand perfectly still for a moment, even as he heard the sounds of pursuit in the distance.

He looked over his shoulder. Were they close? He didn't think so. He took another deep breath through the gag and turned his attention to the bite of the ropes at his wrists.

Ipuky had used Wenatef's own sinew bowstrings, and long experience had taught Wenatef that they were almost unbreakable. If the Nile could pour from the sky, or if he could find a convenient jar of water, he could soak the cords and maybe work them loose... The next choice was to find a sharp stone, but all rocks looked alike in the moonlight and Wenatef did not have time to rub the bowstrings through. He cursed through the gag, a full-hearted, pungent curse upon all evil men and evil chances and all people skilled with knots and all animals that supplied tendon for bowstrings. And then, despairing, he wrenched at the cords.

They parted with a dry snap, like breaking wood.

Wenatef tore the gag from his mouth and stared at the broken bowstrings. What had they been, then? Single strands of dried grass? He knew himself to be strong from years of drawing powerful bows, but certainly not strong enough to break a bowstring by himself! Not unless the bowstring had frayed or somehow become damp and rotted. But Wenatef was an archer of skill and pride, and he kept his equipment in perfect condition.

He heard a shout behind him. He dragged air deep into his lungs and took to his heels, running as he had never run before, blindly headlong, praying that his pursuers were not wise enough to try to fan out and trap him.

He stumbled, fell sprawling among the sharp-sided rocks and scrambled to his feet after a moment of sickening pain. He could feel a warm tide of blood flowing down his shoulder and knew that he would weaken if he couldn't dodge his pursuers. He spared a second to peer over his shoulder in the moonlight, but he could see nothing.

He took a deep, sobbing breath, and ran once more.

** ** **

Later, he could never remember how long he had been running, whether it was hours or only minutes filled with the throat-catching, tearing fear of the pursued creature trying to evade its hunters and fighting the strange urge to surrender to them. His breath tore through his chest; his heart seemed

91

to hammer until his body was filled with its pounding.

The desert of the Necropolis seemed to stretch endlessly before him even as he felt the strength draining from his body with his blood. He was almost spent; he came to a fork in the path, wavered, and started down one of the branches.

A rock-hard, powerful hand gripped his arm. His knees buckled and he sagged against a strong body, sobbing for breath, numbly aware that he had been captured again.

But he was hoisted to his feet and steadied, and after a moment he was able to look up at the man who bent over him. The face was shadowed, but the moon glinted from gold about his neck and his arms. A faint, fresh scent clung to him, as though he had been walking among lotus blooms, or through fields of sweet herbs.

Your way lies there, the man said, pointing toward the other branch. *Go now. You will be safe.* His voice seemed to come from far away.

And then he was not there.

Wenatef would wonder, later, if the man had been only a dream born of exhaustion and fear. He found new strength, though, enough to enable him to run again. And then, suddenly, buildings loomed to either side. He had reached Deir el Medineh.

He reeled and half-collapsed against the nearest wall, rested for a moment, then pushed himself away and groped along the wall, seeking a doorway, somewhere to be safe.

He looked back toward the approaches to the village, his thoughts veering between despair and hope. He didn't hear the door open beside him. Someone took his arm and pulled him inside. He heard words but could not understand them.

He tried to speak but his voice was thin and gasping, the words taking second place to the urgent need for breath. "- After me - from the tombs - dangerous -"

A voice spoke to him, but the pounding of his heart drowned out the words. He heard another voice, sharp and commanding. The first voice answered; he could hear anger.

His shoulders were circled by strong arms. He slumped against a slight, dry body, and then crumpled to the ground, gasping.

He was pushed to a sitting position. "You'll have time to catch your breath," he heard the first voice say, and his head was pushed downward against his knees. His vision cleared after a moment, and he was able to look up and speak with less difficulty.

Thutiy was bending over him, his face even more shriveled by the light of a single oil lamp. His son and grandson were behind him. They both seemed disheveled and winded, their white in the lamplight.

Wenatef shook his head. He did not want this old man to get into trouble. "Tomb Robbers," he said. "I came across them on my way home from the Tomb. I escaped just now. They're after me, close behind. If I can get away -"

"They'll be chasing you in relays," Thutiy said, throwing an unreadable look at Nebo and Ipy. "You'll have to lose them here."

"But I'm in the town -" Wenatef protested.

"They'll think nothing of coming in after you," Thutiy said. "You'll have to hide for a few minutes. Nebo - Ipy -" he raised his voice, "Bring sacks of natron from the storerooms. "You -" he shook Wenatef's shoulder, " - are you better now? You're wounded and bloody, but I'll tend that later. We'll cover you with rags. There's a tub in the embalming room that'll serve very well. Wrap these rags around your head and face when you lie down, and try to keep perfectly still."

Wenatef followed him into the embalming room, looked at the large clay tubs lying side by side with the corpses just visible beneath the natron. There was one empty tub, and Thutiy told him to lie down in that one. Nebo and Ipy came in then with armloads of cloth.

"Cover him up," said Thutiy. "I'll let you know when it's safe."

Wenatef nodded, and then lay still as the two men piled the cloths over him. They were soft and cool, like the soft earth beside the river, with a scent of sun and wind. All sound was suddenly muffled, and he was immobilized. He felt as though he were in the middle of a beautiful dream of coolness and rest after the panic and exhaustion of the night.

The past and the present blurred... He was at Semna in Nubia again, the only surviving officer in the besieged fortress. They had repulsed wave after wave of attacks for over a month, despairing of rescue and, when that rescue finally came, almost too numb with exhaustion to recognize it. There had been a moment when, standing on the high ramparts of the great fort with his men around him, reeling with fatigue, praying for the Army of Upper Egypt to arrive, Wenatef had felt the moment stretch into eternity.

He would always be like this, he had thought, fighting endlessly without hope of rescue, awaiting death and continuing the battle only because it was right to resist the rebels and wrong to capitulate, and death had to be endured if it was the price of steadfastness and loyalty.

And then the Army of Upper Egypt had come with the dawn, smashing through the besiegers, shattering their despair like the sun's first rays bursting through the blackness of night. The siege had been lifted, the rebellion quelled, and Wenatef had been awarded the Gold of Honor for heroism.

"What is heroic about performing my duty?" Wenatef murmured as hands patted his shoulder in congratulations and the warm old walls of Semna took on the glow of dawn...

"You can sit up now, Commander," a voice said as the glow faded to blackness. Wenatef had been dreaming. He opened his eyes to darkness and fleeting panic, then he remembered. Thutiy's workshop.

He pushed himself to a sitting position as rags cascaded from his shoulders and slid down his chest. He lay back against the edge of the tub overcome with dizziness.

"We'll tend to you now," Thutiy said from above him. "How badly are you hurt?"

Wenatef slowly got to his feet.

"Nebo is preparing a bath for you in the back room," Thutiy said. "What's this blood from?"

Wenatef looked. In addition to the long, thin cut inflicted by Unas, a gash ran down his upper arm from his shoulder. Another scored his ribs. Stone cuts from his second fall. They were still bleeding freely. Now that the danger was past he felt them.

Thutiy poured some wine into his palm and gently washed the gashes with it. His touch was as deft as a physician's.

"I can tend those when I get home," Wenatef said. "I'm only endangering you."

Thutiy gave a derisive snort and caught Wenatef as he stumbled over the edge of the tub. "There," he said. "Now that the danger is past you feel your hurts. Relax for a moment. You can wash off the sweat and blood. I have beer and bread and cheese for you. Poor lad! Look at your wrists! Were you tied, then?"

Wenatef looked down at his wrists. They were badly torn, the flesh purple with bruising. Had the bowstrings done that? He thought they had snapped like dried grass. The cuts certainly hurt now.

"Out with you," Thutiy said. "You can bathe and then we'll dress your wounds in an inner room."

** ** **

"I interrupted a tomb robbery," Wenatef said as Nebo and

Ipy tended his hurts. "I was walking home late after enjoying the sunset and the moonrise from a hill near His Majesty's tomb. My chariot had been taken back earlier - there had been an accident... Anyhow, I interrupted the robbers - I thought they were a search party - and I was foolish enough to pause and take a closer look. I escaped through sheer luck, and I don't know how I managed to break the bowstrings they tied me with. I ran here. I - I think I was too tired to even know where I was going..."

"You were almost dead of exhaustion," Thutiy said. He looked up at his son and grandson. "Bring food and then leave us."

This was done, and Wenatef busied himself with devouring two small, flat loaves of bread, a bowl of raisins, and some beer and cheese. Thutiy watched him eat, expressionless in the lamplight. When Wenatef had finished he said, "Now tell me what you found: Tomb robbers? Where?"

"I don't know for certain," Wenatef said. "I could probably find the place again. It was near the tomb of Thutmose IV, I think, but I can't swear to it. They had dug directly down into the chambers. Their knowledge of the site must have been very precise."

"You saw them go in and come out, then?"

"Yes. They lowered themselves using ropes, and they brought the treasures up in baskets. The gold was torn off and tossed into a pile. I don't know what they did with the base parts. Buried them, I suppose. I don't know. But they -
"

"Did you see any of these robbers? Would you know them again if you did?"

"I saw two or three of them, as well as Unas," Wenatef answered, frowning with the effort of remembering. "There were a lot of them, and they were organized. I wonder... One of them was named Ipuky, I recall. And there was one named Khai -"

Thutiy looked thoughtful. "What were they planning to do with you?" he asked.

Wenatef lowered his head. He was beginning to shake. "Question me and then kill me," he said. "Unas wanted to do the honors. They thought there were others with me investigating them. I didn't contradict them."

"Are there?" Thutiy asked, leaning forward.

"There may be," Wenatef answered. "I don't know. I told you: I stumbled across them. I guard His Majesty's tomb while it's being constructed. There are others whose job is to stop robbers. But I didn't dare tell them that. They would have killed me out of hand and tossed my body in the desert, the victim of another 'lion'."

Thutiy nodded. "You were wise," he said. "It's dangerous for you to remain here. Leave Thebes. You told me once that you longed for other lands. There is nothing for you here, you said so yourself. The only thing awaiting you here is your death. I'll give you gold and silver enough to take you there. It'll be a gift; I am your friend, after all. But go."

Wenatef shook his head. "I can't accept it," he said. "Now that I've put my foot in this, I can't leave until it is stopped. I'll stay here if it means my death."

Thutiy's fists clenched. "Why should you be killed defending the property of long-dead kings from their living, starving subjects?" he demanded. "Who would your death benefit? His inept Majesty, who pens love poems in Memphis and is undeserving of the loyalty of a pet monkey, much less the death of a hero such as you?"

Wenatef smiled in spite of his fatigue and the pain of his injuries. "His Majesty is my King," he said. "I am sworn to serve him."

"Folly!" Thutiy snapped, "We have no king, our only

97

crops are ignorance and strife. When Pharaoh dies the lands will split apart and Egypt will be no more! There are monsters abroad, men twisted by greed and hunger to the point of sacrilege, willing to kill all in their way, like dogs quarreling atop a heap of offal! And you would set your precious life between them and the trash that lies beneath the ground! Nothing is worth that sacrifice!"

"I think it is," Wenatef sighed, pushing himself to his feet and biting off a gasp of pain as the gashes on shoulder and ribs were stretched and broken by the motion.

The almost inaudible sound stopped Thutiy in mid-spate. The old man gazed at Wenatef for a long time before he lowered his eyes at last and spoke more gently. "You don't know what you're saying," he said. "Consider my offer tonight. Come to me in the morning and we'll discuss it further. But I say this: leave this alone. Leave this land. Send a message to the Vizier - I'll deliver it myself - but leave the country. Please. Don't give them a chance to kill you."

Wenatef looked down at the remains of the loaf of bread in his hand.

Thutiy set a gentle hand on his unwounded shoulder. "Think about what I've said," he told him. "I would say nothing different to my son or my grandson. I would tell them to stay away from this, to send a letter perhaps, but to leave the city. I would say that they would be killed if they became involved in this. Think about it. Tell me your decision tomorrow."

CHAPTER XIX

"No, I can't believe it!" Thutiy exclaimed the next morning. "It is folly! You're stepping into the most dangerous situation of your life - and it may be the last! Nothing but evil can come of it!"

Wenatef merely looked down at the golden lion's head on its thong about his neck. Gold of Honor, won at Semna. What could be more deadly than that lonely fight in Nubia against overwhelming odds?

Thutiy's brows drove together. "I am serious!" he snapped. "You're merely carving your own tomb if you remain here!" His voice gentled, became pleading. "Do as I suggest. Write the letter of warning. I'll take it for you. I am not a poor man. See: here is the silver and the gold. Take it for my sake and the sakes of all who love you."

"Save your breath, Master Thutiy," Wenatef said. "I'm a man of wealth, too. I can't ignore this."

"You're a fool!" Thutiy exclaimed. "You have courage - have you thought that it would be improved by the addition of a little sense? Listen: if you don't leave this place and go far away, you will die."

Wenatef frowned. He could have died fighting the Tjehenu the past week. How could facing an organized gang of tomb-robbers be any more dangerous if he went against them with allies? He said so.

It brought Thutiy up short. "No!" he exclaimed. "I know what I am saying. I have seen..."

He stopped as though choosing his words very, very carefully. "I've seen what you have seen. I have. You are lost if you ignore me. This isn't a threat. You will die." He leaned forward, his bright eyes fastened on Wenatef's, his thin hands clenched like the claws of a bird.

But Wenatef only smiled again. "Is that supposed to frighten me? Isn't it better, when I face the Scales of Judgment to be able to say, 'I haven't turned aside from good' than to admit that I turned and ran the first time I encountered a criminal? I'll stay here and do what I can. I am not descended from a line of cowards who shout warnings over their shoulders as they flee. Criminals must be fought. I'm sorry, Thutiy. I can do no less."

Thutiy stared long into Wenatef's eyes. Finally he lowered his gaze and sighed, and touched Wenatef's shoulder. "I expected nothing less from you," he said, "But I had so hoped..."

His hand was on the cuts from the night before; Wenatef flinched.

"You still hurt," the old man said in a different voice. "Take off that shirt and let me put fresh ointment on these, and a clean, sturdy bandage to protect them..."

Ipy came into the room and looked inquiringly at Thutiy.

Thutiy looked up from gently dabbing ointment on Wenatef's shoulder. "The Commander will be going to the stables, son," he said. "Go before him and take his bow. It'll be one less thing he'll have to carry with his injuries. Oh, it's with your chariot now?" He looked at Wenatef with raised eyebrows. "So much the better. Have them make the chariot ready, Ipy. I'll tend his hurts for him."

"It isn't necessary," Wenatef said, shrugging off Thutiy's hand. "A little sun won't harm me, and these aren't severe enough to kill me. You've done enough for me already, and I have much to do, quickly." He meant the words, but the coolness of the balm against his shoulder and side was soothing, and he closed his eyes.

Thutiy's smile was wry, though Wenatef could not see it. "A little sun won't harm you - though it won't help either. But a little sand, a few flies, being torn afresh - all these can lead to an infection, which could kill you. You need a good, firm bandage. Humor an old man who cares for you and doesn't want you to be hurt more than necessary. I'll tend these another day or two. It would ease my mind."

Wenatef nodded and opened his eyes to smile up at Thutiy.

The old man smiled back at him and, surprisingly, bent to kiss his forehead before turning to his son. "Good," he said. "Ipy, go to the stables and have them harness Commander Wenatef's horses. Then you and I must do an inventory of our spices this morning, so come straight back after you've done what is necessary. I'll be finished by then."

Ipy left. Wenatef had been disturbed by his expression, which had seemed almost vicious. But Thutiy's ministrations were soothing; he was almost lulled to sleep, and only Ipy's return saved him from that.

He rose, thanked Thutiy, promised to return when he could, listened patiently to Thutiy's pleas that he be careful, assured the old man that he would, and left, making sure that no one had seen him leave Thutiy's establishment.

CHAPTER XX

Wenatef had learned long before that the best way to seem like a fugitive was to look furtive. He walked boldly down the main street of the town on his way to the stables, pausing to smile at a pretty girl who was watching him from beneath her lashes.

She smiled back at him, her cheeks blushing a more delightful pink. Wenatef would ordinarily have paused for a little pleasant flirtation, but he had too much to consider at the moment, so he bade her good morning and, suddenly decisive, turned away from the stables and headed down the main street toward Dhutmose's house.

He had slept very little since leaving Thutiy's house, spending the few hours before dawn weighing his choices. This was what had so horrified Merihor, and had occupied the minds of the captains of the village ever since. This was the fear that no one had wanted to discuss openly: wholesale, organized robbery in the necropolis, possibly involving members of Deir el Medineh itself.

What should he do? If the two Foremen, the Scribe of the Village, and His Majesty's Architect were afraid to proceed openly, then they must fear that the scandal reached into the clerical hierarchy - wasn't Nuteruhotep responsible for the presence of Unas and Roy in the Necropolis Police? And could it even reach to Herihor himself?

Perhaps. They certainly had more to fear than Wenatef, who did not move in the same circles as them. As an officer high in His Majesty's service, he could bring pressure to bear from places the others could not touch.

His eyes narrowed. As his father's son, he had an old score to settle with Lord Nuteruhotep. As a start, he could swear out a warrant for the arrest of Nuteruhotep's nephew, Unas, and serve as a witness against the robbers. It would be a beginning, and it might be enough to mire Nuteruhotep.

But first he had to speak with Dhutmose.

He had reached Dhutmose's door. He rapped on the wooden panel and reflected that he was doing the wisest thing possible. It was late in the morning. Duwah, Khons and probably Harmose were already at the Tomb. Dhutmose had told Wenatef that he would be taking care of some village concerns that day. Wenatef could tell him what he had seen, discuss what to do, and then go to the Tomb and speak to the others.

There was no answer. He knocked again and waited. The door was opened after a moment by Hemshire, Dhutmose's pretty young second wife. She smiled at him, invited him within the house, and closed the door after him. Baketamun, Dhutmose's eldest daughter, heavy with her first child, greeted him from her chair, where she sat embroidering fine linen.

Dhutmose was at Karnak that day, speaking with Herihor on the question of his tomb. He would be back late that evening. Baketamun regretted that Wenatef had missed him, but if he wished to leave a message, she would make certain that Dhutmose received it.

Wenatef nodded. Lady Hemshire left and returned with a smooth flake of limestone, brush, and ink. Wenatef considered for a moment, dipped the brush in the ink, and wrote swiftly:

> *I have some disturbing news that I must*
> *discuss with you and the others. It can't wait.*

If you return before sunset, go to the tomb. If not, then come to my home this evening. I think you will agree that this matter is of the gravest importance. It is dangerous for me to say anything further.

He signed the flake of limestone, waited until the ink was dry, and then handed it to Hemshire. "Please see that Dhutmose receives this at once," he said.

The lady Baketamun nodded. "We will do so," she said. She frowned on the bandages on Wenatef's wrists and then raised her dark eyes to his face. "You seem tired and troubled, Commander. Rest here a while - we have freshly baked cakes and fresh milk."

The room was cool and dim, filled with the light scent of musk and the heartier smell of scrupulously washed and ironed linen. The two ladies were pretty and charming, and Wenatef had often enjoyed their company when he was with Dhutmose.

Wenatef refused politely, though he would have liked to return to his own home and sleep. But he had to speak to Duwah yet, and Duwah, Harmose and Khons were at the Tomb. He took his leave of the two ladies and headed back toward the stables, cursing himself.

A bad fate was upon him this day. He should have gone to Dhutmose at once instead of lingering at Thutiy's home and arguing with the old man.

He lifted his chin and considered and then, suddenly decisive, turned back toward the stables. It was not too late to speak to Dhutmose. He only needed to head to Karnak. He was well known there after the skirmishes with the Tjehenu, and he counted Taharka, the Commander of the Temple Guard, as a friend. If Dhutmose was anywhere near Karnak, Taharka would know it.

The weight of uncertainty lifted from his heart and he

approached the stable with an almost jaunty step, bidding good morning to the women returning from the ovens with their day's baking of bread, nodding to an old man sitting in a doorway and sketching on a flake of limestone, and smiling once more at the pretty girl who still lingered in the street.

He was at the doorway of the stable when he realized that he had forgotten his driving whip. He hesitated, debating whether he should go back to his house to fetch it, and then finally shrugged. Brightfoot and Swift needed no whip.

He entered the stable, took two steps into the darkness, and suddenly stopped, his heart pounding. Danger.

He spun around to see Unas behind him, his face twisted with exultation as he seized Wenatef's arm. There was no time to shout for help and no one to come to his aid. Wenatef had a dagger and knew how to use it. He whipped it from its sheath and brought it arcing up toward Unas' ribcage.

The Guard officer arched away from the blade, gasping a curse, and Wenatef took advantage of his shifted weight to pivot on his heel, making himself the axis of a circle, slamming Unas against the wall and shaking off his grip.

He was facing the door, his back to the shadows that were suddenly alive with desperate motion. He spun around to face it and turned directly into a crashing blow to his skull that sent him spinning down into darkness and silence.

CHAPTER XXI

Wenatef opened his eyes to darkness and a silence so intense that it was stronger than any noise, stronger even than the pounding agony in his head. He drew a slow breath, the sobbing intake of air loud in the stillness. Another breath, whimpering with pain and the sudden fear that he was blind. But that fear faded. The darkness was outside him, not within his eyes.

He lifted his head from the floor and then lay back again. He was bound hand and foot; the cords were well tied and thick. A rope was cinched about his upper arms and chest, as well. They were taking no further chances with him.

…Where was he?

It was colder than a house would be, the silence so intense he could almost feel it. He was in the hills, probably in a tomb. The air was heavy with myrrh; he was in a burial chamber.

He struggled to a sitting position, shivering. The effort made him dizzy, and he doubled against his knees, gasping with the sudden, tearing pain that lanced through his left side, bringing the taste of blood to his lips. A wave of weakness washed over him and ebbed.

Merciful Amun! He thought. *I am dying!*

His time was short. He refused to die like this, tied like a steer for slaughter. At least he could meet his end with his back to a wall.

He pushed his way across the floor, knocking jars aside, the clatter of their fall muffled by the tomb's silence. His shoulder struck something cold, square and sharp. The base of a statue, probably a king's. Well, then. He would die at the feet of a king.

It took every ounce of his fading strength to haul himself up on the plinth. He groped behind him with his bound hands and located the statue's feet. They were side by side - a seated statue. He could feel the block that served as the statue's seat.

Wenatef collapsed against the carved legs and stared into the darkness that seemed to be closing about him. He swallowed – the taste of blood was stronger. He was not prepared for the dreadful mystery of death that loomed before him in all its bitter loneliness.

A terrible lassitude was stealing along his limbs, weighting his eyelids, slowing the beat of his heart, drawing him inexorably down into the dark, drugged sleep that would finally end his stay beneath the warm sun of Egypt and cause him to awaken in the West, the realm of the dead.

So just and fair, the words came unexpectedly. *Where fear is not...*

Where fear is not.

His lips moved stiffly as he whispered with the last of his strength,

The span of our earthly deeds is as fleeting as a dream;
But fair will be the welcome that awaits him
Who reaches the hills of the west...

** ** **

...He stood before doors of dark wood that swung inward as he gazed, revealing a sight that chilled him to the bone. He was at the end of a long hallway lined with cloaked, motionless figures. Between the two rows stood a large scale flanked by two indistinct figures, one of them seeming an amalgam of monsters - crocodile, lion, hippopotamus - and

107

the other with the long, thin neck and curved beak of an ibis. Thoth and the Eater of Shades.

Wenatef stepped forward; the doors swung softly shut behind him.

CHAPTER XXII

Wenatef's father had purchased a beautiful and very costly scroll titled *The Book of Coming Forth by Day*, a compilation of the prayers and spells necessary to allow the possessor to journey safely through the lands of the dead until the Judgment Hall of the West was reached.

Wenatef had been allowed to read through the scroll, and at the end of the beautifully illustrated book had been an account of the weighing of the heart and a depiction of the Judgment Hall, showing the gods lining the hallway that led to the scales, with Osiris waiting to judge and Thoth waiting to record the results.

Wenatef had smiled when he read the account of the judgment. He had scanned the forty-two denials, compared them with his own life, and smiled again. He tried not to tip the scales unjustly. He had never murdered, and he would have starved rather than steal from others. Travelers suffered no ill at his hands, and he had a great sympathy for the homeless, having so often been a traveler. Surely, he had thought, the gods would be merciful to one, like himself, who had tried.

He had rolled up the scroll and given it back to his father, not knowing that the scroll, and his parents, would be within a tomb within a few years.

Looking down the hallway, he remembered the scroll and his own serene smiles, and quietly despaired. The scroll had not conveyed the terrible quality of the Judgment Hall, the awe-full silence, the brightness that lay like a mist over everything.

His hands rose and clenched against his heart and he took a step backward, desperately looking about for a way to escape. But there was nothing but blackness behind him, nowhere to go but to judgment.

He took another step backward, his frightened eyes riveted on the darkness behind him, a frantic prayer for help rising to his lips only to die unspoken. The gods were there already. There would be no help from them.

Something touched his hand, warm and solid, like rock or earth.

He gasped and turned and found himself staring straight into the face of Anubis, the jackal-headed god, familiar to Wenatef from his carved shape in the entrance of the Tomb.

Wenatef flattened himself against the door with a wail of dismay, his wide eyes fixed on Anubis' face. It was as though Wenatef were looking at two faces at once, seeing beyond the jackal-visage to another face reflecting the quickness, cleverness and determination of a jackal.

He turned and beat upon the dark doors with his clenched fists. Death. The doorway between the worlds...

"Let me out!" he cried.

Anubis stepped closer, holding out his hand.

Wenatef shuddered away from him, his own hands clenched and hidden behind him. "I'm not ready!" he cried through chattering teeth. "It isn't my time!"

The god's hand was still outstretched, poised with a grace that caught Wenatef's despairing attention. "I'm not ready!" he repeated desperately.

The god's gaze lowered to Wenatef's hands; the hand stretched out once more, inviting, steady.

Wenatef shrank back against the doors.

You are behaving as badly as Merihor, child.

The words, slipping gently into Wenatef's mind, shocked

him to silence.

Anubis had not moved.

Wenatef lowered his head and unclenched his fists. It was useless to resist. What could he do? Remain flattened against the door through all eternity? Wail like a baby? He was an officer of His Majesty and a man of honor and courage. He would be wise to put the best face that he could on this. If he had tried to lead an upright life, surely the judgment would reflect that. It was his only hope.

He moved away from the doors and held out his hand; Anubis gripped it reassuringly as he led him along the frightening short walk to the scales.

Wenatef tried to say the forty-two denials, but he could only keep repeating that he had tried to live an upright life, that he had tried not to hurt anyone or offend the gods.

Now Anubis was placing his heart on one of the pans and gently setting the Feather of Truth on the other. Thoth lifted his palette and dipped his brush in the ink, ready to record the results. Wenatef experienced the double- vision again, seeing the head of an ibis atop a long neck and then, at the same time, seeing a face with the deliberate movement and wisdom of an ibis.

The Eater of Shades growled softly.

Wenatef heard a commotion behind him, a sense of movement and increased numbers. A voice rang out behind Wenatef as the scales began to swing.

He is mine! I speak for him! A hand, solid as granite, descended to his left shoulder and gripped. *Look!* said the voice, and another hand appeared from behind Wenatef, to the right, pointing.

But Wenatef was watching the scales as the pans rose and fell slightly, balancing each other.

The grip on Wenatef's left shoulder tightened. *Look!* the voice said again, and light seemed to flash from the fingertips of the pointing hand.

The scales were still now, perfectly balanced.

O Unnefer, his heart was true! Anubis' voice rang triumphantly through the Hall of Judgment like the call of a great trumpet.

Gentle hands set a diadem about Wenatef's forehead, and the Feather of Truth was placed there.

Look! the voice said again, and now Wenatef could turn and see the face behind him, a face full of command and power.

He turned back and the room was dark. All that remained was the painful pressure on Wenatef's shoulder, and the flash of light off to his right...

CHAPTER XXIII

Wenatef jerked awake. He had slipped onto his side and the statue's foot had been digging into his shoulder. He could still feel the edges, although the pain was fading. Had he been dreaming? It had seemed so real. And he could still hear the command that had forced him upright:

Look!

He looked and then gasped. A finger of light had pushed its way through the wall of the burial room, knifing across the floor to rest upon a long, thin sliver of strange gray metal, streaked and dim, half-hidden in a pool of red within a clutter of dark shapes.

An iron dagger.

The glow faded and was gone as Wenatef watched, though the light now touched one of the jars. Another second and he might never have seen the knife, but he had marked its place. He pushed himself across the floor to it, his heart pounding, cursing the bonds that hampered him. Where had the light come from? Was the burial chamber carved so deeply into the hill that it had come out the other side?

His fingers closed around the knife. Another second and he would not have seen it... He turned his mind back to the judgment hall. His memory was fading, but he could remember the face of the man behind him as clearly as though it were the face of a friend. *Was* it a dream?

The question of the dream could wait, Wenatef's bonds could not, and he did not know how long the shaft of sunlight would last. It took almost no time to free himself. He located a fire drill and materials to use for a torch shortly after. Soon he had a small fire burning in a large pottery tray. The light from the fire showed that the chamber had been ransacked.

Wenatef wrapped a length of linen about the smashed leg of a chair, tied it with another strip of cloth and poured oil over the whole before touching it to the fire. It took some time to catch, but then it burned satisfactorily. He found some vessels that he could use for lamps, and several tall jars held oil. It was not long before Wenatef had a small galaxy of lamps burning throughout the chamber. Now he could look around.

His kilt was dark with dried blood, but there was no mark of a wound. His hand rose to his side, following the flow of dried blood to his fifth rib. The flesh was smooth and whole: had he merely dreamed the taste of blood? He pulled the scraps of cord from his wrists and unwound the layers of cloth that had swathed them. The cloths were stiff and stained with blood next to his skin, but his wrists themselves were smooth and strong.

He was whole now... But he might not remain whole long if the robbers came after him. If he wanted to stay alive, he had to act now.

He pushed to his feet and looked around. He had been right: he was in the burial chamber. An alabaster sarcophagus lay in the far corner with the massive lid cast aside and broken into three pieces. He went over and looked inside. The wooden inner coffins had been opened and stripped of their gold, and he could see the mummy beyond. If a gold or silver mask had ever covered the upper part of the body, it was gone. The face was still wrapped, but the robbers had taken an axe and split the arms away from the body and then hacked at the chest in their search for gold. Wenatef could see the ends of broken bones, yellow in the torchlight.

He swallowed a bitter taste at the back of his throat, found a piece of cloth, and covered the body. A glance at the sarcophagus lid showed him that he could not replace it alone. Even broken, the pieces were too heavy to be lifted by one or even two men. He shook his head and turned slowly. His breath froze in his throat.

He was looking at a face that he had seen less than an hour before. It was the face that he had seen in his dream, but set within the graceful folds of a striped 'sphinx' headdress, atop wide shoulders and an elegant torso that narrowed to slim hips. His eyes returned to the face.

It was a good face, but a pensive, slightly sad one, and the sculptor had meant it to be a portrait, for it lacked the sweet, serene blandness of most formal sculptures of kings. Wenatef moved forward until, standing knee to knee with the statue, he was looking up into the face.

Yes, it was the face of his dream - but who was he? Wenatef looked down at the statue's chest. Beneath the broad collar was a pendant carved with two names, the given name and the throne name of the king. Nakhtamun Nefer-Neferu-Ptah. 'Amun Mighty in Battle ', with the throne name 'beautiful are the beauties of Ptah'. Nakhtamun, firstborn son of the great Seti I. He had died after a co-regency with his father of only six months. He had died in battle, in Palestine.

CHAPTER XXIV

Wenatef was squatting on the floor of the tomb some hours later trying to eat bread and wine and raisins. The bread, over two hundred years old, was the stalest he had ever had between his teeth, and while it was still drinkable, the wine was hardly palatable. After several abortive attempts to eat the bread, he ended up by soaking it in the wine along with the raisins, leaving it there in pottery bowls while he explored the rest of the tomb.

It was large for that of a secondary king with such a short reign. The tomb had been completely excavated and the decorations nearly finished, which seemed to show that King Seti had ordered the construction of the tomb early in his reign while his son was still crown prince.

The tomb seemed to lack nothing that Wenatef could see, though most of the jewelry had been taken. In fact, it contained more supplies there than Wenatef would have thought necessary for a tomb, though his experience with royal burials was limited. But the untidy mound of boxes and jars near the hole in the ceiling through which Wenatef had probably been lowered, indicated that this tomb had been used as a storehouse for goods from other plundered tombs.

While his knowledge of the locations of the royal tombs was not precise, he believed that Nakhtamun's tomb was far beyond that of Thutmose IV in the far southeastern corner of the Valley of the Kings, away from the normal flow of traffic. It was a perfect place to store valuables or prisoners.

Some of his captors had apparently intended to keep him

alive for a time. Wenatef had found a pan of water near the spot where he had lain, and where he had found the knife. A lamp with a large supply of oil was close by, and had been lit at one time. The slight draft from the crack in the wall had extinguished the flame. Now it was lit again.

Wenatef was puzzled by that and several other things that he had discovered, beginning with the extra padding that had been put about his injured wrists. Had they wanted to keep him as a hostage? Against whom? He finally concluded it was time, and turned his thoughts to the question that had been lurking in the back of his mind since he had awakened: whose blood had streaked the blade of the knife and pooled on the floor?

He had been sure he was dying. Blood had come to his lips with every breath, and he had felt the tearing wound in his left side. A path of blood led to the plinth of the statue, and the legs of the statue were dark with drying blood. Yet here he was, the flesh over his ribs whole and unmarked, though the side of his kilt was stiff with dried blood. The flesh of his wrists was smooth and unmarked, as well, though the swathing cloths were bloody. Could he have been mistaken?

Wenatef pondered this for some time, and then abandoned the line of thought as disturbing and a waste of valuable time. He was a pragmatic man at heart. Faced with the unanswerable, he turned his attention again to those questions that could be answered. His captors had obviously wanted to cow him with a few days alone in the tomb before they questioned him. His smile was cold. Excellent. He would not be there when they returned.

He considered piling boxes and furniture to reach the hole in the ceiling, but then dismissed it. It would take a lot of effort, and the goods that had been brought to the tomb from the other plundered burials had all been easily portable.

Diana Wilder

There was nothing big or sturdy enough there to use. He would have to find another way out.

He put his eye up against the crack in the wall and gauged the thickness of the rock. Four feet, maybe, of what felt like friable limestone. Tombs were cut from rock like that. He thought he could easily cut his way out of there. He already had an iron knife that could be used as a chisel, and he had found a carved stone gazelle that he could lash to a stout piece of wood to give it leverage. It would do well as a hammer. He would begin tunneling just as soon as he had eaten and looked through the rest of the tomb.

** ** **

Wenatef discovered another, larger crack in the wall of a smaller room at the very end of the long, straight tomb. The far wall of this room had been cut close to the edge of the hill, and the shifting and settling of the rocks above it had caused a gaping split in the farthest corner. The crack itself was wide enough at the edge of the room to permit Wenatef to crawl into it and curl up. He thought it would take fairly little effort to enlarge it to a tunnel. The room was filled with a jumble of clutter, and Wenatef could easily pile some of that against the wall to disguise his digging. It would be easier to hide there if his captors decided to make an unannounced visit.

He set to work, collecting the stone chips in baskets, working swiftly but with great care. It took some time to learn the proper rhythm for cutting the stone, and he was forever stopping to collect fragments, but the work went quickly. He was exhausted after several hours, and he knew he needed sleep. The tunnel that he had cut was large enough now to allow him to lie down, and since the tomb was full of cloth - rolls of linen, wads of fine, embroidered garments, some neatly folded, some thrown into corners – he was able to make a good sleeping pad. He found a plain head-rest of clay beneath one of the dismantled beds.

118

A Killing Among the Dead

It took a moment to deal with the lamps and hide his tunnel. He closed his eyes and was immediately asleep.

**   **   **

Wenatef awakened to fragrance of lotus, jasmine, and sweet myrrh. They all combined to make a perfume that seemed to permeate his very flesh. The wind blowing softly over him and the gentle rise and fall of the surface beneath him was somehow familiar, as though he were on some sort of ship. The ship seemed immense, vaster than the Valley of the Kings, Thebes, and the desert beyond the city combined. He felt the great wooden planks that lay beneath him, and he could hear the creak and groan of the mast and, in the distance, the plash of oars.

He raised his head, nearly blinded by the brightness that seemed to hover above the ship. And then he realized that the brightness was the ship itself, and he was sailing on the barque of the sun in its journey through the fields of the West.

He was surrounded by men and women bright as the noon sun, of a terrible beauty that made Wenatef's brown flesh seem leprous and insubstantial. And the men and women were so blindingly beautiful that Wenatef fell to his knees on the deck and covered his face.

He could see the radiant planks of the deck beaming through the ghostly outlines of his hands, and was paralyzed by the terror of one who has seen Heaven and felt himself unworthy. He was a ghost among gods. It did not matter that they seemed to wish him well. The thought of meeting the gaze of one of the splendid beings around him was more dreadful than anything he had ever faced. He buried his face against his arms, praying incoherently for something to take him from this place, as if his presence somehow defiled it.

A hand touched his arm as he lay trembling, and the feel of that hand sent him into a fresh spasm of shuddering, for it

119

was as solid as stone and yet warm as the sunlight upon his back. The hand touched his arm again, the grip tightened, and Wenatef was drawn to his feet with a gentleness that he could not fight.

His eyes fell upon the hand that gripped his arm, and he cried out again, for the hand was strong and smooth, flashing like gold, and his own flesh seemed as insubstantial as smoke beside it. "Let me leave!" he pleaded. "I meant no offense!"

Stop it, a voice said. It held the hint of a chuckle, and Wenatef stopped his stammering at the sound. He had heard that voice before. He looked up, past the hand, past the bronzed chest, past the heavy collar of gold and lapis, to the face that he had seen in his first dream and then on the statue in the tomb. It was the face of an ally, even of a friend. Wenatef tried, trembling, to thank him.

Nakhtamun's words were unexpected. *You waste too much time in being afraid*, he said, releasing Wenatef's arm. His voice was clear and kind, but somehow distant. *Come. Sit and take some nourishment.*

He moved toward chairs of carved cedar wood and Wenatef followed, looking around at the other people - gods? - on the boat. Men and women as golden and brilliant as Nakhtamun, and as smiling. He sank into the chair, lowering his head as the brightness and the fragrance rained down upon him, as tangible as motes of sand in a windstorm.

One of the women came to him and offered a silver cup filled with a fragrant wine. *To refresh you,* she said.

Wenatef raised it to his lips, conscious of the smiles of the Bright Ones around him...

CHAPTER XXV

Wenatef opened his eyes, warm and rested. He had sailed along the Nile in his dream until the moment of the sun's rebirth, when he had suddenly been spun back into darkness, the fragrance of the barque of the sun still in his nostrils, ready to continue his work on the tunnel.

He lost track of the time he spent digging. He often worked with half-closed eyes, unsure whether he slept or woke, unaware of the passing of time. When he was completely exhausted he would throw himself down on his bed and sleep. During this time he traveled in dreams to the Land of the West, always in company with the Great Ones, who offered him food and drink that refreshed him. Once he awoke from a dream of lotus fields, and the tomb seemed still to hold their scent.

Nakhtamun was always beside him in those dreams. He often spoke to Wenatef, but he answered no questions.

It did not take Wenatef long to lose his fear of Nakhtamun and the Great Ones, though he never quite lost his awe. They wished him well, and he felt new strength when he awoke from his travels. He had tried once to thank them for that fact. Nakhtamun had actually laughed at him - it was kindly laughter - and had gently touched Wenatef's shoulder. *We should rather thank you*, he had said, and then said nothing further, though the smile remained.

Wenatef had awakened from that dream to discover that the thieves had been in the tomb while he was in the Land of

121

the West. They had obviously been looking for him, knocking over containers, throwing open chests and toppling piles of boxes. The bloodstain had been uncovered; someone had scraped at it, probably with a knife, as though measuring the severity of the blood loss. They had probably decided that he had escaped; Wenatef had a breathing space.

** ** **

The tunnel progressed swiftly and Wenatef broke through on the eve of the fourth day, just as his supply of water ran out. He aimed one last powerful blow of his hammer against the now blunted dagger, sending the point bursting through the stone into sun-warmed air. Rocks tumbled down the hillside with a hiss and a rumble followed by their dying echoes and then silence. The wind pushed through the hole, bringing the scent of the distant river.

He set his hammer down and crawled backward. He looked at his work, a tunnel perhaps ten feet long and three feet in diameter, angled toward the outside so that it was hidden from anyone within the tomb who did not know what to look for. It was big enough to curl up in if he suspected intruders, but could be easily hidden with baskets or boxes. He had probably displaced over a ton of rock, and he had done all this on what he would have termed siege rations in his days in Nubia.

He drew his knees up and wrapped his arms around them. It wouldn't take long to enlarge that hole and be out of the tomb. He could finish it in a few hours.

No. His shoulders ached, he was bone-weary, and it was time to rest. He pushed the dagger aside with his foot, crawled to the pile of folded linen, curled up, and lay for a time watching the light from the oil lamp dancing on the wall.

He had a lot to consider. He had planned to go to Dhutmose, Duwah and the foremen before he was captured. Now he was not sure...

A Killing Among the Dead

He had told the Necropolis Police that the folk of the village knew the locations of the tombs better than anyone else in all of Egypt. That was true, and it was quite possible that one of the villagers had told them where to place Wenatef. He might have been imprisoned by the very men whose help he had sought. How could he be sure?

Even if that weren't the case, the robbers might not know that they were being watched by the village captains. If Wenatef went to Dhutmose, it could place him in danger and possibly wreck any groundwork that he and the others had laid. For that matter, if Dhutmose and the rest were moving cautiously, perhaps they were trying to assemble enough evidence to keep suspicions from being turned against them. What other reason could there be for not going directly to the authorities?

Wenatef did not know, and he was exhausted from digging. He sighed and closed his eyes and let himself drift toward sleep.

** ** **

Night was falling in the Necropolis. Lights were moving about along the hillsides, just as they had been on the night Wenatef had first been captured. He bent toward them, trying to see more clearly, and as though in response to his wish, the lights and the figures were suddenly distinct.

He could see men scurrying about bearing torches, going in and out of a dark opening on the spine of a ridge. He realized what he was seeing, and the sight sickened and enraged him. This was no hurried attempt to find wealth in order to stave off starvation. It was an organized operation, almost military in its precision.

He turned away, filled with helpless fury and stepped backward, startled. He faced the gazes of countless men and women ranged on the hills behind him, glittering in the pale light of the stars. Their hair and garments seemed to be stirred by a wind that Wenatef could not feel on his own flesh. They stood motionless and silent, watching him.

He heard the clash of metal and savage cries satisfaction behind him. He turned toward the dark hole in the cliff. The ridges of stone shivered like wall hangings billowing out before the dry heat of the khamsin. Wenatef stretched out his hands and the stones thinned and parted, no more substantial than cobweb.

He brushed them aside and stepped into torchlit rooms filled with a jumble of tomb goods, splintered rock and gloating men.

The sarcophagus stood against the wall. A fire of dried cow dung was burning hot and fast at its base, throwing shadows of the men in the room into weird, writhing shapes on the wall, grotesquely superimposed on paintings of a queen in the land of the West.

Wenatef could see faces clearly, though he seemed to be looking down from a great height at a huddle of dolls. He recognized some of them from the night he was captured. Unas was there as well, working with a silent, white-faced fury that seemed somehow out of place in that organized, brisk activity.

The robbers were bringing out jewelry and precious objects and tossing them into a pile.

Wenatef's hands clenched and unclenched beside him.

A roar and crash behind him made Wenatef turn in time to see the massive stone sarcophagus splinter as one of the thieves dashed a bucket of water against it. Unas' eyes glinted; Wenatef watched him turn and go to the ruined pile of stone.

The others pulled something large and vaguely man-shaped from the rubble. The coffin, glittering with gold. They ringed it, pushing at it, lifting - and suddenly it split lengthwise in half showing another smaller object like it. This was lifted out and split in its turn, revealing something that glinted in the torchlight. The mask over the mummy itself. But that meant - that meant - He bent forward as a still smaller, man-shaped object was pulled forth. He caught a flash of upraised axes and swords and then the clink of jewelry against rock.

The mummy was a mass of bundled rags and splintered flesh; as Wenatef watched, Unas bent over it and spoke the words of Opening in terrible parody:

You die forever!

He raised his foot and brought it crashing down on the skull. One of the men touched his torch to the body. The dried flesh flared and blazed.

Wenatef tried to shout, but no sound came, and he could only watch in silence as the corpse went up in flames, dishonored, robbed and dismembered.

And then Unas laughed.

It was enough. Wenatef whirled on the silent people behind him. "Stop them!" he cried.

They did not move.

"Don't you see what they're doing?" Still no reply, no movement.

Wenatef turned back in time to see the robbers light the two coffins. He drew a sickened breath and then rounded on the silent people. "You are the Great Ones - the Justified Ones - fight!"

There was no sound.

"If you won't fight, give me a weapon and *I* will fight!"

And then one of the silent people stepped forward, smiling at him. Nakhtamun. He wore the blue war crown, and his eyes seemed to flash. He held a long, powerful bow and a great fistful of arrows.

Wenatef took the bow from Nakhtamun, fitted one of the arrows to the string, and drew the bow until the arrow's fletching grazed his ear. He let fly; and the arrow arched slowly, slowly, like a falling star, dipping down toward the robbers until it touched the burning coffin and exploded in a shower of brilliant stars, spinning him back to wakefulness.

** ** **

He sat up and squinted at the hole that he had dug. The sky was bright and blue and a wind came in through the opening. He could smell baking bread, rushes - all the wonderful scents that he had forgotten during his time in the tomb. He crawled back into the tunnel and pressed his face against the hole, but he could see nothing but stones and hills.

He sighed and reached backward to his dagger and the hammer. The gazelle did not look much like a gazelle any more. But it still looked like a hammer, and that was all Wenatef needed. He went back to the opening, set the dagger in place, and began to pound.

CHAPTER XXVI

The first thing Wenatef did was to throw himself down on the ground, on his back, and stare up at the cloud-scattered sky with a wealth of joy that he had never felt before. The sky was so beautiful! Boundless and blue, the motion of the clouds full of a vast peace! The very patterns of the clouds enthralled him, and he seemed to find strength and rest just watching them.

He rolled onto his stomach after a moment and offered thanks to all the gods he could recall and then, closing his eyes, a heartfelt one to Nakhtamun. That done, he pushed himself to his hands and knees, squatted on his heels, and considered.

Deir el Medineh was not safe for him. He would also be an easy mark in Thebes, if he was right in guessing that powerful interests were involved in the tomb robberies. If he was going to fight them, it would take sound strategy and a lot of luck. He was a target as an escaped captive. It would be safest for him if they continued to think him dead.

He smiled grimly. It was time to die. The easiest thing to do, then, would be to get rid of the fragments of stone from his excavation and fake his death. He planned to maintain residence in Nakhtamun's tomb after he 'died'. They already thought that he had managed to free himself and escape by climbing the piles of boxes to the hole in the ceiling and wriggling out that way. His tunnel would be hidden with boxes and debris, and they would not find it if they were not looking for it.

He stood, brushed the dust from his kilt, and peered toward the tomb of Ramesses XI, wishing that he could speak to Duwah or Dhutmose. His hand closed about the Gold of Honor, which still hung around his neck.

** ** **

That night, naked, covered with blood, filthy and exhausted, Wenatef returned to the tomb and crept inside. His body was sticky and stretched where the blood had dried, but except for the loss of his Gold of Honor, he was content. The blood had belonged to a goat that Wenatef had poached. He had bled the animal, saving the blood in the sac that surrounded the animal's heart. He would have liked to roast the flesh, but he dared not risk the smells and the light from the fire. He had buried the carcass far away under the cliffs.

He had returned to the tomb, then, climbed the boxes to the hole in the ceiling, crawled out, and then headed toward the desert. He left distinct tracks in the sand and rocks, and when he finally reached firmer ground, he hurried to the spot where he had hidden the sac of blood. He shied a few stones at a jackal that had arrived before him, and was sniffing at it.

He had lifted the sac of blood. After finding a suitable spot, not far from Deir el Medineh, he had poured some of the blood on himself and then, holding the sac of blood to his chest, had thrown himself to the ground, writhing and flailing with his arms and legs. He had spilled a great puddle of blood and then, the container leaking down his chest, had dragged himself through the softer sand and gravel to the smooth rock. Then he had stood, poured the rest of the blood out, and smeared it with his foot.

He had pulled his kilt off, torn it with his hands, and then tossed it aside after wiping his feet on it. His last act had been to wrench the Gold of Honor from his neck, hurl it to the ground, put his foot upon it, crushing the lion's head, and then scrape it through the gravel. Wenatef knew that it would be the last bit of evidence needed to convince everyone that he had been attacked and killed by an animal and then dragged away to be devoured. The absence of a corpse would not trouble them if they found the Gold of Honor.

He had stood aside then, and surveyed his work. Not bad, if the people who found it were in a hurry, drunk and blind to boot. Maybe they would think he had been killed by a lion or a hyena and then hauled off, though the absence of pawprints would tend to disprove that.

** ** **

Back at the tomb, he lay down and fell at once into a deep sleep. This time his dreams were fragmented, flashes of vision swiftly crossing his mind and as swiftly forgotten. He was filled with a brooding regret throughout the vision, and it seemed as though all the grief of all men, grief for all that might have been, for all that was lost and could not be found again for all beautiful things twisted and spoiled, lay for that night upon him. The yearning of the exile, the grief of the bereaved, the remorse of the sinner, the despair of the condemned - all burdened his heart, and he could find no comfort.

He sighed in his sleep, tasting salt on his lips, murmuring words of apology, of pleading, until the burden finally seemed to pass and he rested, empty and quiet, watching the mountains that guard the sun's rising and setting in the Land of the West.

The dream was filled with a vast silence. The sun cast a glow on the tawny backs of the mountains, turning them to gold, quivering along their flanks. Lion-like, they seemed to guard as they slept.

And then the great, golden mountains heaved themselves to their feet and stretched, scimitar-curved claws digging deep into the earth, great tooth-studded jaws opening wider and wider and then crashing shut with the sound of falling cliffs.

They *were* lions, Sef and Duau - Yesterday and Tomorrow - guardians of time, mighty- maned and dangerous, with great golden eyes. They transfixed Wenatef with their golden gaze long enough to bore into the very depth of his soul, setting it ablaze with a fierce rejoicing before they turned away, racing to meet the sun.

CHAPTER XXVII

"A lion," said Unas, kneeling by the dark spots in the sandy earth. "Look at the size of that pawprint! There were two of them, by the look of it. Poor fool, I don't envy him. And it looks as though he tried to put up a fight." He raised his head and called to one of his men. "Kenher, come here - tell the fellow from the Tomb Guard that we've found something."

The man named Kenher lifted his hide-covered shield and hurried off as Unas pushed to his feet. He was smiling, but it was a grimace that held nothing of happiness or contentment.

Wenatef, hidden behind a cluster of rocks, saw the smile and longed for twenty minutes alone with Unas and a knife. He consoled himself with the reflection that Unas would probably be dead by the time he had completed his work.

Kenher returned with Ramses behind him, standing to one side as Ramesses looked down at the patch of blood.

"We found a piece of cloth among the rocks," Unas said. "Part of a kilt, I think. Torn and bloody. And we found this." He tossed something to Ramses. The sunlight caught the flash of gold. "There is no doubt that this is his," Unas said. "The search can end here."

Ramses turned the golden pendant over in his hands, smoothing the dried blood from its bright surface. His head was lowered and Wenatef could not see his expression, but tears streaked his face when he looked up. His hand was clenched about the Gold of Honor, and he was suddenly snarling at Unas.

"This is your doing! You stink with corruption! And there are many who have noticed it!"

"Captain Ramses," Unas began.

"Silence!" Ramses hissed. "You understand me! Better than anyone else here! Shall I call them over here and explain it to them? He's kept this area clear of criminals, and now it seems the criminals have killed him!" Wenatef thought there was something very calculated about his words for all his very real grief.

"You saw the tracks of the lions," Unas objected, looking anxiously behind him.

Aha, thought Wenatef. *The rest of the Necropolis Police with you today aren't part of the tomb robbing plot. We have learned something important.*

"I saw the tracks," Ramses said. "I've seen other killings, as well. There are those in the Necropolis Police who're rotten through to their hearts. They're party to all sorts of corruption and abomination, and their actions have not been overlooked. The day comes Unas. The day comes when payment will be demanded - will you be able to afford the reckoning?"

Unas' eyes narrowed. "You speak too loudly and too pointedly," he said.

"Do I?" Ramses said, his voice sharpening. "Then bring an action for slander against me before the Vizier. But don't forget that truth is a defense. There are those of us who feel that I am not speaking enough to the point. So I'll repeat: this is your doing - " he lifted the golden pendant, " - and you shall pay for it. That is all I have to say. I'll bring this to Deir el Medineh. There will most likely be others with much more to say to you." He stepped backward and turned on his heel. It was a magnificent exit. Wenatef, watching, thought of Nakhtamun.

A Killing Among the Dead

Unas also watched Ramses leave, his hands clenched at his sides, and his thoughts obviously not admiring ones. He looked down at the bloody cloth in his hand, hurled it to the ground, called his guardsmen together, and left.

** ** **

Wenatef remained where he was until they were completely out of sight and then waited several minutes longer before making his way across the warm sand toward the bloodstains. They were believable. He nodded and turned to see what had convinced the others that two lions had come and devoured him. What he saw made him drop to his knees and steady himself with one hand against the ground and the other pressed against his heart.

Massive, bloody paw prints, longer than Wenatef's hand with the fingers spread their widest. He set his other hand beside it and his fingers barely covered the marks. He saw two distinct tracks; the paws had been driven deep into the rocky ground, as though it had been soft river mud.

He drew a shaken breath and pushed himself to his feet, looking east, remembering his dream. The lions - the Guardian Mountains - had arisen and gone east to the place of the sun's birth. And so - and so - Wenatef shook his head and forced himself to take several slow breaths. No, it could not be - and yet these tracks came from the west - from the direction of the Libyan desert.

Wenatef looked west and east and then lifted his head. He had to know.

Following the tracks was not easy, for each stride measured well over thirty feet, but at last the tracks ended abruptly. Or perhaps the proper word was 'began'. There were two sets of deep prints, as though the beasts had leaped down from a great height and landed heavily, and then nothing before that. And yet Wenatef was kneeling in the middle of a flat expanse of ground. The nearest piece of higher land was over half a mile away, though there were some clusters of rock jutting above the level ground.

He rose and investigated each in turn, but he could find no further tracks, though he cast about for fifty yards. Those lions might as well have come down from the very sky. He returned to the tracks and stared at them.

A wind rose, scattering loose sand across the prints, and he seemed to hear faint voices. He could not understand what they were saying, maybe they were the echoes of his own disordered thoughts. He looked back toward the east, and he could see only traces of the paw prints.

What could he think, after all? It was time to return to the tomb and plan his next move.

He started to shiver, though the wind was warm. He did not want to return to the tomb. Not yet. He went, instead, to the Nile, to bathe and wash away the dried blood and grime of the past week. It was a long journey - three miles to the river and three miles back - but it would give him time to compose his mind and plan his next move.

He returned from the river and found a spot of shade in the breathless heat that nevertheless did not drive the chill from his heart. He was not afraid or shocked. How could he be terrified when it was made clear that all the forces of Heaven were behind him?

It was time that he, Wenatef son of Hapuseneb, Master Archer, veteran of the armies, and Commander of the Guard of Pharaoh's Tomb, realized that he had been chosen by the gods to act as their instrument of justice.

The discovery might be an exhilarating one for some people; it aroused a vast and almost despairing weariness in Wenatef. All he wanted to do was sleep and forget his responsibility for a time. He curled on his side, rested his cheek on the crook of his elbow and fell into a dreamless sleep.

CHAPTER XXVIII

Wenatef awoke from that sleep feeling refreshed and resolute. He had not bowed before any of the Justified in the Land of the West. He had simply slept, and that sleep had been the very tonic his exhausted body and soul had needed.

He lay for a time gazing up at the sky and thinking. He had been admitted to the ranks of the Justified. Had he not received the Feather of Truth? He had been welcomed among the Great Ones, and been nourished and armed by them. The very mountains of the West had risen to his aid - he was clothed in the strength of the Justified. In that strength he would pursue those who threatened the safety and health of Egypt and destroy them.

The people of Deir el Medineh could only proceed with caution, but Wenatef could go where he wished and learn what he wished, since he had been numbered among the dead. There was a magnificent bow awaiting him somewhere in Nakhtamun's tomb. It would be his weapon, to use against the tomb robbers. He would find it and use it.

Wenatef sat up and squinted at the sun. There was only one problem: he might be one of the dead, but his stomach still considered itself to be among the living. There was food aplenty in the tomb, but it was all stale and dry and of a hardness that could grind granite, much more the teeth of anyone foolish enough to try to eat it. He thought that the gods needed to make some sort of provision for feeding him, since he could hardly be expected to dine on the food

portrayed in the tomb, and he had already learned that any
food he ate in the Land of the West would not fill his
stomach when he awoke in the land of the living.

** ** **

He awoke the next evening from a dream of great beauty
to the reality of grinding hunger. He stilled the hunger with
a breakfast of stale bread and staler raisins washed down
with musty wine, and he debated the wisdom of pulverizing
the raisins and the bread together and making a powder that
could be moistened with water.

It seemed like a good idea, and he spent the next hour
breaking the bread into tiny fragments and then pounding it
to dust with the now unrecognizable gazelle hammer. At the
end of an hour he faced a large bowl of gray paste with gritty
pink overtones. It did not taste as bad as it looked, so he
shrugged and put it aside for his supper, and went to the Nile
to bathe..

Wenatef slipped into the warm water swam out to the
middle of the river, to float on his back and gaze up on the
moon. It hovered above the horizon, its light splintering
upon the ripples of water about him until he seemed to be
bathing in a sea of stars.

Dark shapes converged upon him, gleaming in the light
that revealed every scale, every knob of thick, rough hide.
Great crocodiles with tooth-studded jaws and small,
gleaming eyes that glowed in the reflected light on the
waters. They circled him silently like a fleet of warships,
remaining at a distance, unmoving, presenting no threat.

Wenatef's days among the Blest had made him brave. He
stretched out his hand and touched the nearest crocodile, a
huge patriarch that was twice the length of the others. The
hide felt thick and rough beneath his fingers, and he could
see the jagged line of teeth fringing the upper jaw. The
monster shivered, but made no move to hurt him.

He jerked his hand away, hearing the plash of paddles

against water. The great crocodile rumbled deep in its throat; the log-like bodies moved more closely around Wenatef.

He heard words, the snatches of a sentence spoken half under the breath. ".... . .the tombs are rich there, and the Necropolis Police turn their faces away..." And then Wenatef, peering above the big crocodile's back, saw the faint outline of a papyrus boat. Four men were loaded tightly within it. He saw the flash of knives at their belts before he ducked back under the water.

One of them cried out and pointed to the knot of crocodiles. "Sobek protect us! Look there!"

"The size of them!" another gasped.

Wenatef caught the sound of shaky laughter as the helmsman carefully steered away from the great beasts. The boat grated on the shore and was hoisted up on the bank. The voices faded toward the west.

Wenatef waited until they were well away from him before moving back to the shore. The crocodiles followed him up on the bank and then settled themselves about the thieves' boat. Wenatef smiled as he pictured their return.

Back at the tomb, he knotted a loincloth from a triangle of light linen, wrapped a kilt over it, and then sifted through the boxes until he found one of warm-toned cedar inlaid with ebony hieroglyphs bearing the personal and throne names of Ramesses III. The box was beautifully joined, the hinged top was secured by a length of cord circling the knob at the front of the lid. He unknotted the cord, lifted the lid, and gazed down at the contents.

A shallow tray at the top held a mirror of bronze in the shape of a pretty maiden holding up the disc of the sun. Wenatef lifted the mirror and buffed it on the trailing apron of his kilt before raising it to his face, to take a long look at himself.

The face that gazed back at him was smudged with weariness and half-hidden by a week's stubble of beard. But all in all it was not bad, though Wenatef now could understand the amusement in the Great Ones' faces. He brushed his fingertips across his chin and smiled as he lifted the mirror's tray from the top of the box and looked down at the array of jars and pots before him.

The box was divided into compartments. Thin alabaster bottles held perfumes and sweet oils. Ointments were held in shorter, wide-mouthed jars, and he saw a number of small, squat bottles holding kohl as well as powdered malachite. A separate compartment held tweezers and scissors with handles of gold and blades of bronze. Most importantly, He found two small whetstones and, in a box of their own, two bronze razors.

Wenatef lifted the razors from their boxes. They were wedge-shaped, with handles carved in the shape of bound captives, a Nubian and another with a flat- topped, feathered headdress or helmet, one of the Sea-peoples. The blades were still sharp, but Wenatef stroked them along the whetstone, tested the edges, and then set them aside for the moment and unstoppered a jar of unguents.

It was still sweet eighty years after the death of its owner, smelling of fragrant herbs. He dipped into the jar, smoothed the ointment over his cheeks and chin and, the mirror propped between his drawn-up knees, lifted the razor and carefully shaved, humming a dancing song, his toes tapping against the floor of the tomb.

Now he did not look like such a barbarian. The mouth of his reflection quirked in a wry smile as he reached for a tiny glass pot of kohl and one of the round-tipped sticks used to apply the powder. He paused for a moment to admire the workmanship of the pot before dipping the stick into it, shaking off the excess powder, and then outlining his eyes, drawing out the lines at the outer corners until they almost met his brows.

He eyed the other pots of rouge and red unguents for lips and cheeks as he re-stoppered the kohl bottle. He wondered for a moment if the great warrior-king, Ramesses III, ever used them. He shrugged and took a comb and a pair of scissors and set his hair in order. Now, for the first time since he had been captured, he felt like Wenatef, son of Hapuseneb, Commander of the Guard of His Majesty's Tomb, Commander of One Thousand, Master Archer and Bearer of the Gold of Honor. He replaced the pots in their niches, set the mirror atop them, and closed the box.

He devoted the rest of the night to finding the composite bow that Nakhtamun had given him in his dream. He could see it clearly, the grip overlaid with ivory and ornamented with bands of gold, the golden tips, and the layers of horn and wood beautifully oiled and gleaming. He had always longed for such a bow, even when he had commissioned the bow he had used in Nubia and Deir el Medineh. He had longed for that bow from the moment his father had first put a child's bow in his pudgy hands when he was only six years old.

A thorough search of the tomb revealed countless things that other men would consider treasures - rich garments, precious ointments, jewelry, cosmetics, implements to make daily life easier or more elegant - but the bow eluded him and he finally went to his bed and lay down with the dagger beneath his shoulder.

He sat up a minute later, cursing fluently. He was a fool! He knew where the bow was - he should have known it all along! Where would a soldier keep his weapons? Within easy reach beside him, of course!

Wenatef went to the sarcophagus, still cursing himself. He pulled aside the cloth that he had used to cover the mummy and frowned down into the coffin. Shreds and tatters of linen wrappings littered the inside of the sarcophagus; Wenatef scooped up a handful and thrust it aside. There was nothing there.

That didn't trouble him. The filth who had robbed the tomb had defiled Nakhtamun's coffins, and if they had seen fit to chop the mummy itself apart, they would have had no qualms about discarding something as useless to them as a bow. They weren't archers. A knife, the weapon of stealth and treachery, would be their chosen weapon. The sight of a bow would move them to nothing more than scorn. They had probably thrown it aside. It would not be far.

In fact, it was not. Wenatef found it as he turned away from the sarcophagus: a plain, long box of dark wood. The box itself, once fine, was scarred and battered, though none of the dents or scrapes were new. Someone had carried that box on long journeys, had polished and smoothed the dents with loving hands. Wenatef knew every dent, knew the size and heft of the box without ever having touched it, for his own bow had been stored in just such a box, dented from traveling and campaigning.

He knelt beside the box and touched the lid, then gripped it and lifted. He was engulfed in the nauseous smell of spoiled leather and aged oils. The thieves had obviously opened the box, been repelled by the stench, and had thrown the box aside. The thought made Wenatef smile as he touched the roll of leather that lay just beneath the lid. It cracked; had the bow been damaged by the dryness, or had the leather protected it?

He lifted the roll from the box and carefully eased the crumbling leather away. The scent of sweet oils grew stronger and the leather felt more supple, more moist near the center of the roll.

Another twist of leather and the bow lay before him, strong and intact, glistening with oil. Wenatef lifted the bow in his hands and blessed the man who had packed that bow away, all in one piece, without ritually 'killing' it by breaking it, so that it would not harm the spirit of its owner. The oil was sticky, but a good half-hour of rubbing would remedy that. His hands shook as they touched the ivory grip, the golden tips, the rich wood and horn.

He still had bowstrings with his clothes. He retrieved the pouch and took one out, then rose and strung the bow. Yes. It was still supple, still strong.

It felt good to draw the bow. Wenatef sighted along an imaginary arrow, pictured it speeding to its mark. He remembered his dream. He knelt again and found the arrows beneath the sliding panel at the base of the box. They too were magnificent, the arrows of a king, with a quiver of stiffened, oiled leather, and a silver bracer for his wrist.

Wenatef sat down and sighed with delight. He was armed again - and with such a bow! There was no enemy that he couldn't face with that bow, no target that he couldn't hit. Now he was almost invincible.

He drew a shaking breath, expelled it, and looked down at the box again, and then frowned and looked closer. He could see a speck of blue in the corner, beneath some bits of leather. He pushed the dry fragments aside with his finger and found a little ring of blue faience.

It was too small to fit on his finger. He lifted it. Yes, it had been worn once, and a name was painted on it: 'Nakhti'. For Nakhtamun?

Wenatef looked at the bow again, then at the ring, and he had to swallow a sudden taste of salt. He knew who had placed the bow in that box, so carefully wrapped. Who but a father would swath a bow so lovingly in well-oiled leather and then tuck a child's trinket into the box along with it? Who but a father gazing with bleak eyes at the wreckage of the future? Who but a father renouncing his hopes of being laid to his own rest by the hands of a strong, grieving, beloved eldest son?

Wenatef took the ring, rose, and went to the sarcophagus. He tucked the ring among the folds of linen surrounding the mummy, then turned, took up his bow and arrows, and went into the tunnel, to move the stones aside and peer out into the darkness. The sun was about to rise, soon it would be daylight and time for him to sleep.

He rearranged the boxes at either end of the tunnel, smoothed the pile of folded sheets that made his bed, positioned the headrest beneath him, and closed his eyes. He would go after the robbers the next evening.

CHAPTER XXIX

Now that everyone thought him dead, Wenatef decided that it was safe to go about and observe things. Sleeping by day and patrolling at night was the best option. He began to prowl the Necropolis armed with Nakhtamun's bow and arrows.

His nights were dull at first. Merihor's panic and Wenatef's supposed death had drawn too much attention to the Valley. For the moment, at least, the robbers were leaving the Valley of the Kings alone, although he found evidence that the thieves had been within the tomb and deposited some of their loot there once while he was away. His own exit tunnel had remained undiscovered.

He suspected that the robbers had most likely drawn back and gone after the tombs in the Valley of the Queens or the burial places of the nobles. The people buried there had been powerful, and their tombs were probably rich. Wenatef decided to follow the thieves there.

** ** **

He saw a steady glow of light from what appeared to be a doorway. A torch flickered among the rocks. Voices came to him, carried by the faint night breeze. Snatches of words like 'dig' and 'find' and 'carry', were enough to make Wenatef stiffen and draw an arrow from his quiver and move closer to the lights. No one was there; he drew closer, moving carefully.

He was on the crest of the ridge of the Valley of the

Queens, looking down into the narrow valley running behind the graves. He could hear the sound of vessels scraping across the earth and items being taken from them. Spoils from the tomb, no doubt, Wenatef thought, narrowing his eyes. Men emerged into the open after another moment, carrying torches and baskets.

Wenatef's recognized one of them: Khai, the man who had guarded him when he was first captured. His mouth thinned: he had hoped that the man had been killed as punishment for letting him escape. Khai was turning to another and laughing, and he was holding a statuette of a woman in one hand.

Wenatef nocked his arrow and slowly rose to a kneeling position. He felt no compunction about killing a tomb robber who had been caught in the act. The death he would deal out with his arrows was a kinder one than that which would await them at the hands of the authorities.

He drew the bow, sighted along the shaft of the arrow - and then slowly eased the bow back. Something was moving between him and the robbers. He watched as another man crept closer to them, behind a screen of rocks. Three men were about to converge on him from behind, two with drawn knives and one with a length of thin rope in his hands.

Wenatef's heart lurched. It was Ramses who was watching the tomb robbers - and doing a wretched job of it, too! Ramses whose father had been killed by 'lions' and who had sworn vengeance in Wenatef's hearing. And only a very young man would go about matters in such a brash way.

The three men had almost reached him. Wenatef took a deep breath and cried, "Run!"

Ramses reared upright, saw the men surrounding him, groped for his knife, and then froze as the three fell, struck down by Wenatef's arrows. One of them cried out before he died, bringing a panicked stream of men shouting from the tomb.

It was like slaughtering cattle in a pen. Wenatef killed another five of them. Silence fell. He looked around at the ground, scattered with dead men. Ramses was gone.

Wenatef made his way to the robbers. He retrieved his arrows from the corpses and then thrust their own knives into the wounds, thinking that the less people to know that an archer was at large, the better it would be.

He cleaned the last arrow in the sand and straightened, wondering if any others were still hiding inside the tomb. He would go in and see, but he would have to do it slowly to allow his eyes accustom themselves to the light within the tomb...

He cast a quick glance around him.

Ramses was standing on the ridge, looking down at him, his face in the moonlight showing fear and joy, his stance uncertain.

"Get away from here, you fool!" Wenatef said. "This isn't your quarrel."

Ramses still seemed to hesitate.

Wenatef fitted an arrow to his bow and half-turned toward the tomb. "Go now," he said. "Before you're involved in something greater than you can fight."

Ramses lowered his head and turned.

"Run!" Wenatef ordered.

Ramses disappeared, and Wenatef turned back to the dead-strewn ground. The air was full of the metallic reek of blood. Still no sound from the tomb, though he could see a faint light within it. He raised his bow.

** ** **

Wenatef came through the tunnel into warm light and a vision of the gods and goddesses welcoming a queen to their midst. Wenatef paused, filled with a sense of strangeness: he had been in this tomb before, in his dream. He looked

145

around at the wall paintings once again.

The queen was the fairest woman he had seen, alive or in a painting. She was slim and young, with a gently smiling mouth and a wealth of hair that fell to her waist from the fillet of her crown. She clasped hands with Horus, bowed to Hathor, presented offerings to Osiris, sat at a senet board with one playing piece poised, as though she were awaiting another player. She seemed to be smiling at him, and for one dizzy moment Wenatef almost felt that he could step into the painting, take the seat opposite her, and play senet with her.

The smile seemed to deepen...

He wrenched his thoughts away. This was folly. He was alone in a tomb that might yet harbor enemies. But he smiled at the queen, and she seemed to smile back at him before he turned away.

No one was hiding in the disordered antechamber, though a twist of rag floated in a bowl of oil, giving a fitful, stinking light. Wenatef passed through the tunnel leading into the burial chamber and frowned at the sarcophagus that lay opened and splintered, just as he had seen. He stirred an untidy swath of ashes and bones with his foot. A ruined, blackened skull lay at one end. It was all that remained of the mummy. He could still see the queen's smile within his mind.

Had he heard a sound? He froze, lifting his head and looking from side to side, his eyes narrowed. He decided that he had been mistaken and went back to the opening.

The queen still smiled at him; her name was effaced, and he did not know who she was. He blew out the lighted wick as he passed into the night that was turning toward morning. It was time to return to his tomb and sleep.

** ** **

He had not seen the man cringing in terror behind the sarcophagus, hidden by a jumble of linen wrappings, scarcely daring to breathe. This man, a poor peasant lured by the tale of riches available to anyone for the digging, had come downriver seeking Khaemwase, an outlaw from Koptos with a reputation for knowing of such things. He had told Khaemwase's lieutenants a sad tale of failed crops and a starving family. He had been put to work.

The thought of robbing the dead had frightened him at first, for he was a superstitious man. He had also been filled with horror and fear by one of the leaders who had shown delight in smashing the faces of the dead, in dismembering them, and, in the case of the queen whose tomb they were plundering, burning the corpses and scattering the ashes, destroying any hope of Heaven for the unfortunate dead. Surely a terrible fate awaited such evil!

But he was desperate and there was no way to live besides doing what he was doing, and the sight of so much wealth when he and his family were trying to scrape along from one meal to the next had eased his fear. Until that night.

He had heard the cries outside, but when the others went charging out into the blackness, he had hidden, hysterically mouthing prayers to the gods of his village. They had hidden him, he was convinced of it. He had cowered, staring wide-eyed at the heavenly being of wrath that had silently entered the tomb.

It was Montu himself, god of war from the Land of the West, come to earth to wreak vengeance upon the despoilers of the dead! His flesh seemed made of bronze with the breath and pulse of life itself underlying the skin. He glistened in the dim light of the tomb, and the dark chamber was filled with an awful radiance that flashed and glittered like the reflection of rippling waters cast by the sun upon a wall, turning all that was not part of that brilliance and radiance into blackest shadow.

He had been tall and mighty, his shoulders spanning and surpassing the width of the burial chamber, and it was as though the tomb walls themselves were merely shadows, cobwebs that circled his shoulders but could not confine him. The god carried a great bow; an arrow like a bolt of lightning was fitted to the string, and the god's gaze swung back and forth across the chamber, swift as a striking snake, slow as the journey of the sun across the sky. The peasant caught a glimpse of the terrible eyes. They were as deep and as blinding as the sun itself, and the peasant had felt himself seared and laid bare by the glance.

He had drawn a quick, awed breath, and the god had heard him. He had despaired, then, feeling the god's gaze pass over him, narrow and then sweep across him once more. And then the god had turned and moved away, sparing him. His feet had made no sound upon the floor, but the very walls of the tomb had seemed to shake with his passing. He had departed in silence, casting the tomb into darkness.

The peasant stirred, whimpering a little with gratitude. He would never, never rob another tomb, not though his family starved! The gods had been generous to him, and he would not test their generosity any further. He would take with him nothing that he had stolen, would tell all who asked him that only fools robbed the Great Ones, and fools met the fates they deserved.

He was disoriented; it was some time before he found the doorway leading to the antechamber, and he had to crawl on his hands and knees. Once in the antechamber he found the tunnel easily by the faint glow of moonlight at its end. He passed through the tunnel and came out into the night.

He paused, breathing the cool, pure air after the reek of the tomb, troubled by a sense of past disaster and the ominous smell about him, but feeling once again the beauty of simply being alive. He thanked his gods for delivering

148

him, and then looked down.

A body sprawled at his feet, and the moon flashed from a dark puddle beneath the contorted limbs. Other bodies lay here and there. All his companions. Now he understood the cause of the scent, for it was the smell of a slaughterhouse.

He drew a long, , shaking breath and then ran. He would tell Khaemwase about the archer god and warn him not to meddle in the affairs of the dead. Khaemwase would be angry, of course, but if the peasant did not tell him that he planned to desert, then he would have no reason to kill him, would he?

No, the peasant decided, he was not a fool. He would leave while Khaemwase was looking the other way...

CHAPTER XXX

Now that he had probably discouraged further midnight depredations for a time, Wenatef decided that he could look into the other tombs and see how extensive the robberies really were. He had a half-sick feeling that they would be extensive indeed, since the thieves were reduced to plundering the burial places of the queens and the nobles.

He took a handful of raisins from the ones he had soaked in wine and tucked them into a pouch at his waist. Some of the bread, also soggy, went into the pouch with them. He measured out a small container of water from his store, reflecting that he would have to try to hunt for some decent food, since the gods as yet showed no inclination to feed him properly.

Everything was in place in the burial chamber. He ducked out through the side opening, pulling a basket against the wall behind him and then covering the opening with several flat stones.

Merihor had been terrified after coming from the tomb of Thutmose III. It would have been the first the thieves struck, since the king had been the greatest that Egypt had ever produced, the conqueror who had brought her to the pinnacle of her glory. The treasure buried with him must have been magnificent. Wenatef decided to go there first. Being familiar with the thieves' methods in Nakhtamun's tomb, he knew what to look for.

** ** **

Ten minutes later he was standing in the hollow of the

A Killing Among the Dead

Valley looking up at the tall, pillar-like clefts and hollows of the cliff face. Thutmose III's tomb was within those vertical gashes, and Wenatef's suddenly sensitive eyes could detect a faint irregularity halfway up. The entrance was there, most likely, but impossible to reach except by a rope let down the face of the cliff. The thieves' entrance was probably at the top of the cleft, away from the edge.

He found it after some searching, carelessly hidden by several large stones. It was easy to move them aside and crawl into the entryway. The tunnel was not large enough to allow Wenatef to stand; he fit within it on hands and knees, but there was no room to spare. The steep slope of the tunnel forced him to crawl down backward with the torch in his mouth, his provisions bumping against his knees and the ground.

He reached the bottom of the passageway after what seemed like hours, drew a deep breath of the stuffy air of the tomb, and settled on his knees, fumbling for his coal-carrier. He found it, opened it by feel, nearly scorching a fingertip, touched his torch to the coals, and hid his eyes as it flared into brilliance.

A jumble of broken boxes and furniture leapt into his sight. The steepness of the tunnel had made it necessary for the thieves to cut away the precious parts of the tomb provisions, since most of them were too bulky to carry up intact. His torch picked out flakes of gold and bits of glass and fine stone that had fallen from the mutilated goods.

He looked around, his mouth wry with disgust. Because the tomb had been dug deep into the hillside and, unlike Nakhtamun's tomb, had been constructed in the shape of an L, the entryway had come into a small side room. To Wenatef's appalled eyes, the entire chamber seemed filled from floor to ceiling with rubbish. He could catch the heavy, bitter taste of anger in the air, and he could not escape the feeling that the disorder had been the result of a fantastic orgy of malevolent destruction.

The torch was still too bright; tears streamed from his eyes and he wiped them away with the back of his hand as his vision slowly became accustomed to the light. It was better after a moment, though the details of the destruction were now distressingly clear.

He would look through the rest of the tomb. He rose, still shading his eyes, and took a tentative step forward. His foot bumped against something dry and light, like ancient wood. He opened his eyes wider and bent down with the torch before him.

Teeth grinning at him, yellow in a blackened face, like a chuckle from the depths of the tomb, amid withered, wizened flesh. Clenched, desiccated fingers leapt into his vision and bones stood out, knobbed and grotesque beneath shreds of what had once been muscle. And the face - the face -

Wenatef yelled and dropped his torch, and yelled again as the flame struck splintered wood and flared into a leaping, crackling blaze, throwing the face and the teeth into sharp red light. He seized some cloth with a wail of dismay and beat at the fire and then lifted the torch. Some tongues of flame still hissed and crackled among the litter of wood and cloth on the floor. He extinguished them at the cost of another scorched finger. He put his fingers in his mouth and sat down, trembling.

He looked to his left after a moment and jumped. He had forgotten the face. He closed his eyes for a second and then forced himself to look. It was not so terrible, after all, he decided. The expression was almost benign. He looked about the chamber and saw two more pieces of the body.

Someone had dragged the corpse of the great Thutmose III into this room, stripped it, and then torn it apart in the search for gold. And then, after all this had been done, someone had taken his fist and caved in the bridge of the nose with a single blow.

Unas. Why did he have such a hatred of the dead?

Wenatef's reactions were complex. He was looking for the first time upon a mummy - a preserved body that was expected to house the soul throughout eternity. This wizened mass of meat that might have been dried fish, except that it was molded in a human form! This - this! - was what lay beneath the layers of bandages, within the golden mask that covered the head and shoulders, nestled within three gold-sheathed coffins, locked away within a great stone sarcophagus. All the care, all the fear, all the precautions taken to preserve the body resulted in this! But it was madness!

He remembered snatches of superstition. Tear the body apart and you have destroyed the afterlife. Cut off a hand and the spirit will be hand-less. Smash the nose even of a statue and the spirit won't be able to breathe... Preserve the body and all will be well... By that line of thought, then, the Fields of the West should be filled with shriveled, brittle shadows.

The thought of shadows jolted him. It had not been the dead - the blessed ones - who had appeared as shadows in the Fields of the West, but Wenatef. They had been pulsing with life, as filled with light, as the Nile is filled with water. And yet the bodies they had worn in their lives were undoubtedly shriveled like this one. Someone had hacked Nakhtamun's corpse with an axe - and yet the spirit that had once been housed in that split, hacked corpse, had been strong and whole, more real than Wenatef.

The mummy's hand was near his; he set his own strong, brown one beside it and gazed down at them side by side. His living flesh was more real than the dried, withered flesh beside it, just as Nakhtamun's spirit seemed more real than

153

Wenatef's living flesh. Pure flesh was less than flesh and spirit combined, and when flesh and spirit submitted to death, they passed into something greater than both. All the fear, all the worry, all the elaborate precautions taken to protect the body were unnecessary.

Wenatef moved his hand, closed it and held it against his heart, transfixed by the thought and unable to halt its progression from conclusion to conclusion.

It did not matter what happened to the body, for Wenatef had seen the bodies of the Blest, and they had been whole and unblemished. There was no need for embalming, no need for an elaborate tomb, no need for the grave-goods, no need for anything but the honor and virtue, courage and generosity that was in his own heart, to secure his place among the *Akhu*. That was all that was needed, and all the rest was a childish, frantic scrabbling after that which was unnecessary.

No one in the world could harm those in the Land of the West. They had passed beyond the reach of evil men.

Wenatef remembered all his comrades who had died in Nubia in the siege of Semna, remembered their hacked, battered bodies hurriedly wrapped and buried. The besiegers had dug up the cemetery near the fort, torn the bodies apart and scattered them over the desert in a gesture of defiance. He remembered his own agonizing fear that his parents' embalming had not been done well, and the dream that had haunted even him, the veteran of wars, of encountering them in the Land of the West, wandering maimed and hungry through the wastelands, the prey of other, stronger ones. He had awakened from those dreams with a pounding heart and a bitter taste of tears in his throat. And now, it seemed, the tears and the fear had been unnecessary.

He doubled against his knees, his face buried in his hands, trembling with emotion too deep for laughter or for tears, whispering something over and over, but not hearing what it was that he was saying. The conflict was too much to bear in silence, and the exposure and negation of all the fears and superstitions that had held him from childhood was a painful freedom.

Minutes passed before he finally raised his head, brushing at unaccustomed wetness on his cheeks. He covered the face of Thutmose the Great, drew a shaking breath and rose.

He was weary, he decided, weary and hungry. So much had happened to frighten or overawe him, and he had not had the sort of food that would put heart into him, either. There was much to do, and if his heart ached with a freedom that he could not yet understand, the best cure for that ache was   work.

CHAPTER XXXI

Wenatef set about exploring the tomb. It was simply laid out, and seemed bare of decorations, unlike the tomb Duwah was excavating. He could catch the impression of simplicity, even amid the signs of wholesale destruction. The room was rounded, the smooth corners harboring no shadows in the light of his torch. He carefully stepped over the huddle of dry flesh that had been Thutmose III and paused in the doorway that seemed to open into black nothingness.

He raised his torch and stepped forward. The light flashed, stabbing upward along a column of white to scatter across a star-flecked ceiling, painted to resemble the night sky. Shadows quivered around the litter of boxes, beds and chariots that flashed with gold. Chips of wood were scattered everywhere, and an adz lay at Wenatef's feet.

He frowned and bent down to examine the hacked wreck of a fine, gilded chair. The gold had been stripped from it in little chips, revealing the elegant form beneath the bright metal. Beyond the chair were other furnishings, treated the same way. The work appeared to be ongoing.

The white shape caught Wenatef's attention; he stepped forward, stretched out his hand and touched the stark, square shape of a pillar. Beyond the pillar loomed the dark shape of the sarcophagus with the broken lid lying just before it.

The tomb chamber itself was rounded and long, and the walls that reflected the light of the torch were the color of sand and pink granite. They seemed to teem with activity, their surface filled with slender, elegant figures moving in the hours of the Amduat, the sun's journey through the realms of the night. The king fighting great serpents, vanquishing the foes of the sun, while above him brooded gods with falcons' wings and the scarabs of the sun.

The text of the Amduat followed the drawings, the borders representing the sand of the horizon below which the sun carried on his battles. Wenatef saw the sun descending below the horizon, lighting the netherworld, the congregation of gods... He blinked and turned away, suddenly uncomfortable.

It was as though he were reading a message meant for another. He lowered his head and touched the cold smoothness of the sarcophagus before turning his attention to the wreckage of the tomb.

The jumble of grave-goods made Wenatef shake his head. The thieves had been in a hurry, and they had thrown the contents of chests on the floor, smashed furniture, strewn cloths across the floor and emptied pots and jugs indiscriminately. Desiccated steaks from a long-dead steer lay at Wenatef's feet. He kicked them aside and then realized that he was standing in the middle of a mound of kohl and other cosmetics. A puddle of unguents lay close by, staining the air with their fading sweetness.

The disorder disgusted him. The thought that this had been the site of an orgy of destruction occurred to him again. Maybe they had been drunk. He looked about in search of wine jugs or jars of beer, and he found them. Not old ones, but new, with seals dating from Wenatef's time. He examined the seal of one jug of wine. It came from a vineyard that Wenatef was familiar with, and the vintage mark was that of the past harvest season.

He lifted the jug and sniffed at it, and then upended it. A small quantity of wine spotted the floor before him. It had evaporated to the thickness of blood. How long would it take for wine to evaporate in that tomb? More than a week? Less? And the unguents were beginning to dry out as well, from the feel of them.

Another wine jug lay smashed on the floor, and the condition of its shards seemed to indicate that someone had opened the jug, tasted it, and then hurled it on the floor and stomped on the pieces. Wenatef bent to read the notations on the jug and then grinned in spite of himself.

This was some of His Majesty's finest wine. Older than Nakhtamun's wine by a century or so, and probably that much worse. The thieves had probably opened the jar, tasted the 'nectar', and gone into a rage.

The thieves had come into the tomb recently, probably within the past two weeks. And maybe Merihor, seeing something that had sparked his interest - some irregularity in the familiar hills, perhaps - had come into the tomb as well. The sight of Thutmose III's broken, defiled corpse had certainly shocked Wenatef. He could guess the effect it would have had on someone with Merihor's uncertain temperament.

Wenatef went back into the burial chamber and sat down on the lid of the sarcophagus. He opened his pouch of lunch and ate the soggy bread and hard raisins in thoughtful silence, looking around the chamber, trying to pierce the darkness that shrouded the corners. One of the pillars showed the king being suckled by a tree. Isis herself, transformed to the shape of a graceful sycamore, as she had done during the terrible battles between Horus and Set.

Wenatef stared for a moment and then nodded and went on eating. A tree, indeed! He stopped smiling after a moment.

There was nothing to smile about, really. Someone had stolen, which was bad enough, but he had mutilated and smashed. Wenatef could not ignore the malice and the insult. It did not matter that the one so insulted was a king. He would have been just as enraged if he had discovered that someone had done this to the humble tomb of Sobek the potter or Nedjmet the fishwife, or even Wenatef's own parents.

That thought made his eyes widen and his heart lurch. His parents - ! What if someone had defiled their tomb? By all the gods - !

He made himself take a deep breath. He would go to his parents' tomb the next night and make certain that no one had disturbed it for the sake of the modest wealth buried with them by their grieving son. Until then there was nothing he could do about it. And in the meantime there were monsters at large - human monsters - and he was the only one who could fight them.

** ** **

It was very late before Wenatef returned to Nakhtamun's tomb. He had walked to the Nile to bathe and wash the defilement of Thutmose's tomb from his flesh. It had taken some time, but he was at last clean and very hungry.

He looked around carefully, saw no one, and hurried to the side entrance to the storage room. No one there. He slipped inside, found tinder and flint, and quickly lit an oil lamp and then hid the opening from sight. And then he paused.

A scent had come to him, a faint aroma of onions and fresh fruit and warm bread. His stomach protested; he pushed the baskets carefully aside from the tunnel entrance and looked into the tomb. Onions, lettuces, fruits and breads spilled from their baskets like the overflow from a dream of delight, filling the air with their savor, making the memory of rock-hard bread, stony raisins and musty wine seem like the echoes of some hilarious tale Wenatef had heard at a banquet and then forgotten.

He knelt before the mound of food, eyeing each morsel with fresh joy. And then he closed his eyes and said a heartfelt thanks to the gods for providing him with palatable food at long last.

At *very* long last, he decided as he selected some lettuce and two persimmons. He ate where he knelt, savoring each bite and finding the pleasure almost unbearable. When he was finished he sat back against the wall with his fingers laced across his stomach, yawned contentedly, and set about deciding how the food had come to be in the tomb in the first place.

He knew from his own experience that the gods hear prayers. But that same experience had also taught Wenatef that the prayers were generally answered through the actions of people. That food had not simply appeared in the tomb. Someone had carried it inside, and by the look of things he had had to make several trips.

He inspected the storage chamber, where he had dug his tunnel. No, there was no doubt of it. Whoever had brought the food had entered that way and not through the ceiling of the burial chamber. And that person had tried to make things look as though he had never been inside the tomb. The baskets had been piled against the opening almost exactly as Wenatef had piled them, and the only difference that he could find was one box which had been tipped over and come open, spilling its contents, blue clay ornaments of little value, across the floor.

Ramses. Wenatef said the name aloud. No doubt about it. He grinned. Besides, who else but a young man would think of bringing food to a friend who was unable to forage for himself, go to great lengths to bring the food through a hidden entrance, carefully disguise the entrance so that the tomb robbers would not find it - and forget to hide the food as well?

The grin changed to a chuckle as Wenatef carefully put

the provisions away in the tunnel and then penned a message to Ramses:

Thank you, Ramses. Next time, though, please try to hide the food so the robbers don't find it.

He left the message, written on a large chip of limestone, in plain view atop a basket of bread, and then placed boxes and baskets full of trinkets before the entrance, so that he could hear if anyone tried to come in that way again. He decided to sleep with Nakhtamun's bow strung and ready beside him, with arrows within easy reach

.

CHAPTER XXXII

The wind was whistling through the rocks and the valleys of the cemetery with the sound furtive voices whispering secrets in the night. It swirled about Wenatef, tugging at his kilt and tunic, tweaking his hair, pushing at his shoulders, and always whispering to him of hopes brought to nothing, of fears realized in darkness and despair, of gnawing loneliness and heartbreaking grief. It seemed to take the black pain that filled Wenatef's heart and cry it aloud, sending the echoes ringing through the valleys and along the hills.

Wenatef turned his back on the wind and climbed the hillside, past the dark, silent doorways of tomb chapels. His parents' tomb was just beyond the next opening; he could remember the day he had gone with his father, Hapuseneb, to inspect the site. They had stood by the doorway, where Wenatef stood now, and looked over the swell of the hills down toward the Nile. *This is a good place*, Hapuseneb had said, *I'll be happy to sleep here.*

And there he and his wife had been taken to sleep through eternity. Wenatef could remember the day. He had been numb with the double blow of their deaths within four days of each other. They had died in his arms during an epidemic that had decimated Thebes. The last words for each had been the other's name.

Seventy days later Wenatef had stood in the courtyard and watched as the priests performed the ceremony of the Opening of the Mouth on both coffins. He had ordered a funeral feast for all the mourners, paid and otherwise, but he had been unable to eat or drink, himself. He had remained outside the tomb after the others had left, his knees against the ground, his unseeing eyes fixed on the river, while the funerary workers in the depths of the tomb wrestled the two coffins into the burial chamber amid laughter and jests and then filled in the pit. He remembered, as clearly as though it had happened just the night before, how their laughter had stilled as the workers came past him.

Wenatef looked toward the Nile, coiling in the distance like a stream of moonlight. This was a good place to sleep, just as Hapuseneb had said. He squared his shoulders, fighting back a chill of foreboding, stepped into the tomb chapel, and lit the small oil lamp that he had brought with him.

The tiny flame threw everything into stark light and shadow, playing over the straight edges of the false doorway with its offering table, slanting across the remains of an offering-feast of bread and meat, touching the feet of the statues of Hapuseneb and his wife, the Lady Neitneferti.

Wenatef could feel their eyes on him in the darkness. He turned and went slowly to the statues, then raised the lamp and gazed up into their faces. Hapuseneb had commissioned the best sculptor in Thebes to carve the statues out of the living rock of the tomb. The sculptor, Nakhtmin, had owed a favor to Hapuseneb, who had been Chief of the Granaries of Mut. He had carved the statues as repayment and had counted himself the gainer.

Nakhtmin had done a good job. Wenatef, looking up into the carved faces of his mother and father, seemed to see them as they had been in life, smiling, happy, their arms about each other, festively garbed, Neitneferti's hair dressed in ringlets, Hapuseneb sporting a gala kilt and wig.

They blurred before him; Wenatef turned away, shaking

in the grip of remembered grief that seemed to clutch at his throat. His had been a loving family. He blinked back the blur, went to the table, and gazed at the offerings laid out upon it. He had paid Ka-priests to perform the proper ceremonies at the tomb, and they had been faithful.

He turned back toward the statues, trembling. He had come to the tomb prepared to find destruction and desecration. He had been ready to wreak vengeance upon those who had disturbed his parents' rest - and found it intact. His heart was certain that all was as it should be. All was most well and his fears had been unnecessary.

He looked at the paintings on the walls of the chapel, aware at the same time that the sealed, undisturbed tomb of his parents lay far below his feet. He saw himself portrayed on the wall, crouched beneath his father's chair, playing with their pet kitten. Aboard a papyrus skiff, hired for the day, he stood wearing the sidelock of childhood and nothing else, clinging to his father's leg while his mother's hand steadied his shoulder. Hapuseneb was about to hurl his boomerang at a flock of ducks... Yes, Wenatef remembered.

He smiled, but the smile was unsteady, and the hand that held the lamp was shaking as he went back to the statues.

Hapuseneb and Neitneferti seemed to smile back at him, and he almost saw their living flesh over the beautifully carved stone. All was well. No one had torn their bodies apart and scattered the wrappings about the floor of their tomb. All was well.

Wenatef would have pursued his vengeance calmly and thoroughly, but the lack of that necessity unmanned him for a moment. He dropped to his knees before his mother's statue, buried his face in her lap, and sobbed. It seemed to him that he wept for all the desecrated tombs, for all the broken corpses, for the greed that warped the souls of thieves, and for the grief of all those who had buried their loved ones far below the earth and away from the kind light of the sun and could not understand what he now knew.

Had he felt a hand upon his hair? His mother had soothed him like that when he was a little boy.

He raised his head and gazed up into the smiling, carved faces, and it seemed as though the world had shifted about him and he was viewing the wreckage of the tombs and the desecration of the bodies through new eyes. There were monsters abroad, there was no denying it - but what of the thousands of people in Thebes and in the rest of Egypt who had not robbed tombs?

The tally of those who had not bowed to greed far outweighed that of those who had. It was easy to forget that fact amid the horror of the acts of the guilty. Wenatef had lost sight it for a time, but now it was as though he were surrounded by a great, silent multitude: the honorable and faithful ones who had not done wrong. It made him feel almost as he had when he had stood on the ramparts of Semna and watched the Army of Upper Egypt smash through and scatter the rebel besiegers.

And as for the innocence of those of the village whom he liked and trusted - why did he demand proof? What could be proven, after all, that was of any importance? Everything important had to be taken on trust. Wenatef had not thought the village captains were involved in the robberies, and there was no new evidence to show that they were. Wenatef had trusted the village chiefs; why not rest on that trust and affection?

And, finally, the mutilation of the corpses, the destruction and looting of the tombs could no more harm those of the West than scribbling the word 'darkness' on the wall of a room could extinguish the light of the sun. The gods still reigned in the heavens, the *Akhu* were unhindered by the vicious actions of madmen and superstitious simpletons. Had Wenatef found all in chaos here in his parents' tomb, he would nonetheless have known that Hapuseneb and Neitneferti his wife walked healthy and whole through the Fields of the West.

Wenatef bowed his head against his mother's knees once more. He still wept, but it was with joy too deep for laughter. All was well. He could pursue the thieves with a lightened heart, knowing that he was not alone, that fading, dying as Egypt was, she still harbored men and women with true hearts who walked upright before the gods.

He arose after a time, finally at peace, but exhausted by the storm of thought and emotion that had filled his heart. All was most well. He placed fruit and bread on the offering slab and left the chapel.

** ** **

He was actually whistling as he walked to the Nile to bathe and then make his way back to the tomb. His heart felt as light as it had when he was a carefree child running along the riverbank, playing tag with his pretty little mother, who had usually let him win.

The crocodiles were there again, led by the monster that had protected him some days before. Wenatef tossed them the food he carried with him, and used the biggest crocodile as a sort of buoy while he bathed. The beast had become something of a pet; he had not seemed to mind.

Afterward, refreshed and clothed once more, Wenatef settled the quiver of arrows more comfortably at his shoulder and once more became little Weni, the beloved son of Hapuseneb and Neitneferti. It was good to forget the Commander of One Thousand for a time, to forget that he had ever been a hero at Semna, or Commander of the Guard of the Tomb of His Majesty, and instead to walk along the Nile, picking up handfuls of pebbles to scatter across the moonlit river.

He watched them sink into the water, leaving ripples behind them. Sowing ripples of moonlight. That is what his mother had called it, standing beside him and sowing the ripples, too. How smooth her slender hands had been then! He had thought her the most beautiful of women when he was a little boy.

Wenatef paused to raise his face to the sky and smile at the moon. It was the first time that he had been able to remember his parents without grief. The heartbreak was gone and the memories were good once more. It was as though he had come back to them after a long and wearying journey.

** ** **

"Now do you see what I mean? Someone's been in here!"

"You're imagining things." The second voice was quiet and flat.

Wenatef heard the voices as he came slowly awake in his tunnel. They were coming from the burial chamber, low and quiet, as though the speakers were afraid of being overheard.

What time was it? He squinted out the passageway toward the sky. Light. They were very sure of themselves to come by daylight. He silently reached for his dagger and settled it in the waistband of his kilt.

"I tell you, things have been rearranged!" The first voice's slightly higher pitch was increased by dismay. "See: the bones have been covered again."

"If someone's been here," said the second voice, "Who do you suppose it was?"

"It was him, that's who."

The voices were familiar, but Wenatef could not quite place them. He inched toward the entrance to his tunnel and frowned toward the burial chamber.

The speakers were approaching.

"How can that be, you fool?" The second voice was scornful. "You heard Unas' report. He was killed by those lions. Everyone saw the blood!"

167

"Yes, but how do we know it was him? Did anyone see his body?"

"That Gold of Honor that he wore - "

The first speaker snorted. "Don't forget that was the second time he was supposed to have been killed!"

There was a long silence, then the second voice said, "What are you talking about?"

"I'm talking about Unas," said the first voice. "He said he came back here to make certain of him the afternoon after they brought him here - "

"That warped little liar!"

"Yes, well... But I happen to believe him this time," said the first voice. "He told me he took his dagger and gave the death-stroke below the fifth rib. He said the knife went in and came out and the blood came as well. And look, you - "

Wenatef heard the sound of boxes scraping across the floor. " - here's the spot. You can see the bloodstains. It took a lot of blood to make a stain this size. And see, there's a trail to the foot of that statue."

"Unas made a mistake. The knife must have struck a rib and slid off."

"Oh no. Unas knows how to kill. You've seen him, yourself. Weren't you in the army? No one loses that much blood and lives."

"Then how do you explain the lions?"

"I can't. That's what troubles me. There is too much that can't be explained."

Wenatef suddenly knew who was speaking. Roy of the Necropolis Police. Roy, who had been part of Nuteruhotep's private guard.

"You're as fanciful as a pregnant woman," the second voice said.

"That may be. But what of that little peasant and what he saw in the Valley of the Queens after that massacre?"

"The one who was so scared, he cut and run without

waiting to get his share?" asked the second voice. "Hysterical."

"Maybe so. You'd be hysterical too if all your friends were killed - but that's another thing: who did the killing? Not the Necropolis Police, or I'd have known of it. Not the army, not the Karnak Temple Guard, not the Theban Municipal Police. So tell me, Seneb: who did it?"

There was no answer.

"And he said he saw Montu himself. Explain that."

"Superstitious, that's all. He told tales he remembered."

"What story has ever described a god as towering above and through solid rock? None that I've ever heard!"

"I tell you, he was hysterical!"

"Maybe so," said Roy. "And maybe I am as well. And maybe I'm taking the same course of action that he did."

"What's that supposed to mean?" demanded the second voice."

"It means that I am leaving this plot," said Roy. "I was wrong to join it in the first place. I won't fight against the *Akhu*."

"Now you're being foolish," said the second voice. The speaker was close enough for Wenatef to see now. He recognized Seneb.

"No, I am being sensible for the first time in weeks," said Roy. "Listen to me: I got into this plot because I was greedy. I chose to believe that this life is all there is, and when it ends it ends. That vast complex that we call Karnak was erected by men to honor something that they made up in their own minds, and it means nothing to those of us who can think - "

"Well?" Seneb said with amused tolerance.

"Well, I haven't been easy in my own heart since I came to join you in this. I've been thinking, and my thoughts tell me that I was wrong. I've been doing evil, and I regret it.

I've come a long way from what I once was - and shame to me for that! - but I can try to turn back."

"You can try," Seneb said. "But I don't give much for your chances of survival. *He* takes a dim view of traitors."

"I'll take my chances," said Roy. "And so should you. We've been friends for years, Seneb. Think about it: come with me and leave this plot. Save yourself before it's too late."

The silence stretched out, punctuated by the sound of papyrus-sandaled feet moving through the tomb.

"Well," said Seneb at last. His voice had altered slightly, to Wenatef's ears. "Things have certainly been moved. Someone's moved them." He paused and added with scornful emphasis, "Probably the Akh of that fellow Unas failed to kill. He seems to come in regularly."

"But he isn't in here," said Roy. His voice was flat. "Is he?"

"Not right now," said Seneb. "But he will be. I'll set a trap and wait for him to fall in."

"You go right ahead," said Roy. "Set the trap. And then see if you like what you catch." He paused and added, "You could leave with me, you know."

"So you say," said Seneb. "I'm not so sure. And when you do go, what will that do to the rest of us? You hold our lives in your hand."

"I wouldn't betray you."

"Wouldn't you?"

"We're friends, Seneb. I wouldn't harm you." Roy was silent for a moment, waiting for a reply. When none came, he said, "Come on, let's leave this place."

The two men went back to the burial chamber, and Wenatef heard them climbing up the knotted rope that had been let down through the opening.

He considered, frowning, then went silently out his tunnel and watched as Seneb and Roy emerged from the tomb and stood on the rocky outcropping overhanging the cliff below.

A light chariot had been tethered near the hole; Seneb went to the horses' heads and gazed down the cliff and into the valley while Roy coiled the rope.

"Will you at least think about what I said?" Roy asked.

"Yes, I'll think about it," Seneb replied. His gaze, trained on the valley below, became more intent. "Come here and look at this," he called.

Roy tossed the rope into the chariot and came around to stand beside Seneb. "What is it?" he asked.

Wenatef suddenly understood. He drew a swift breath, meaning to shout a warning, but Seneb was too fast. He seized Roy by the shoulders and gave him a powerful shove that sent him hurtling headlong down the side of the cliff, crashing against loose stones and scree, sliding the last few yards to come to a rest, tangled and torn, at the foot of the escarpment.

"I'm sorry, Roy," Seneb said. "I've thought about it. I'll catch that ghost tomorrow." He stepped into the chariot and drove away along the path.

CHAPTER XXXIII

Wenatef sat down to a meal of bread, onions and beer in Nakhtamun's tomb and set his mind to the question of what to do next. He had gone to Roy and found that the man was dead. The fall had broken his neck. Seneb had probably gone careering back to Medinet Habu with a tale of an accident. From what Wenatef had been able to observe about Roy, no one in the Necropolis Police would be terribly upset. Roy's murder would go unavenged, Wenatef thought, but his repentance had not been in vain.

He turned his thoughts to Seneb. There was a lot that man could tell him about the plot to rob the tombs, starting with the people involved. It was easy to guess one of the names: Unas. That young man had seemed a menace from his first appearance after Merihor's fright. The defilement of corpses was that young man's own personal signature. But Unas could not be the leader. He was too young and too vicious. Someone stronger and more dangerous than Unas was leading the robbers. Wenatef had a very good idea of the name of the leader, but he needed to be certain.

Was Seneb the leader?

Wenatef sat back against Nakhtamun's knees and frowned at that question. He finally shrugged. Anything was possible, he supposed. Seneb was a wealthy man by all reports, able to support two wives and a concubine. But Seneb was not intelligent or courageous enough to manage such a far-reaching plot as this one. The man could not lie convincingly, and he was incapable of hiding his thoughts.

172

A Killing Among the Dead

When he and Roy had gone through the tomb looking for
Wenatef, Seneb had said *'He takes a dim view of traitors.'* It
had to be someone more powerful and more intelligent,
someone he and Roy both feared, but who?

The thought of Herihor's possible involvement came to
Wenatef again, but he dismissed it. Herihor had lifted his
eyes toward the throne, perhaps – or toward royalty. But
Wenatef had dealt with General Herihor when he was at
Semna, and the activities of an organized tomb-robber did
not fit his impression of the man. He doubted Herihor would
have changed so much. If he had in fact raised his ambitions
toward kingship, as the successor to all the kings who had
gone before - as Horus the son to Osiris the father - he would
have the care and safety of their tombs and their bodies
firmly in his mind, for appearances' sake, if nothing else.

That left the villagers. For intelligence and
resourcefulness, Dhutmose was quite capable of leading a
gang of robbers, and so was Duwah. Any of the village
leaders were.

Wenatef lifted the onion that he was eating, took another
bite, then a bite of bread and chewed them together. He
washed the mouthful down with beer.

The villagers certainly had the opportunity and the
knowledge. The Deir el Medineh masons and artists had
been constructing the tombs for half a millennium. They
considered themselves guardians of the tombs and their
goods. Wenatef dismissed their involvement. For a plan
like this to prosper someone with connections, high in
society, would be needed to help recruit the other members.

He looked at the bread and the onion in his hands and
drew a long breath. Seneb had said, 'He is coming...' He
knew who one of the leaders of the plot was. He had known
who that man was almost from the first, from the day
Merihor had gone into his fit and Captain Taharka of the

173

Karnak Temple Guard had sent that letter. It only remained to find confirmation, and he could get that the next day. And perhaps that information would give him the name of the other leader.

** ** **

After he had eaten, he made his way along the main path to a tomb some three hundred yards southeast of His Majesty's. He had discovered it when he first came to the valley, open and empty. The tomb had certainly been violated, but he did not know who had occupied it, since the inscriptions had been mutilated and it was completely bare. The sarcophagus was in the tomb, but it was open and empty, the names of its occupant hacked from its surface. Any furniture or supplies that had been there had been smashed or removed long before.

Wenatef brought food enough to last a week and placed it in the sarcophagus chamber, along with bedding material. The ceiling was high, there was nothing for anyone to stand on to reach the entrance hole in the ceiling; it would be the perfect place to hide a prisoner.

That done, Wenatef returned to Nakhtamun's tomb and snatched a quick nap. In the afternoon he would go to the hillside armed with a mace - he had found a magnificent one marked with the names of Thutmose III - and await Seneb.

** ** **

Wenatef heard someone approaching the tomb. He crouched motionless behind a boulder on the hillside and watched as Seneb came up to the thieves' entrance and looked around, his sword drawn, a lit torch in his other hand. He had driven to the tomb; his chariot was pulled by two very fine horses, of a quality that a mere officer of the Necropolis Police should be unable to afford.

Seneb reined the horses in, cursing under his breath as the sword and the torch interfered with the reins, and then stepped down from the chariot. He paused to hobble the horses before walking up to the hidden indentation that marked the entrance to the tomb.

"Come out in His Majesty's name!" he cried.

Wenatef smiled grimly and smacked the mace soundlessly against his palm. 'His Majesty', indeed!

Seneb paused a moment longer, then took a coil of rope from his chariot, secured it to the harness-tree, and tossed it into the tomb entrance after looking around to make certain that no one had observed him. He tossed the torch into the tomb and then lowered himself hand over hand with the rope. A faint glow marked the opening of the tomb. It faded as Wenatef watched.

Wenatef raised his eyebrows. The Necropolis Police were not terribly bright, he decided. This furtiveness was about as unobtrusive as a man waving a red cloth before an angry bull. And he must be amazingly confident in his aim, to risk setting the boxes ablaze with that carelessly tossed torch. He sighed, shook his head, and hurried to Seneb's chariot, pausing only to pat the horses before silently hauling up the rope. He wished that he could see Seneb's face when he discovered that the rope was missing.

Then he crept into the tomb through his tunnel and waited at the end as Seneb moved through the rooms. The man's head turned from side to side while the torch sent shadows along the walls and among the jumbled boxes, jars and pieces of furniture that crowded within the tomb.

Seneb passed the tunnel opening and paused to peer into the corners of the room before continuing.

Wenatef stepped silently out after him, raised his mace, and tapped the side of Seneb's skull, and then caught the torch as the man fell like a sack of stones.

He set the torch carefully on the ground and kicked the man's dislodged wig aside before turning Seneb on his stomach, pulling his hands behind him and securing them with thin, sturdy cord. He improvised a gag with a piece of wood and a length of linen, and then dragged Seneb from the tomb and dumped him in his own chariot. So far so good, he decided as he clucked to the horses and enjoyed the feel of a chariot beneath his feet after almost two weeks.

Once at the empty tomb Wenatef tied a rope around Seneb's chest and lowered the man, who was showing signs of awakening, through the ceiling. He then lowered himself hand over hand, as well. He tied Seneb's feet and removed the gag, then took out his supper, sat down with his back against the wall with the torch beside him, and proceeded to eat.

CHAPTER XXXIV

Seneb took a long time to groan his way back to consciousness. He looked around for a time in a dazed fashion and after his eyes opened, as though he could not understand who or where he was.

Wenatef finished his supper and waited with placidly folded hands as Seneb's gaze wandered about the room once more before fastening on Wenatef and then widening.

Seneb choked on words, then he struggled to sit up and fell back against the ground, his eyes fixed on Wenatef in sheer terror that seemed oddly out of proportion to the threat Wenatef knew he presented.

"Yes, Seneb," he said gently. "I see you remember me." He watched Seneb for a moment. "No, you won't be able to free yourself, and you'll only make the knots tighter if you fight them. I have some questions for you and I want answers to them. I don't wish to hurt you, but I'm not squeamish and if I have to do it in order to get those answers, I won't hesitate."

Seneb's eyes dilated. He fought the knots once more, then lay back against the floor, panting.

Wenatef smiled.

** ** **

The sight of Wenatef unnerved Seneb more than any threats. His wide, fearful eyes fixed on Wenatef's face, he told everything he knew, and some things Wenatef had not thought to ask.

177

"I lead nothing!" Seneb gasped. "I wish I'd never heard of this plot in the first place!"

Wenatef lifted the flask of wine to his lips and drank, then set the flask down again. "No?" he said. "Then who is the leader?"

Seneb flinched at the motion, as though it hurt his eyes. "Khaemwase," he said through chattering teeth. "Khaemwase is the commander. He supervises the tomb robberies and the division of the spoils from his base in Koptos."

"Do you advise him?"

"He doesn't consult me," Seneb said. "Khaemwase does whatever he sees fit to do. He takes no notice of what others say. He kills those who displease him."

Wenatef lifted an eyebrow and nodded. "There is a lot of merit to that approach," he said. "When did you join this plot?"

"Six months ago," Seneb answered. "Roy approached me and spoke cunningly of wealth and opportunity under the protection of powerful people..."

"Such as his master, Nuteruhotep?"

"Yes!"

Wenatef paused, considering. Given who else was in the plot and what he knew of the man, he had suspected Nuteruhotep. But Seneb had agreed very easily, and might well be clutching at straws. He had already shown himself adept at mixing lies and truth.

"When did you learn that robbery was involved?" asked Wenatef.

"Not till much later. I didn't get involved in it! You have to believe me!"

"As it happens, Seneb, I don't," Wenatef said. "What you've told me is exactly opposite what you discussed with Roy yesterday."

Seneb closed his eyes.

A Killing Among the Dead

"From what I saw and heard, you were the one to approach Roy and speak cunningly of wealth and opportunity. And I suspect it was you who had Si-Iset killed. Did you wait until you got him to Tanis? Or did you kill him outside the city?"

Seneb stared at him with white-rimmed eyes. He moistened his lips. "How... How could you possibly know?"

"You would be surprised at what I know," Wenatef said. "Now tell me: what was your part, precisely?"

Seneb flinched again. "I keep track of patrols. Sometimes I help with the digging."

"You're a spy, then," Wenatef said with scorn.

"I've never actually killed anyone," Seneb said.

Wenatef frowned for a moment. "I think you consented to my murder by Unas."

"No! Please - let me go! Have pity - !"

"Pity?" Wenatef repeated. "I have nothing to do with pity. I'm concerned only with facts. You'll have to plead with the others. And you'd best keep to the facts!"

"The - others?" Seneb faltered.

Wenatef did not explain. "You were speaking of Khaemwase," he said. "How does he oversee things?"

Seneb licked his lips and shook his head. "He comes to Thebes from time to time to supervise matters and confer with Nuteruhotep. He'll be coming to the tombs in two days. His headquarters are in the Valley of the Nobles near Sheikh Abd el Kurna, in the tomb of Djeser. He's been upset by reports that his men have been killed."

"As well he might be," Wenatef said with a dark smile. "Tell me more of these killings."

"One of the men went to him at Koptos with a tale of a rampaging archer-god whom he had seen with his own eyes. He had been terrified. Khaemwase wanted to interrogate

179

him more forcefully, but he escaped and no one knows where he's gone. Khaemwase wants to get to the bottom of the disturbance."

"He will," said Wenatef. "Soon. Tell me: how did the robbers know where to dig?"

"I don't know," Seneb said. "I just make sure the eyes of the guard are turned away."

"And for *that* you receive a share of the spoils?" Wenatef said.

"It wasn't enough!" Seneb said. "I was going to leave the plot-"

"Really?" Wenatef said. "And risk making make Khaemwase and Unas your enemies?"

"Just so!" Seneb said.

Wenatef's eyes narrowed.

Seneb flinched again as though his eyes hurt him. "If you'll let me go, I'll swear never, never again to rob another tomb!" he said.

Wenatef remained silent.

Seneb licked his lips and said, "I'll even help you to capture the robbers! Or else - " he hesitated, his expression shifting, " - or else I can give you a share of the profits - there is plenty of wealth here in the Valley. All you need to do is release me."

Wenatef rose and stood looking down at Seneb. "You snake!" he said. "You said you'd promise never to rob another tomb! I can see how deep your repentance runs! You face a terrible reckoning. I pity you from the bottom of my heart." He lifted the mace beside him.

Seneb flinched.

"No, I won't kill you," Wenatef said. "You're safe in my hands. Tell me about Unas."

Seneb shivered. "I'd heard tales of his dismissal from Karnak for sacrilege, but I hadn't believed them until I joined this plot. It was Unas who smashed Thutmose III's face -

that was terrible to watch! He rejoices in destruction. It's as though he's being strengthened... Curses, ghosts and evil spirits don't frighten him - maybe because he is one of them. It isn't safe to know him."

Seneb's eyes narrowed into the distance for a moment and then returned to Wenatef's face. "If you are interested in finding Unas alone, I can help. Unas said that he'll be plundering the tomb of King Seti I. It hasn't been touched yet. He offered me a share of the spoils if I helped him, but I-" He broke off to swallow. "I refused. If you release me, I can show you how to get to the tomb."

"Didn't you just tell me you had nothing to do with robbing the tombs?" Wenatef asked.

Seneb stared at him.

Wenatef's smile remained. "No," he said. "You're staying here. You'll be safe enough."

He bent over Seneb, who shrank back against the floor. "Hold still," he said as he turned him and cut the ropes about his wrists, then stepped quickly back. "There," he said. "You see bedding here, and I have left oil lamps, tinder and flint. I've given you food enough to last a week, if you aren't greedy. I think you'll be comfortable until His Majesty's men come for you."

"No, wait - I had no choice - ! This plot -"

"You could have refused when you were first approached," Wenatef said. "But you can explain that to His Majesty's lieutenants when they arrive, along with your reasons for murdering Roy as I watched."

Seneb drew a shaking breath and turned, if possible, even paler than before.

Wenatef's smile was cold. "Yes," he said. "The *Akhu* have eyes."

He went to the rope and hauled himself up to the top, and shouted down as he coiled the rope, "You can untie your feet

Diana Wilder

now, Seneb. There's no use trying to get out, since I've left nothing for you to dig with, and the ceiling is too high for you to reach. You'll be comfortable until I get back."

He left and drove back to Nakhtamun's tomb. Once there, he lashed the horses with the end of the rope and watched them go careening back toward Medinet Habu.

** ** **

Wenatef went to all the tombs of the Great Ones over the next two days, and except for three instances, he found that all had been entered, robbed and defiled in the same manner as the tombs of Nakhtamun and Thutmose III. He was shocked by the robberies, but he was more appalled by the destruction wrought by the thieves, especially on the bodies of the kings. Many times the heads had been snapped from the bodies, and in one instance - Horemheb - the lower jaw had been wrenched away, for reasons Wenatef could not even guess. The robbers had torn away the grave-clothes in their search for jewels, and many times limbs were broken or slashed with knives or axes.

Another puzzle was the discovery of traces of older tomb robberies, indications that someone had entered the tombs some years earlier and selected objects of lesser value, leaving the greater part of the wealth of the tombs behind, to be scattered and broken by the later robbers.

The entrances made by the later robbers had been easy for Wenatef to locate, since he knew their methods. And yet, when he had gone into the tombs - always by night - he had found other entrances carefully cut into the rock and cleverly hidden from the outside. Whether carefully done or executed in a hurried, brutal fashion, the entrances were all stunningly accurate, since they almost invariably led right to the burial chamber. It was almost as though they had access to a map.

The robbers, whether neat or untidy, had often brought in refreshment, usually in the form of jars of beer. But there were also jars of wine, open and empty, in the tombs. He had found two jars bearing seals dating them from the last years of the reign of Merneptah, the son of Ramesses II. That reign had seen the beginning of chaotic times, almost of civil war, while the succession was disputed between two of his sons, Seti II and Amunmesse.

Wenatef had found the earlier jars empty and carefully set out of the way of the rest of the objects in the tombs, while the later jars of wine and beer had been left where they had fallen, some of them not even empty, judging from the stains on the floor of the tombs.

Wenatef made notes of his findings, writing as neatly as he could, using the empty jars of beer or wine that littered the tombs, carrying them back to with him, to be stored in the passageway. Pharaoh's lieutenants would find them valuable, he knew, when it came time to set matters to rights.

CHAPTER XXXV

Wenatef watched the sun rise above the Nile, changing the sky from the deep blue of lapis to the pink of a lotus blossom and, finally, turquoise. The stray wisps of cloud remaining from the night blazed crimson and then faded to insignificance. The last stars paled and then vanished into the brightness of the day. The river flashed in the sun, a stream of molten gold that gentled to silver as he watched.

He drew his knees to his chest and rested his chin on them, drinking in the beauty. Soon he would leave Egypt and never again see the sun on the Nile, and though he deplored the decay and disintegration of his people's proud civilization, he would mourn his departure from the land of the Nile.

He shifted his position, watching the flash of the sun upon the river. He was seated at the very top of the Peak waiting for the workmen to make their way to the tomb. It would not be long now. He had gone there to watch the constellations wheel across the sky and count falling stars. He had slept and dreamed of walking among the stars, of taking them into his hands like bright blossoms, cool and faintly sweet. A wind had blown through his hair, and he had stood above the Valley of the Kings and the villages lining the Nile, his feet treading the sky, his path guided by the light of the stars. He had awakened to gaze at the sunrise and yawn contentedly.

Now he sat with his knees drawn up to his chin, a smooth stone at his feet with a message for Ramses: .

A Killing Among the Dead

I must speak with you tonight.

In a few more minutes he would make his way toward the Tomb and find a way to give Ramses that message. Wenatef needed assistance, and Ramses was the only one who could help him.

** ** **

That had been easy, Wenatef decided as he slipped in through his tunnel and arranged his cot. He was still tired, and he was asleep almost immediately, smiling over the ease with which he had delivered the message - a smooth, accurate toss of the stone - and the expression on Ramses' face as he had read the words.

** ** **

A sound awakened him: the tiniest click of one stone against another. He was immediately alert, holding his breath. The sound came again. Someone was in the tunnel. Wenatef took his bow and dagger and moved soundlessly to the sarcophagus chamber, carrying the tiny oil lamp with him.

He took up a position behind the jumble of boxes beside Nakhtamun's statue, well hidden from the view of someone coming into the burial chamber, but affording a good view of the intruder and, most importantly, giving him room to use his bow.

A growing glow at the doorway of the burial chamber was reflected from the storage rooms.

"Commander Wenatef?" The voice was young and slightly unsteady.

Wenatef silently lowered his bow and took the arrow from the bowstring.

The glow blossomed into a flower of flame on a black stalk, held in Ramses' strong hand. He entered the chamber, frowning into the corners, the light running in hot streams from his shoulders and glinting in his eyes.

Wenatef stepped from behind the boxes. "Hello, Ramses," he said gently as the young man turned to face him, startled, "I've been waiting for you."

** ** **

Ramses took a handful of dates, put them in his mouth, and chewed with enjoyment. He shifted the pits to his cheek and said, rather thickly, "Seneb is your prisoner? Where?"

"There's an empty tomb beside His Majesty's. You can't tell it's there. It's deep within the hillside, bare of any goods, and there's no way to escape unless he can jump fifteen feet straight up. He has food enough for a week, and unless he's afraid of *khefts* - and I hope he is - he'll be fine there. I don't envy him. The *Akhu* are hospitable only if you have a clean conscience. I wonder how well Seneb will sleep."

Ramses shivered and rose. He went to Nakhtamun's statue and gazed into the carved face. His hand shook as he raised it, touched the face, and then his own.

"There's a resemblance," Wenatef said.

"How can you tell from a statue?" Ramses asked.

"I've seen him face to face," Wenatef said with a smile at Ramses' look of astonishment. "It *is* his tomb, you know," he added. "How did the village take the news of my death?"

Ramses sat down on the plinth beside Wenatef. After a moment he frowned and shook his head. "Those lion tracks..." he said. "The village has been in terror for a week, and I think the thieves have been scared away as well. The lions must have been huge. Did you get to see them?"

"I saw the tracks, myself," Wenatef said, "The lions that made them must have been as big as... mountains. What happened when they discovered I was missing?"

"We sent out search parties," Ramses answered. "Dhutmose seemed especially upset - I thought you might have told him something, or he might have received some word from or about you"

"I left a message for him just before I was captured."

A Killing Among the Dead

"That explains it. He directed the searches and refused any assistance from the Necropolis Police, though Seneb and Roy and Unas - may they rot in hell! - offered several times to lead searching parties. Your Gold of Honor was discovered by Unas - I thought at the time he might have planted it there, though I couldn't explain the lion tracks. I gave him a piece of my mind."

"Yes," Wenatef said. "I was there. I heard you. It did my heart good, but I was sorry at the time that you didn't land a punch on that young snake's nose as well. I imagine you were itching to do it."

"I was. I still am." Ramses shook his head, then shrugged. "Well. I brought the Gold of Honor back to the town. I took it to Duwah first, since you were friends together from childhood. He was terribly shaken... He's begun to build a cenotaph for you. It'll be magnificent; the entire village is contributing to it."

Wenatef smiled. "That should be interesting," he said. "My parents' tomb is near here. There's room for me there." He looked back at Ramses, who was spitting the date pits into his palm. "What did you do after you were almost killed at the Valley of the Queens?" he asked. "Did you tell Duwah that I was alive?"

Ramses shook his head. "I wanted to," he said. "I would have done it, except I kept thinking that if you had wanted them to know you were unhurt, you would have gone to them yourself. I did, however, go to Duwah and suggest that he might want to delay construction of your tomb. He didn't say much in reply, but I thought his heart had been lightened."

He deposited the pits in a piece of cloth and wiped his hand. "Then I went to Dhutmose," he continued. "I told him two things. First, I told him that I had tried to follow tomb robbers and had actually seen them working in the Valley of the Queens. We came the next day, in daylight, but the bodies were gone, and there was nothing to indicate that there had been any robberies. We didn't look too hard for the thieves' entrance. We did find some bloodstains that had been hurriedly covered. Dhutmose became very quiet, and we left quickly. Afterward, he gave me a rare tongue-lashing for taking upon myself the duties of His Majesty's police. He also read me a lecture on the wisdom of doing dangerous things only when in the company of two or more strong men.

"I told him, then, that I asked leave to draw your allotment of supplies. I didn't say why I wanted it, and he didn't ask, but it seemed to me that his heart, too, had been lightened. He gave me what I wanted and let me use one of his own donkeys to carry the food. He offered to come with me, asking no questions, as a guard. I refused. He said that I might have any assistance that the village could offer."

"But how did you know where I was?" Wenatef asked.

Ramses shrugged. "I remained hidden and watched after you told me to run away," he said. "I saw you enter that tomb, and I remained where I was and counted my heartbeats. If you had stayed within beyond two hundred, I would have followed you and fought. I didn't have to. I saw you come out again and leave. So I followed you at a distance, and I saw where you went. My father told me I am a good hunter, but you're hard to track."

"And you decided to help me by bringing food?"

Ramses grinned. "Well, I went into the tomb - I had wanted to talk to you, but you weren't there - so I sampled your provisions. His grin widened. "My father spent some years in the Royal Army before he returned here to marry Mother. I remember him saying that a soldier travels on his stomach. I don't know how you traveled even a cubit, Commander. I decided to bring fresh meats, vegetables and breads to you. I had to go to Dhutmose, but he didn't question me. I do think he guessed. I was careful coming here and leaving. Is - is there a reason you wanted me tonight? I brought more food."

"Excellent. Seneb has most of mine, though I think we'll be taking him from that tomb before much longer. No, Ramses, I don't need any more food - or not much. I want you to do something simple for me that I can't do myself."

Ramses raised his eyebrows, and Wenatef was once more reminded of Nakhtamun.

"I want you to take my bow and arrows and hide them in the second side chamber in His Majesty's tomb. The small storage room. Do you know the one? It must be done tomorrow evening, after everyone is gone. I'll have other tasks. But if you'll those for me, I'll be grateful."

"I will," Ramses said, frowning a little. "But isn't there anything else I can do?"

"There is. I may be killed tomorrow night. Return here with Dhutmose and the others two nights from now if I haven't come to you before then. If I'm not in this tomb, then clear the side tunnel. I've made notes on these jars covering all that I have found in the necropolis. I've told where the thieves' entrances are, how I located them, and what I found when I entered the tombs, from room to room, and what I did to set things straight. The ink is primitive, and Dhutmose or Butehamun would smile at my writing and call it a scrawl, but it is all there and all legible. Give the information to Dhutmose and tell him to bring it to Herihor and His Majesty. Will you do that?"

Ramses lowered his head, still frowning. "But can't I come with you and fight?" he asked.

"No. I won't be alone. Besides, you're the only one who knows of my hiding place. What if we're both killed? This is childish talk: I don't intend to be killed. If I do die, then I'll be taking quite a few with me."

CHAPTER XXXVI

Khaemwase had been named for Prince Khaemwaset, the son of Ramesses II, who had been Vizier of the North and High Priest of Ptah at Memphis and, for the last half of his life, Crown Prince. The prince had been revered as a good and wise man for over a century. Khaemwase's parents had given him that name in the hope that he would be as clement, powerful, and wise as his great namesake. Their hopes were realized in the last two items only, for Khaemwase, though a powerful and cunning man, was utterly merciless.

He had come from petty nobility north of Thebes, from the great town of Koptos. He left the city of his birth shortly after becoming a man. He had wanted to be a great warrior like Thutmose III or Ramesses II, and he had found plenty of fighting on the Nubian border. He returned to Koptos at the head of a group of trained fighting men who had developed a taste for luxuries, and were not particular about where their luxuries came from.

It was three years previously, during the period of civil war that began in the twelfth year of the reign of Ramesses XI, that Khaemwase learned of the riches in the tombs of the kings at Thebes. Some of the rebel soldiers had told him tales of treasure a short time before, but he had encountered difficulties in getting to it. But then, some months later, matters changed for Khaemwase. He turned his suddenly intent gaze upon the Valley and listened with growing interest to the high-ranking member of the Theban priesthood who had approached him with a very interesting proposition.

The Thebans had heard of him by this time. He had associates along the Nile, men who paid tribute to him in return for protection from river pirates - usually his own men. He was known to trade with the marauding Libyans, selling them food and supplies in return for their labor in his concerns. He owned many farms along the Nile, whose former owners had either fled or met sudden ends.

Though Khaemwase's career had spanned more than a decade, none of his adversaries knew what he looked like. The stories were varied and fearsome, improved by frightened imaginations. The Necropolis Police and the Theban Municipal Guard had tried for years to break his power, but they had been unable to capture the man, though they had caught several of his lieutenants.

His Majesty had exerted his influence to have Khaemwase captured, but his attention had been caught by the revolts to the south and the encroachment migrating tribes to the north. Nevertheless, he had sent messengers throughout the land announcing a reward in pure gold for the capture of Khaemwase. His Majesty paid the reward twice, and each time the prisoner turned out to be a petty criminal sent by Khaemwase himself in a gesture as superbly insolent as that of a man tossing a bit of meat to a chained lion.

** ** **

Wenatef paused at the entrance to Khaemwase's headquarters. He had spent hours near the tomb of Djeser, in the Necropolis of Sheikh Abd el Kurna, moving carefully, fearing an encounter with the guards who undoubtedly were there. He had watched the entrance for over three hours, tallying the comings and goings, learning what he could of the robbers' movements before going into the tomb, himself.

He was unarmed except for a dagger, but he wore a bronze and gold corselet and a kilt of the finest linen he could find in Nakhtamun's tomb. He had painted his eyes and anointed himself with costly oils from Nakhtamun's store. He had found a gold circlet hidden in Nakhtamun's tomb, and he had set an ostrich feather in it. If Khaemwase was half-expecting a god or one of the *Akhu*, Wenatef did not plan to disappoint him.

A group of men left the tomb. No one else was about.

Wenatef took a deep breath and ducked into the entrance. As with the queen's tomb, once Wenatef had passed the small opening, the tunnel became high enough to allow him to stand almost upright. He looked down the tunnel and saw a glow. An oil lamp, probably several of them. He moved silently toward the light.

He had been right. Six lamps were scattered throughout the tomb chamber. He had to look away and allow his eyes to grow accustomed to their brilliance before he could peer at the chamber from his vantage point, half hidden in the shadows. He had devoted a great deal of thought to the amount of time it took healthy eyes to grow used to sudden light after darkness.

The lamps lent life to the bright paintings in the tomb. The room was neat, with beautiful furnishings looted from grander tombs, judging by the names carved on them. There was no jumble of broken, open boxes and jars. The sarcophagus was closed, the floor neatly swept. A fire burned on a wide expanse of bare floor. A man sat before the fire and roasted a chunk of meat.

Wenatef looked the man over from his square, strong feet to his well-shaped, shaven head. He was powerfully muscled and relatively unmarked with scars. His face was handsome, almost benign, and he ate with elegance and economy of movement. Nothing about him suggested a ruffian, but Wenatef had no doubt that he was gazing at Khaemwase himself. This man was Unas' companion on the day that Merihor had run mad.

192

A Killing Among the Dead

The man half-turned to select fruit from a tray beside him. An ornately carved chair sat by the doorway, a throne from a king's tomb. Wenatef stepped silently into the room and sat down in it with his hands gripping the carved finials. A footstool was before him; he set his elegantly shod feet on it and waited.

Khaemwase saw him after a moment. His eyes widened in surprise and the meat in his hand fell unheeded to the floor as he seized his knife. And then he relaxed and smiled. It was a cold smile.

"Well," he said, and his voice was deep and soft, "You must be the archer god."

Wenatef smiled with equal coldness. "And you must be the leader of the thieves," he said.

Khaemwase looked him over and then bent to retrieve the meat from the floor. He frowned at the dirt and set the meat aside. "The archer god," he said again. "You terrified that little peasant. But you're only carrying a dagger. What do you want of me?"

"I need information," Wenatef answered.

"You know that I can have you killed," Khaemwase said. It was not a question.

"It'll take some effort," Wenatef returned. "I have a dagger, as you've noticed, and I am considered a good fighter. I am also armored. You're bigger than me, but that is sometimes a disadvantage. I am also more powerful than you might think."

He smiled at Khaemwase's suddenly perplexed expression. "But do we need to talk like this?" he asked. "You can wait until your men come back to have me taken and killed, and in the meantime you can answer my questions. I won't attack you if you don't move first. If you capture me, you can do as you like. What do you say?"

Khaemwase's smile had some warmth in it now. "That's

193

an interesting proposition," he said. "You'll be killed, you know. Unless you care to join my men? No? You will be killed. I'm sorry for that, especially if you're the man who's been courageous and skillful enough to wreak havoc among my men. But tell me: how did you manage to convince everyone that you had been killed by lions?"

Wenatef returned the smile. He was surprised to find himself liking this man. "Perhaps I really was killed," he said. "Killed, judged and admitted to the Land of the West. Don't look so dismayed, Thief. Did you think the tales were myths? But you are to answer my questions, if you recall."

Khaemwase inclined his head. His eyes flickered over to the entrance for a moment, then returned to Wenatef. "Ask your questions," he said.

Wenatef permitted himself a secret smile. "Are you the leader of the tomb robbers?"

Khaemwase spread his hands. "I?" he asked. "Come now, Archer. Someone came to me and said that he knew of treasure for the taking and customers willing to purchase treasures that are - shall we say? - worthy of kings. There were others as far away as Bubastis or Hattushash or Tanis. I learned of those who owned a map of the necropolis and knew the ways leading into the tombs. I supplied the manpower and others supplied the information."

"Who?"

"Who persuaded me to come to the Valley of the Kings?" Khaemwase said. "I'll give you one name, but one that is worth many: Nuteruhotep."

The robber's fine, cold eyes narrowed at Wenatef's lack of reaction. "Yes," he said gentle emphasis. "The Steward of Amun himself. He likes gold. He was the one who invited me to the Valley. I sold him a magnificent golden necklace just over a week ago. It was taken from the body of Thutmose III himself and bears his names on the underside. I understand His Excellence is pleased with the piece. For the rest, the mind boggles: who else did Nuteruhotep bring into this matter? He is a friend of Prince Sekhemkhet. He is a direct subordinate of Herihor and high in the Temple hierarchy. He is well acquainted with Prince Smendes of Tanis: who could be with him? That troubles you, Archer, doesn't it?"

"Not as much as you seem to expect, Thief," Wenatef returned. "I can deal with Nuteruhotep. I've known of his involvement for some time. Did he supply you with the information on where to dig?"

Khaemwase's eyes narrowed and he looked off into space for a moment. "Not precisely," he said. "Though he was influential in procuring it. I wasn't the first to operate in the Valley of the Kings. There were... other interests...there before me. We clashed, then came to an agreement. It was all very discreet, and I never saw the man face to face. I don't even think I know his name - 'Nakht' is the name I was given, and I think it was a false one - "

Wenatef frowned. "'Nakht'?" he said.

"Yes. Very smooth, very cunning, but then so am I. Still, the man is a force to be reckoned with. But Nuteruhotep, now..." Khaemwase paused and his smile became malicious. "A man with an obsession is a man with no scruples. He covets gold... He met me in the Valley himself - "

"*He* brought you to the Valley?"

"Yes," Khaemwase answered. His voice grew cold with distaste. "Unas was with him. He is a dangerous man. I believe he is unclean..." Khaemwase shuddered, as though caught by a memory.

The robber met Wenatef's stern gaze and said, "I don't give mercy and I don't expect it. But give me credit for this: my actions are open and clean. I don't wear the mask of piety before all men and desecrate the gods in secret. What I

195

do I do for all to see and know, and I abhor hypocrisy. But Unas, now... He is a sickness and a contagion."

"The man is as good as dead," said Wenatef.

Khaemwase's eyes lightened, but he shook his head. "I regret that I'll have to stop you."

Wenatef sat back with a smile. "Wait and see," he said. "How did he get to be involved?"

A crease appeared between Khaemwase's brows. "There are crimes that I don't countenance," he said. "Nuteruhotep wanted a tool. His sister's son was an acolyte at Karnak. Nuteruhotep approached him and was refused. And that is when Nuteruhotep unmasked all the ploys of priestcraft. The statues with hinged mouths, the tricks of ventriloquism, and the works wrought upon the gullible. He showed it all to Unas and I think it drove him mad. Unas left the priesthood and came to the Necropolis, and in the time that I have known him, he's lost no opportunity to vent his anger upon the dead."

"And all because of statues with hinged mouths..." Wenatef said. "My father was very high in the priesthood, and I had once thought to follow him before I went into the army. I've seen such statues and understood their purpose. They're merely puppets, symbols, to be used in ceremonies, and no one thinks otherwise. Surely Unas, with a priest's training, realized - "

"He has nothing to help him realize," said Khaemwase. "He is unbalanced. He is like a wounded beast in a cage, and the kindest action would be to kill him."

"Perhaps so," Wenatef said. "And yet he made a choice once... Maybe he could reject it..." He looked up after a moment. "I want to know the names of the others involved in this tomb robbing, and how long they have been in it," he said.

Khaemwase frowned. "Nakht has been taking goods from tombs here for several generations. I've heard the stories..."

His eyes strayed once more to the entrance. He seemed increasingly impatient, but he curbed his voice to gentleness. "Several generations. Very gentlemanly, no one hurt. Nakht was a fool. He could have stripped the tombs, but he did not. We will."

"And who in the Necropolis Police is working with you?"

Khaemwase scowled, as though remembering an unsuccessful campaign against valiant and stubborn enemies. "No one but Seneb, originally," he replied. "Nuteruhotep planted Roy and Unas there. But that corps is thickheaded and absurdly loyal. It was the same with the Karnak Temple Guard and the corps of priests. I had better luck with the workers at the mortuary temples here, but there was precious little they could do aside from lending the strength of their arms, which weren't terribly strong after lifetimes of soft living. If only I had the Necropolis Police under my thumb, now... Or the Guard of His Majesty's Tomb..." He flicked a surprisingly rueful glance at Wenatef, who bowed.

"What of Deir el Medineh?" asked Wenatef.

"Solidly honest. Though, come to that, I do suspect that Nakht comes from there. I can't prove it, though. Two of my men come from that town. A father and a son. They work as my couriers. I pay them well."

He looked up at Wenatef, swiveled an impatient glance at the opening to the tunnel and said, "Well, Archer-God, it appears that you can pose a few more questions, but it won't be for much longer. Get ready to fight."

"The sooner the better," Wenatef said. He ignored Khaemwase's quizzical expression. "I had a subordinate named Merihor. That man was killed a little more than two weeks ago. I suspect you ordered it. Why?"

"The screamer," Khaemwase said. "I remember him. He found the opening to Thutmose III's tomb, went inside, and surprised us at work. Unas was... looting...the body. Merihor screamed and ran, and Unas and I went after him -" Khaemwase broke off. "It was you," he said after a moment. "You who were with him then... I remember you."

Wenatef bowed again. "And I remember you," he said. "But Merihor..."

Khaemwase nodded. "He was a dead man from that moment. I ordered Unas to take and kill him - and I commanded that the death be quick. It was, if that is any comfort to you."

His smile became cold again and he stiffened and then turned back to Wenatef. "And now I think I hear my men - " He rose, his knife in his hand.

He said nothing further, for Wenatef had sprung to his feet as Khaemwase rose, took two quick steps forward and brought his knife down slicing down across the man's face.

Khaemwase choked on blood, reeled, and was felled by a backhanded blow from the pommel of Wenatef's dagger that splintered his teeth. A swift, sideways kick sent him spinning to the side with a snapped knee joint. Wenatef darted to the side of the tunnel, and flattened himself against the wall.

Khaemwase's hand reached his dagger. He hurled it and then fell back, blinded with blood, roaring with pain as the men came pouring through the opening. Wenatef stood silently as they swarmed into the room, trying to shield their eyes from the glare of the light. Once they were past him, he darted into the tunnel.

"After him!" Khaemwase shouted as Wenatef emerged into the cool night air. He saw another five men approaching him and took to his heels, running as though all the demons of the underworld were after him.

CHAPTER XXXVII

Wenatef would often dream of that chase. Every moment of that headlong race across the harsh, barren land that fringed the Necropolis, the rhythmic beat of his feet against the hard, rocky ground, the sound of the night wind in his ears and his own labored breathing came back to him again and again in his dreams.

He would look back over his shoulder and see torches - close to him, so close, and gaining with each step. And then he would turn and look ahead of him and see the Valley, and know that it was still far away... And yet, when Wenatef awoke from that dream in later years, in high, beautiful lands that had never heard of the Nile, among proud, pale-haired folk who burned their dead and fought with weapons forged from the dark gray metal they called iron, he was not frightened, for it was not death that chased, but death that led in that race toward the tombs, and his pursuers were drawn after him by their own fates, to meet their own ends...

** ** **

They were too close. Wenatef abandoned all caution and ran toward the entrance of His Majesty's tomb with the robbers close behind him. His chest hurt with the urgent need to draw breath and his legs felt weak. He would be safe if he could only get to the storage chamber where Ramses had hidden his bow and arrows.

He reached the tomb entrance and then stopped, his hand against his pounding heart, drawing air into his lungs in sobbing gasps. He could go no further, and he was a dead man if they caught him now.

He heard footsteps on the pebble-strewn approaches to the tomb. They were moving slowly now, sure that he was cornered and willing to take their time and make certain of him. Excellent. He would take his time and catch his breath before going into the stifling atmosphere of the sarcophagus chamber.

He pushed himself away from the wall and then fell to his knees. He was closer to exhaustion than he had thought, and if they came upon him now -

He gasped a prayer to all the gods and all the Great Ones buried in the Valley: *Help me, or else stop them long enough to let me get back my strength!*

The sound began as a rustle, the faintest of sounds, gradually building in intensity and pace until it was all around him. He heard cries as though from a distance, and the notes of a trumpet and galloping hooves. It came from deep within the tomb, and Wenatef, turning toward it, saw a wave of shadow coming from the depths of the tomb, filling the white passageway, coming closer, moving with the swiftness of clouds before a storm wind until the sounds surrounded Wenatef and engulfed him, passing on toward the tomb entrance. The voices were clearer and he could make out snatches of words and sentences as full of power and history as the tatters of a once splendid banner: names of kings and battles, and above it all the ringing of the trumpet.

And then the sounds were behind Wenatef. He turned toward the entrance, and for a moment he thought he could see chariots vanishing against the night sky, ranks of bowmen and rearing horses. And then they were gone from his sight, though he still seemed to be within a river of shadow moving endlessly past him.

He breathed his thanks and got to his feet He was no longer panting, and his heartbeat had steadied. He made his way down the corridor toward the storage room, feeling his way in the darkness.

Voices behind him, from the entrance to the tomb. "What was *that*?"

Shouts of fear and then a voice that Wenatef recognized as that of Ipuky, the leader of the gang of robbers who had first captured him. He sounded calm and certain. "Sons of asses! Have you never heard bats? Into the tomb with you! We have him cornered!"

Wenatef ran as fast as he could, not caring about the amount of noise he made, so long as he could get to the storage chamber. Down the hallway, along the corridors, past preliminary drawings of the Ritual of the Opening of the Mouth, to the small side chamber. The light of his pursuers' torches made the doorway seem like a pit into blackness.

Wenatef ducked into the room. The bow was there, neatly strung, right where he had told Ramses to leave it. The young man had also left a lighted torch and another, unlit, beside it. Wenatef lifted his bow, settled the quiver between his shoulder-blades. Now he was almost invincible.

He extinguished the torch. The sound of his breathing was harsh in the silence. He heard the sound of feet, but he could see no light approaching him yet. He took his bearings and retraced his path to the main corridor of the tomb. A quick glance up the hallway showed that his pursuers were still near the entrance of the tomb.

He looked around. Just past him, he knew, was a flight of steps leading to a square room with four pillars. The burial chamber. Beyond that was another smaller room with two square pillars, reached by three short steps. He went in there, against the inner wall adjoining the lintel, where he would be hidden in a pool of black shadow. He could remain there or in some other secure hiding place and pick off the robbers one by one. And if they kept their torches with them, they would be the easiest marks he had ever aimed for.

He gazed out toward the four-pillared room, his eyes wide and straining in the dark. Noises were unnaturally loud in the utter darkness. He forced himself to breathe quietly, through parted lips, the bow with its nocked arrow held ready before him.

The sounds of pursuit stopped. Wenatef held his breath. If they went away and came back with more people - or posted a guard - Seconds passed, painfully slow, timed by the pounding of his heart. The complete silence was almost suffocating.

Wenatef drew a cautious breath and raised his shaking hand to his forehead, pushing his sweat- dampened hair from his eyes, waiting...

The sounds started again. The tap of rush sandals against hard-packed floor, whispered conversation. The metallic hiss of a knife drawn from its sheath, then silence again.

Wenatef could almost see them, huddled together around the torch, staring down into the dark passageways, with the drawings of the king coming to startling life around them, wondering where he was, straining for some flicker of motion, the hint of sound...

He heard murmuring, then the footsteps started again. Men moving toward him. How many? Hadn't he seen eight? Or were there more? He could not remember.

What was taking them so long? Had they been unnerved by the sounds from the tomb?

Wenatef remembered a snatch of conversation with Duwah and Dhutmose at that very spot: *You can't fight them as you are. You'd have to go to the Land of the West and return with an army.* Well, it seemed as though he had. He smiled ironically and then froze. Someone was speaking.

"There's no light here or farther down. I thought I saw a

torch when we first entered."

"There can't have been tunnels made already. This tomb isn't even finished. Is there another way out?"

"What if he is a *kheft*?" a third voice asked, shaking. "We all heard those sounds at the entrance. I heard one say - "

"Don't be a fool, Meri!" This was said loudly, and Wenatef recognized Ipuky's voice. "We know how he escaped from that tomb - through the top, as we came in. We saw the boxes piled up."

"But how did he escape the lions? We saw his footsteps - we followed them! And then we found where he had been killed by the lions - "

"Stop it!" Ipuky's voice was contemptuous. "You're making yourself panic. Maybe it wasn't him that got killed. Maybe the lions didn't kill him. There are too many questions. And we did see him leave Khaemwase tonight."

"And we saw how he left Khaemwase," another said. "He's a *kheft*!"

The voice was cut off by the crack of a hand against flesh.

The light came closer. Wenatef raised his bow and flattened himself against the wall - The light withdrew. They had entered the four-pillared chamber, cast a quick glance about, looked into Wenatef's room - and had not seen him concealed in the pool of shadow beside the jamb. Now they were moving toward the end of the tomb.

Wenatef considered for a moment, made his decision, and silently left the chamber, hurrying up the two flights of stairs toward the front of the tomb, and out into the bright, starlit night.

A strong wind pushed at his damp hair, chilling the sweat on his shoulders, and the world suddenly seemed large and brilliant after the closeness and pitch-blackness of the tomb.

He shook his head in the wind and breathed a prayer of

thanks to all the gods that his pursuers had not had the wit to leave someone at the entrance to the tomb. Now it only remained to pick a good, sheltered spot and kill them as they came out.

No. Better not kill them in the open. They might shout for help and someone might hear them. He went back to the top of the entrance stairs and waited.

** ** **

It was over in minutes. They had found the torch but they had not found him, and they concluded that the workmen had left another way out of the tomb.

They were talking loudly, confidently, and they did not hear the twang of the bowstring. Three were killed outright, two more as they milled about, shouting in dismay, and the last three in the hallways of the tomb as they fled him. They had not had the wit to throw away their torch.

Wenatef went from corpse to corpse retrieving his arrows. It would not do to have them found, since their design and richness were too striking. They would be recognized as kingly, and that would cause some unhealthy interest on the part of the Necropolis Police.

He shook his head and knelt beside the body deepest within the tomb. The arrow protruded between the man's shoulder blades. Wenatef could see from its angle that it had come perilously close to missing the heart. He shook his head. This sloppy shooting was beneath him. He shook his head again, seized the arrow, gave the shaft a twist to loosen the barb, and swiftly pulled it out. And then he froze, for the man had whimpered with pain.

Wenatef turned the man and found himself looking into Nebo's pain-filled eyes.

The young man's chest rose and fell with the effort of breathing. A pink foam was rising to his lips. "Please..." he choked.

Wenatef bent over him and wiped the foam away.

"Nebo."

But Nebo's eyes were focused fearfully on the wall behind Wenatef's shoulder. "Please," he said, his voice faint and thready. "I don't want - I don't want - "

Terrible, heartbreaking thoughts were crashing into Wenatef's mind all at once. He seized Nebo by the shoulders. "You are in this plot! And your father must be, too! And your grandfather?"

Nebo's eyes closed and he tried to moisten his lips with his bloody tongue even as he clenched his teeth against a gasp of pain.

The man was dying, and there was nothing further to learn. Wenatef released him and eased him back against the ground, looking him over with the knowing eye of one who has seen many battles and many wounds. He took the young man's hand in his. "I'm sorry, Nebo," he said. "The pain will be gone soon, and you'll be able to sleep." He remained until it was through, thinking that no one deserved to die alone and terrified in the dark.

He retrieved the rest of his arrows and his torch when it was over, and then turned each body face-up. As he had thought, Ipy was there. Unas was nowhere to be found.

Diana Wilder

CHAPTER XXXVIII

Wenatef sat on a large stone and looked away toward Thebes. After he had left His Majesty's tomb, he had come to the summit of the Peak to gaze down over the shrines and offering stelae that covered its slopes to the river below him and, beyond that, Thebes itself. He could see the great temples of Karnak and of Luxor lying beside the river, glowing faintly with the light of torches even in the dark watches of the night.

He had triumphed over his enemies that night, but he was filled with a terrible weariness and a vague feeling of defilement. And he had still to fight Unas.

He drew a deep breath. This sense of sickness would pass, he knew. He had to give himself time. He had won this battle, but there were other battles still to plan. Until the war was won he could do nothing but fight on and let his foes fall by the way. He would fight Unas in time. Fearing the fight was useless.

The pallid moon was sinking westward behind the Libyan mountains. Wenatef cast a quick glance over his shoulder at it as it sank, and then he turned his attention back toward Thebes and the dull ache in his heart.

Nebo and Ipy.

He had known that they disliked him, but it made no sense that they should have been there among the dead robbers. Why should they become involved in tomb robbing when the rest of Deir el Medineh had not? Now that he had seen them he understood that they had been Khaemwase's messengers, and it must have been easy for them, since Ipy journeyed regularly to Koptos, the Faiyum and the northern cities for spices and rare herbs. Khaemwase's base was Koptos, and their travels would have fit in well with his needs. But how could they have become involved with a man like Khaemwase or, worse still, one like Unas?

Unas again, Wenatef thought. And suddenly, as though the floodgates of his memory had been opened, he could hear his father, Hapuseneb, speaking again, telling him of a tragedy that he had tried to avert.

He was an acolyte at Karnak. An innocent, idealistic young fellow, eager to learn of the God, seeking almost desperately to hurl himself into the bright abyss of the God's love. My heart was gladdened by the sight of such innocence and such fervor. He came to me at times to speak of - of priestly things - and I saw at those times that while he was an intelligent youth he was too...

Wenatef remembered that his father had paused to search for words.

Too easily made glad and too easily cast down, he had said. I dealt gently with him, and in time he would have resolved that tendency, but he was given no time. Someone - Hapuseneb's fine features had grown cold and hard, *- took him and twisted him and in one destructive afternoon turned love to hatred. I tried to help him, perhaps to heal him, but in the end he was discovered in the holy of holies, trying to defile the image of the God - as though, Weni my son, defiling the statue could somehow damage the God. He was expelled at*

*last, and he took some promising youngsters
with him. A very great pity. And how can one
gauge the magnitude of the crime of the one
who twisted him? I thank the God that I will
not have to answer for that before the Throne
of Judgment.*

Had Nebo been one of the acolytes who had left? And
had he somehow involved his father in the robberies?

Wenatef took a deep breath and leaned back on one
elbow to stare at the hills beyond Thebes, visible only as a
black outline against the star- flecked night sky and gave the
matter some thought.

If Nebo and Ipy were involved with Khaemwase, he
reasoned, then where did that leave Thutiy? The possibility
that Thutiy was old and senile entered Wenatef's mind only
to be dismissed. And there was something odd about the
attitude of the villagers toward Thutiy...

Wenatef paused. Khaemwase had spoken of 'Nakht'.
'Nakht' had opposed him. 'Nakht' figured in village legends
as a great hero. And yet he was also a thief. Wenatef had
found those indications of earlier tomb robberies.

Was Thutiy 'Nakht'? It was possible. But that did not
explain Nebo and Ipy's involvement, or Thutiy's continuing
friendliness.

The line of thought was painful. Wenatef turned his
attention to Nuteruhotep. The man was an avid historian and
a connoisseur of art. His scholarship was impressive, but his
morals were not. He had survived Herihor's purge of the
priesthood at Karnak due to his powerful connections.

But long before Herihor's arrival in Thebes, during the
reign of Ramesses IX, Nuteruhotep had locked horns with
Hapuseneb over the accounting of the temple's grain stores.

Hapuseneb, who had been fifth-ranking priest at Karnak
the Chief of the Granaries, had caught Nuteruhotep writing
down less than had actually been reported, intending to add

the difference to his own considerable wealth. The confrontation with Hapuseneb had been sharp and dramatic. The conflict between the two men had gone up through the hierarchy until it had reached His Majesty, himself, where the matter finally died.

Wenatef and his mother had been sent far to the north, to her family in Memphis, for a time - he learned later that Hapuseneb had feared for their safety and had hoped to block any attempts to harm them. But there had been no threats and no injury due, Wenatef later realized, to Hapuseneb's fine reputation in Thebes and his friendship with Prince Imseti, Pharaoh's cousin and the Commander of the Theban Guard. Nuteruhotep was not dismissed - his family was too powerful for that - but it had been made clear that Hapuseneb was not to be touched.

With such a matter in Nuteruhotep's past, Wenatef thought it was not surprising that he was involved in this plot. Nuteruhotep would think nothing of greasing the wheels of the plot, but to even consider setting his sister's son on the path to madness and damnation—

The thought of such evil was sickening. Wenatef turned and gazed at the waning moon, hanging huge and pale above the western horizon. But he did not see it. Instead, he was remembering the night he had first been captured.

He had broken free, had run to the point of exhaustion and collapsed against Thutiy's house - and Thutiy had been there, awake and alert. He remembered Nebo and Ipy's appearance shortly after. They had been winded and disheveled. They had probably been among the men chasing him.

And, too, he remembered Thutiy's expression at the last supper they had eaten together, when Ipy and Nebo had questioned Wenatef on his involvement with Merihor's misfortune. Thutiy had watched and listened as intently as

Diana Wilder

they had.

And then there was the day Wenatef had been captured and brought to the tomb. Thutiy had sent Ipy ahead of him to order his chariot at the stable. He had even asked about the whereabouts of his bow. Wenatef remembered that conversation: *Go before him and take his bow. It'll be one less thing he'll have to carry with his injuries. Oh, it's with your chariot now? So much the better.* And then Thutiy had said, even as he salved Wenatef's hurts, *Ipy, go to the stables... Come straight back after you have done what is necessary...* And what had it been necessary for Ipy to do? Was Wenatef really fool enough to pretend not to know?

Bleak eyed and heavy-hearted, Wenatef followed his train of thought to its conclusion, rose, and returned to Nakhtamun's tomb.

210

CHAPTER XXXIX

Wenatef returned to the tomb by the back route, slipped through his tunnel and then pulled the baskets back in place. That done, he sat down and inspected the bow and arrows. No blood on the arrows, and none of the shafts bent or splintered. Very good, indeed.

He unstrung the bow and set it carefully aside, with the half-suppressed wish that it were really his. He took two loaves of bread, broke them into manageable pieces, and sopped them in Ramses' wine. It did very well and soon he was satisfied. He looked around at the burial chamber, at the scenes of the king being greeted by various gods and goddesses. Nothing more needed to be done in the chamber. He was tired; soon he could sleep. And he could plan a way to deal with Nuteruhotep and Unas.

It was so unfair. He had thought to have the robbers discovered and rounded up that evening. Or else so disposed that he could find them whenever he needed. Now he felt as though he had merely scratched the surface. Tanis, Bubastis, Hattushash, Babylon! Nuteruhotep's involvement widened the plot. He had suspected the man, but suspicion is far different from confirmation

What other mighty lord might be in this? He had been wary of Khaemwase. Nuteruhotep with his far-reaching influence and his high rank was a thousand times worse. His involvement meant, effectively, that Wenatef would be tackling the entire Theban hierarchy, from Vizier to High

Priest. And if Prince Sekhemkhet -

He forced himself to stop. He was behaving like a green soldier before his first battle, seeing enemies behind every rock, hearing their footsteps in the sigh of the wind through the rocks. He tried to wrench his thoughts to matters that he could bear. But he could find no comfort, for with the easing of his fear came the conviction that Thutiy had betrayed him.

Wenatef lay down at the feet of the statue. The stone feet made a satisfactory head-rest, and he did not think that Nakhtamun, the kindest possible host, would object. He was hurt and lonely and exhausted, and the nearness of a friend, even one carved of stone, was a comfort.

He put out the torch, set it in a large pottery tray, and turned his eyes to the patch of sky visible through the wall of the tomb. And then he sighed and settled his head more comfortably against Nakhtamun's feet. The stone was cold; he curled more tightly on his side and pillowed his cheek against his wrist - and paused as the bracer chafed his lips.

Suddenly he sat up, staring at his shadowy hands, remembering the layers of soft cloth that had protected his cruelly torn wrists from the bite of the ropes. Someone had sought to spare him pain. Why?

He drew his knees up, wrapped his arms around them, and forced his tired mind to confront the matter squarely.

Assuming that Thutiy was involved in the plot to rob the tombs, assuming that Thutiy had helped his sons to capture Wenatef, assuming that Thutiy's friendship had been a sham - then why had Wenatef been taken to the tomb alive? There had been no reason to imprison him, no reason to provision him or to save him from unnecessary suffering. The logical course of action would have been to kill him at the stable and dispose of his body. There had been no need at all to keep him alive - unless someone in a position of power had stepped in to protect him.

He began to smile. Yes, there had been someone with power. He could see that man in the eye of his mind, standing between Unas' drawn knife and Wenatef's senseless body. Wenatef should have been killed then, but he had not been. And the one who had spared his life had done so knowing that he was putting himself in danger. It did not take a great leap of imagination to conclude that the one who had spared Wenatef's life had been one of those who had dug the earlier, more skillful tunnels and had committed the earlier, careful robberies.

'Nakht'.

Wenatef's smile gentled. He lay down with a sigh, pillowed his head upon Nakhtamun's feet, and gazed at the sky beyond the crack in the tomb wall. He was sleepy from the escape of that evening and the very good wine he had drunk with his supper. The stars were bright and sparkling like the surface of the Nile at noon, and he could almost hear the sweet, cool chime of the wind as it crossed them...

** ** **

...It was noontime, the air heavy with the scent of lotus blooms, filled with the music of the river. Wenatef was in a field of ripe grain beneath the bright sun, gazing down at the river, now brighter and bluer than he had ever seen it, scattering light from its surface.

He bent to the harvest, moving with a rhythm that seemed ageless, and as he worked he realized that he was not wearied, not thirsty, not bored, but filled with a vast peace and joy that seemed to melt the grief that he had felt, a joy almost too vast for his mortal heart to contain. The sun did not burn him, the air held no breathless heat, and the wind that blew across the fields seemed to blow into Wenatef's very soul and awaken a spark of something untamed and fearless.

Rising in the morning without ceasing

213

Diana Wilder

Not wearied in labor...
When thy rays are visible
Gold is not considered.
It is not like thy brilliance...

The words were all around him and he found himself joining in their repetition as though they were engraved within his soul.

The wind stirred again, and the light seemed to splash across the fields like molten gold. The wild sweetness stirred again in Wenatef's heart, and he laid his sickle aside and straightened. The countryside rolled away from him with the vast blue river running through it, and far away in the distance a mighty range of mountains with a glow behind them, as though they were awaiting another, greater sunrise.

Wenatef was surrounded by people, millions of millions of people, and yet there was no noise, no crowd, no conflict of race with race or nation against nation, only the music of the river and the sweet peace over all.

'For none may tarry in the land of Egypt;
None there is that passeth not thither.
The span of our earthly deeds is as a dream;
But fair is the welcome that awaits him
Who has reached the Hills of the West.'

Wenatef heard the voice behind him and turned.

Nakhtamun was holding the bow and arrows in his hands; as Wenatef bowed before him, he raised his hands and offered the weapons across his palms. *Take them,* he said.

Wenatef obeyed. Their hands were side by side for a moment, and once more Wenatef saw the difference in their substance, as though Nakhtamun were flesh and he, Wenatef, merely smoke. As though Nakhtamun and the fields and the people in the fields were all part of a deeper reality, which Wenatef had not yet joined.

The thought sent a stab of pain through his heart. He

214

loved the fields, the peace, the multitudes working in harmony beneath the brilliant sun. He loved the shimmer and ripple of the grain before the wind. This was his true home, this the land of which Egypt in all its beauty was only a pale distortion. This was the land that satisfied his wanderlust, the land that he could at last call home for all time.

He raised his eyes from the bow to Nakhtamun's face. The king was bareheaded and smiling in the sun.

'None may tarry in the Land of Egypt', nor may you, my son, when your task is ended. His voice was as clear as the wind that blew across and between them, as kind and warm as the voice a wise adult uses to speak to a very young child. *Your heart is set on other, younger lands. You shall have your heart's desire - and our blessing until we meet face to face in your true home.*

Wenatef did not want to understand the words. "But there is so much that must yet be done, King! I've killed the villains who defiled the tombs, but their leader - And Unas - I must still fight Nuteruhotep, and maybe even Sekhemkhet, King! They are great lords, and their influence reaches beyond Egypt, while I - "

You're wasting your fear on mortal men, said Nakhtamun. *How can they hurt you?* But his gaze gentled even as he spoke, and his voice certainly was warmer. *Go to the High Priest of Amun. He will help you to finish this fight.* The words were spoken with warmth, but also with great firmness.

The fear rose up again. "But King - "

Nakhtamun's hand rose, forestalling protest, soothing fear. It touched Wenatef's hair in a caress that contained within it the power of a blessing. Wenatef felt as though he were made of smoke. The touch remained against his temple, cool and gentle, as the wind rose, and Wenatef

215

suddenly thought that it was the touch of the King that kept him from blowing away like a wisp of mist on the back of that powerful wind.

Battle nerves, Commander of One Thousand? Nakhtamun said with the hint of a smile. *This isn't such a terrible conflict. Go to Herihor and take courage. We will be with you and you'll be safe.*

And then Wenatef was falling, falling, spinning downward, ever downward, lighter than a falcon's feather on the winds of time, and the touch was still against his hair, blessing him with coolness...

** ** **

Wenatef sat up. It was morning, and a finger of wind had pushed its way through the crack in the wall to stroke Wenatef's hair away from his face. The feet of the statue were warm, and the bow and arrows were propped against the wall, within his direct line of vision. Nakhtamun's carved stone face smiled above him in aloof serenity.

CHAPTER XL

Wenatef walked briskly toward the tomb of Ramesses XI in the bright sunlight of mid-morning. He held Nakhtamun's bow strung and ready in his right hand, and a quiver of arrows slanted between his shoulder-blades. His face was freshly shaven, he was clean and anointed and he had eaten well.

He was returning to his friends. He knew he should be happy, but uppermost in his heart was the bleak realization that he was returning to a world that he had outgrown like a garment. He was trapped in a smaller, narrower dispensation, like a hawk within a cage, and it would be like this for the rest of his life.

Wenatef could hear the sound of chisels and good-natured bickering, and he heard a deep voice raised above the other sounds, roundly cursing someone and then shifting to laughter. Yes, Duwah was there.

He passed the entrance of the small, unfinished tomb beside that of Ramesses XI, and he paused. Six bodies lay in the sun, their faces covered. Six of the eight that he had killed. Where were the other two? Probably at Deir el Medineh, at Thutiy's establishment: Nebo and Ipy.

He walked past the bodies without another glance and continued toward the tomb entrance, waiting for the echo of the warning trumpet.

The echo never came. Instead, faces appeared at the tomb entrance and people stepped out into the sunlight to

217

watch his approach. He could hear excited whispers, and then his guardsmen came forward, their bows in their hands. They, too, were staring with a mixture of awe and fear, and some of them raised their hands to shield their eyes, though the sun was behind them.

Wenatef could see Ramses standing high on the hillside. The young man raised his hand in greeting and then hurried down to the tomb entrance.

Wenatef paused to look up at them and note their expressions, then squared his shoulders and began to ascend the hill toward the opening. Several of the men fell to their knees, their hands about their protective amulets.

Wenatef saw the motion and paused. *They don't know*, he thought with a sudden lurch of his heart. *They'll never understand, even if I explain...* "Don't be stupid!" he snapped.

He heard a hiss of indrawn breath, and then the workers began to smile and call greetings.

Wenatef started up the hill toward the opening, toward the plump, balding man who had appeared in the doorway and was watching him approach.

Duwah seemed to be having trouble controlling his mouth, for it shook slightly and could not seem to remain in a straight line. His eyes were very bright; suddenly they overflowed and he stretched out his hands as his smile broke.

"Wenatef - My Weni! - It really is you!" He seized Wenatef by the shoulders, savoring the reality of his flesh. One hand slanted upward to Wenatef's hair. "Oh it *is* you! You are alive! Oh, the gods are good!"

It was good to be among mortals again. Wenatef tried to swallow the knot in his throat, but without success. He let his bow slide to the ground; the years vanished and he was standing before the friend who had shared his misadventures so long before, with whom he had once broken the spirit of the meanest priest in Thebes.

A Killing Among the Dead

They embraced, laughing and crying at once, with Duwah blessing all the gods and cursing Wenatef for a stiff-necked fool who did not have sense enough to keep out of matters that might kill him. The others crowded around, adding their greetings and embraces, all demanding to know where Wenatef had been and how he had managed to escape the monstrous lions.

Wenatef pulled away and wiped his eyes. "You'll just have to wonder, you sons of asses!" he said, and his voice was shaky even though he was smiling "And as for my so-called guards, I have a few choice words on the subject of my command that the alarm be sounded whenever anyone approached! Has my absence made you all so slack? Shame on you!"

There was a moment of awkward silence. "W-we thought you were a god," someone said.

The words surprised Wenatef, who looked around to find the speaker. No one came forward. Finally he said, "Then you've been out in the sun too long."

He was surrounded again by laughing men, and Duwah cried, "We've done enough for one day! There is no more work to be done today on this tomb! Close it up - and take the carrion away to the desert! Let's go home!"

** ** **

They made a tumultuous entry into Deir el Medineh. The children of the town saw them and ran before them, crying the news. People came out from their houses to shout greetings and join the procession that wound its way to the house of Harmose, the elder foreman.

** ** **

"Then none of you knew that I was alive?" Wenatef asked, looking from Harmose to Dhutmose.

The Scribe was smiling broadly. He had hurried from his house as the procession passed, calling for Butehamun to

219

Diana Wilder

join him, and then had walked beside Wenatef, laughing with delight at his return.

"We suspected," Dhutmose said, "Especially after Ramses came to me with a story of robbers at work in the Valley of the Queens. Did he tell you? We went together to the larger branch of that valley, and while there was nothing obvious there to see, I found signs of blood that had been hurriedly covered up. We got out of there and I went to the Necropolis Police. By the way, Seneb investigated the area and, he said, found nothing amiss."

"I'm not surprised," Wenatef commented.

"Yes, well..." Dhutmose's smile was ironic. "Then Ramses came to me and asked for your allotment of food. He wouldn't explain why he needed it, but the fact that he had asked for your share, specifically, was indication enough. I gave him what he wanted and offered help if he needed it. He said he did not."

The Scribe looked down at his hands for a moment, then raised his eyes to Wenatef's face. "I am so glad that you're safe," he said. "I am sorry that you were harmed in any way. You know that I would have done all I could to prevent that. I'm sorry. You, whom we all called outsider, you've done more than any of us could to halt the robberies, and I am ashamed... If I can assist you - if any of us can help you in any way, you have only to ask."

Wenatef smiled at him and then looked around at the others. Ramses stood beside the door, his arms folded. Duwah was lounging in the only really comfortable chair in the room.

"I thank you all," Wenatef said. "I understand now why you were all so hesitant to confide in me. I'll have a request to make in a moment. But tell me first: what happened when the bodies were discovered this morning?"

"It was a strange thing," Dhutmose said, frowning. "Several of the men had gone early to the tomb to try and get

220

a head start on the cutting for today. The rest of us came later, about an hour before you arrived. We found the men huddled together outside the tomb, claiming that there was a ghost army inside. And indeed, I seemed to hear voices, though when I entered with a stonemason's mallet in one hand and a torch in the other, there was nothing to see."

All eyes were on Wenatef. Furtive hands were again raised to amulets. Wenatef saw the motion and sighed. "Stop it," he said. "I am a man like you, the same one you've obeyed and complained about for a year. There was nothing to fear but your own imaginations. Now tell me: what of Nebo and Ipy? What did Thutiy say and do when he saw them?"

"We summoned him from the town." Duwah answered. "He seemed stricken, as though he had expected something like this to happen, but had hoped it would not. He took the bodies back with him. Is - is he implicated in this?"

Wenatef noted the expressions around him. "No," he said. "He isn't involved in this."

There was a collective sigh of relief. Wenatef pretended not to hear it. "Now, Dhutmose," he said. "You can assist me. Take me to Herihor. Immediately. I must speak to him today."

** ** **

The town leaders wasted time arguing over strategy. Harmose said it was too early to bring the matter before Herihor. They needed time to gather their information and discuss their plan of attack. Khons said it was too risky to strike at that moment.

Wenatef listened, folded his arms, and then shook his head. "You said that you would assist me," he said. "This is the assistance I want. I must speak to Herihor immediately. Do you refuse to bring me to him?"

"No one refuses," Dhutmose said. "I am the one to take

you to Herihor: I'll do it gladly. Do you want me to remain with you when you speak with him?"

Wenatef's frown relaxed. "Remain, if you wish. Can we leave for the temple at once?"

"At once," Dhutmose answered.

CHAPTER XLI

Herihor, High Priest of Amun, had also held the titles of Commander of the Army of Upper Egypt and Viceroy of Nubia. He had marched on Thebes at the head of his army five years before when Libyan marauders, acting with the connivance of Amenhotep, the High Priest of Amun, had almost overrun the western approaches to the city.

Herihor had stormed the fortified temple-palace of Medinet Habu, putting the Libyans to rout and commanding Amenhotep to find his own way to the Lands of the West. He had then assumed the title of High Priest of Amun and set in motion a purge of the priesthood that was still the subject of shocked whispers.

A time of calm had set in, then, as Herihor assumed control of the greatest office in the land, commanding more wealth, more manpower, more prestige than any other position except that of the King, himself. He had not even been disheartened or deterred by a lack of priestly training, for Herihor knew how to delegate authority. He ruled the south of Egypt, while the north was controlled by the Prince of Tanis, Smendes, who had married a daughter of Ramesses IX.

Ramesses XI lived in his palace in Per-Ramesse, in the delta, penning love poems and philosophical treatises and taking a hand in ruling the land, but it was clear, not least of all to Ramesses himself, that the Ramesside dynasties were coming to an end. In fact, his reign would continue for another fifteen years. After his death Herihor and Nesubanebdedet, who was also known as Smendes, would both rule as kings, dividing Egypt - 'The Two Lands' for the first time in millennia.

** ** **

Herihor was a strong, well-muscled man, growing slightly thick about the middle, but with no loose flesh. He was often seen during the hours of Amun-re's morning office, driving his chariot and shooting arrows at copper targets. He had been pleased with the results of one such shooting match and had had the target hung in the temple with the arrows still transfixing it.

He had added to the building at Karnak and had caused his name to be carved on the walls of Karnak enclosed in a kingly cartouche, or border. Wenatef, loyal to Pharaoh, had been angered by Herihor's presumption that seemed to mark the end of His Majesty's power. But now, gazing on the man, he found himself thinking of beginnings and not of endings. It was impossible to feel jaded or hopeless when standing before him, for he seemed to radiate vigor, and his more than fifty years had touched him very little.

Herihor watched Wenatef rise from his obeisance, inclined his head to acknowledge the bow, and then fixed Dhutmose with his clear hazel eyes. "Who is this?" he asked, and his voice was deep and calm as his eyes flickered over Wenatef once more.

"Holiness, this is Wenatef, son of Hapuseneb, who was Chief of the Granaries of Mut before his death two years ago. Wenatef commands the Guard of His Majesty's Tomb. He has been awarded the Gold of Honor for valor - "

Herihor had leaned forward to gaze more closely at Wenatef. "At Semna," he finished for Dhutmose. "I remember you." He smiled suddenly. "Yes, I remember you, Commander of One Thousand. I remember you well... You were the only officer left alive in that entire garrison, yet you rallied the defenders and held the fortress firm, prepared to die if need be, rather than to surrender. It is good to know that such men still live in this land... But where is your Gold of Honor?"

"It was lost in a struggle with tomb robbers, Holiness," Wenatef answered.

The High Priest blinked. "Tomb robbers?" he repeated.

"Yes, Holiness."

Herihor looked from Dhutmose to Wenatef. "Explain yourself, Commander," he said. Wenatef did, and Herihor's expression grew more thunderous. Finally he said, "I've heard enough of this filth to last the rest of my life! You say that you have proof of this? What proof is that?"

After having walked among the Blest for the past two weeks, Wenatef was unmoved by Herihor's fierceness. It was rather like listening to the growling of a kitten after having lived among lions.

Dhutmose raised a hand. "He's no crank, Holiness," he said. "This is something the chiefs of the village had suspected long before this - "

"And you didn't bring your suspicions to me?" Herihor asked, dangerously quiet.

Dhutmose paled and raised his hands in protest as Wenatef frowned at Herihor. "We can explain, Holiness - " he began.

Wenatef cut in on Dhutmose's protests. "They were prudent enough to avoid coming before you without proof," he said. "They were afraid they'd get just such a reception as this from you. With good cause, it appears. I have proof. I have Khaemwase within easy reach - "

"Khaemwase!" Dhutmose and Herihor shouted the name in unison.

"Yes. Khaemwase. He is at Abd el Kurna, in one of the tombs. I can draw a map for you. He is alone and injured, if

225

not dead - "

"Your doing?' Herihor asked.

"My doing," Wenatef said. "He won't have gone far: I left him in no condition to escape. I also have the bodies of eight tomb robbers available for your viewing, if you wish. I would imagine that some of them might be known to the various corps of Guards in Thebes.

"There is another prisoner, as well: Seneb, a Necropolis Police officer. He should be able to shed considerable light on this question of robberies. And finally, I've written my observations covering my findings in the tombs of the Necropolis."

"Where are they?" asked Dhutmose, suddenly intent.

"They're hidden in one of the tombs. I had little to write with but makeshift brushes and ink, and I had to use empty wine-jars for writing space, but the information is there and it is accurate."

"Very well done," Herihor said, speaking calmly, though a deep line slashed downward between his eyes. "Well done, indeed! Where is Khaemwase?"

Wenatef told him, then told of his battle against the tomb-robbers. He said nothing of his time in the West. Herihor was a soldier. Tales of a sojourn in the Land of the Blest would only make Wenatef seem like a dreaming fool. Wenatef needed Herihor's confidence.

And so Wenatef related his fight against the conspiracy from the moment that he found himself buried alive until his return to Deir el Medineh that morning. He told it swiftly, compellingly, as a soldier might report to a commander, all the while watching the emotions reflected in Herihor's hazel eyes, reading them as a skilled scribe might read the words of a scroll, judging the proper moment to make his demand.

** ** **

"...And so I returned," Wenatef said, "Past the defiled tombs, with the cliffs rising on either side, up through the valley until I stood before the bodies of those I had slain. I have made my report to Your Holiness. I am at your service in whatever way is needed."

Herihor sat back with a deep sigh. "It - it is almost too much to believe," he said. "I thank the gods that you halted this matter in time! We are truly in your debt! You shall certainly be rewarded... I will consider your information and take what steps seem necessary. His Majesty will pay a reward to you for capturing Khaemwase - " He actually grinned for a moment. "That is, if you can convince the royal counselors that the man actually *is* Khaemwase. The reward is well-deserved."

"I want no reward, Holiness," Wenatef said, rising. "I only have one request to make of you."

Herihor's brows drew together, but he said quietly enough, "What is that?"

"I have the name of a man high in this plot. The man who brought Khaemwase to the valley in the first place. He must be arrested and brought to justice."

"You didn't tell me of this before?" Herihor said.

"The time was not right," Wenatef answered.

"It is right at this moment." Herihor said. "We must stop this abomination before it spreads. Name the man!"

Wenatef took a deep breath, his eyes locked on Herihor's. "He is Nuteruhotep, the Steward of Amun," he said.

Herihor had been sitting forward. At the sound of the name he recoiled so violently that his chair rocked backward. "Nuteruhotep!" he gasped. "What's this? He is my representative here and abroad for all matters involving the cult of Amun!"

"I mean that Nuteruhotep is behind the tomb robberies and the murders," Wenatef said quietly.

Herihor pushed himself to his feet. "Then the priesthood of Amun is implicated in this? No, I can't believe it!" He looked from Wenatef to Dhutmose. "There must be some mistake!"

"I am sorry, Holiness," Wenatef said. "I wish it were not so. But he has been named by Khaemwase, and by Captain Seneb of the Necropolis Police." He said again, "I am sorry."

Herihor sank into his chair again. "My right hand man," he said. "I have trusted him with everything, even with matters touching my honor." He raised his eyes to Wenatef's. "You are a man of honor and truth. Tell me honestly: can there be any mistake?"

"If the man is your right hand," Wenatef said, "Then you're familiar with his character. Is it possible that he has the courage and resolve to be involved in this scandal?"

Herihor lowered his eyes. "It...is possible," he said. "Must he be arrested?"

"No," said Wenatef. "He will have a chance to speak for himself first."

"I will conduct an inquiry," Herihor said.

"This must be settled at once.," Wenatef said. "You've heard my account of desecration and robbery in the tombs. You have heard it corroborated by a man who is known to you personally. Nuteruhotep was named by Khaemwase himself. My prisoner, Seneb, will also name Nuteruhotep. What reason can you possibly have to doubt me?"

Herihor was unused to being addressed so directly. He scowled at Wenatef and said, "I'll look into matters. It is enough."

Wenatef stepped away from Dhutmose and faced the two men, seeing them through strange eyes, as though he were above and beyond them in space and in time, while they were huddled below him, somehow smaller and younger

"Wenatef - " It was Dhutmose, stretching a hand up to him.

Wenatef leveled his gaze at Dhutmose and said, "No.

228

Listen to me, both of you. I found things to make all men bow their faces to the dust in shame and horror.

"Thutmose III rests in his House of Eternity, torn into fragments, his face laid bare and smashed by the blow of an evil fist! Nakhtamun was stricken with an axe. Horemheb's jaw was torn from his face. Ahmose-Nefertari has been desecrated - and still there are others!

"I fought the slaves of greed and the monsters of hatred and destruction and slew them by the strength of my arm alone and unaided."

Wenatef's voice rose, clear and strong as the cry of Anubis from the Hall of Judgment. "I come to you now, seeking your help in the one final matter concerning this plot - and you want to delay it. Nuteruhotep leads this plot, and I can prove it. Will you give me the assistance I require to capture him and end this menace of greed and destruction?"

The world was strange, slightly blurred, for a moment. His last words seemed to echo in the beautifully carved chamber of the God. The men standing before him were pale and silent, moving stiffly as though emerging from a paralysis of fright.

Dhutmose took a hesitant step forward, his hand stretched out, almost touching Wenatef's shoulder, but pausing just short of the contact of his hand upon Wenatef's flesh.

Herihor lowered his head. "I will do as you ask," he said. "And I will pray that you are wrong, for this is a very great shame to me and mine."

Wenatef gazed at him for a long moment. "No," he said. "No shame can ever touch you, no matter who else in involved."

Herihor raised his head and met Wenatef's smile. His expression eased and he nodded.

"Now," said Wenatef. "I know that Nuteruhotep is here at the temple. I want him to be brought to me, and I must speak to the man alone."

"But then how - " Herihor began.

"Let me finish, Holiness. I must talk to him alone. If he thinks no one is with me, he will speak freely. He'll probably think that he can kill me. So much the better. I want two trustworthy men of your own choosing who can listen to what is said. And I want the best scribe you have, one who can write swiftly and well. He'll sit and record what we say, word for word, as best as can be done. They can be easily hidden, I am sure."

Herihor was frowning again, but it was a frown of approval and even admiration. "There will be four records," he said, "Three heard and one written: It'll do. Dhutmose, send for Captain Taharka. Tell him that I want him to find to Petamenophis and Mentemhet. And tell him, also, to summon Thutnefer, the Senior Scribe of the God, from the archives. Tell him it is urgent. And then tell Taharka to bring a squadron of his guards to the lotus audience chamber with the other three men. I'll send to Lord Nuteruhotep and tell him that his presence is required."

When Dhutmose had departed, Herihor turned to Wenatef and inclined his head. It was almost a bow. "I know what you plan," he said. "It will be a bold stroke if it works."

CHAPTER XLII

Clerestory windows let the sun down into the audience room in slow streamers that lay across the floor like ribbons of gold. Gold glinted as well from the hinges of the cedar door, glittered from the grillwork at the windows and flashed, hot and blinding, from the winged goddesses, carved in high relief, that flanked Wenatef's throne. The walls about him were painted with lotus flowers in cool shades of blue and green, and bright, jewel-like birds darted between the blooms.

Wenatef set his arms along the gilded arms of the chair, his hands resting atop the twin carved lion heads. He remembered the lion guardians and smiled at the thought of their might and their size. How they would terrify any evildoers who saw them!

The two witnesses and the scribe were behind a screen to his left: the scribe, Thutnefer, had lifted his palette and his brushes, smiled at Wenatef and bowed low to him, and said, "Good luck," before stepping behind the screen.

Wenatef had been warmed by the words, but he had no need of good wishes, for he felt the power of the Land of the West upon him and he knew now that whatever happened in that audience chamber could only end in victory.

Nakhtamun had said, *We will be with you and you'll be safe.* Wenatef could feel their presence about him. They surrounded him, rank upon rank, unseen but not unperceived, silently watching and judging. Their presence made the room almost seem to hum with power, with a sense of awe and a dread far greater than that inspired by the ghostly army in His Majesty's unfinished tomb.

He set his feet upon the gilded footstool and raised his head as the sound of footsteps approached the doorway. The room grew still.

A Nubian guard entered the audience room and brought his fist to his heart in a salute. His eyes widened and he faltered backward a step, his eyes darting to the corners of the chamber and then to Wenatef's face. He saw no one but Wenatef; he composed himself with a visible effort and said, "The Lord Nuteruhotep."

Wenatef had seen Nuteruhotep when he was a child, at the time that Hapuseneb had accused him of dishonesty. He had always remembered Nuteruhotep as a giant among men, filled with menace. Hapuseneb and Neitneferti had never voiced their fears to him - he had been too young at the time - but Wenatef had known that Nuteruhotep was a man who could have his father killed. He remembered the flight to Memphis with his mother, and the weeks when he lay awake at night and listened to the quiet sound of his mother weeping. Now he watched the man enter and wondered why everyone had been so afraid.

Nuteruhotep was a portly man with a proud face beneath a heavy shawl wig. A collar of intricately wrought gold beads lay round his neck. Wenatef remembered it from Khaemwase's description. The necklace of Thutmose III. Wenatef's eyes fastened on the collar, then rose to Nuteruhotep's face and narrowed.

The Steward of Amun had followed the Nubian guard into the room and, like the Nubian, had come to a dead stop, his eyes wide, his chest rising and falling with the swiftness of fear. He looked around the room, caught sight of Wenatef, and strode forward with an appearance of confidence, but with his shoulders slightly hunched.

He stopped before Wenatef and looked him over with angry hauteur. "I was summoned to you," he said. "Who are you?"

Wenatef inclined his head to the man and then addressed the guard. "You won't be needed for a time," he said. "You may leave for now."

The Nubian bowed and left.

Wenatef turned back to Nuteruhotep. "Steward of Amun," he said, "You have been summoned to answer for your actions in the Valley of the Kings."

Nuteruhotep's arm jerked once, then he was still, but with a rigidity that had not been there before. "What do you mean?" he asked. "Is it because I inquired about building a tomb? But that would be somewhere besides the Valley of the Kings! Negotiations aren't complete at any rate. And what business it is of yours is beyond my understanding! I am a busy man with little time." He turned on his heel and started toward the door.

"You are not dismissed," Wenatef said.

Nuteruhotep whirled and stared at him. "What did you say?" he demanded.

"You are not dismissed," Wenatef repeated with a smile.

"You make it sound as though I am on trial," Nuteruhotep snapped.

"You are," Wenatef said. "You face grave charges. You have been granted a hearing - "

"Before you, I suppose!"

"Before me," Wenatef agreed. "There are others who will hear you and judge. Can't you feel them around you even as we speak?"

Nuteruhotep's eyes shifted to the corners of the room and then returned to Wenatef. "You're quite mad," he said. "There is no one here but you, and no one to force me to stay."

"If you truly believe that, then turn and walk through that door," Wenatef said, reflecting that the necklace alone would damn the man. The necklace coupled with the testimony of Khaemwase and Seneb would triply damn him. There was no real need to trap the man in his own words. No need except Wenatef's conviction that for whatever reason there could be, the Great Ones wished to give Nuteruhotep a chance to speak for himself.

The Steward of Amun turned and took a step toward the door, and then halted as though dragged to a stop by a powerful hand. He was very pale when he turned back to Wenatef. "Pretending that there is a tribunal reviewing my actions," he said, " - which I don't for a moment admit - what charges do you bring against me?"

"I charge you, Nuteruhotep, with conspiring with Khaemwase of Koptos to rob the tombs in the Valley of the Kings. I charge you with the crime of bringing Khaemwase of Koptos to Thebes for that purpose. I charge you with the crime of receiving and selling stolen grave-goods. I charge you with recruiting conspirators and giving them orders, with corruption and murder."

Two spots of color rode high on Nuteruhotep's cheekbones as his lips blanched white. He was silent as he paced to the door again, but he made no attempt to leave. His hands were clenched behind his back, but his expression was calm once more. "Who has told you these lies?" he asked quietly.

"You are accused by Khaemwase of Koptos, himself," Wenatef answered. "Seneb of the Necropolis Police also accuses you. You are convicted by their testimony, and there will be others."

"Khaemwase is a thief and a murderer!" Nuteruhotep exclaimed.

"That gives us all the more reason to question your involvement with the man," Wenatef said.

Nuteruhotep's eyes narrowed.

"Let's not bandy words, Steward of Amun," Wenatef said, leaning forward. "I have Khaemwase in my custody and I have Seneb of the Necropolis Police. There is other evidence as well. You're lost. There is nothing about your movements that is not known."

Nuteruhotep came back to Wenatef and frowned at him, his hand hovering at the hilt of his dagger. "Then why did you summon me?" he asked.

"To give you a chance to defend yourself," Wenatef answered.

"And who are you to judge me?" Nuteruhotep demanded.

"I am the one appointed by those whose tombs are lying open and defiled. I have been judged and justified. I came back from the West to slay the defilers and the evil ones. It was through me that Seneb and Khaemwase were captured. I have the information that will convict you, and it has been given to those who judge you. But there is still a chance to speak in your own behalf."

"To you?"

"To me. There are others who will hear and judge, as I said before."

Nuteruhotep's eyebrows almost met above his nose. He moved his lips soundlessly.

"Come, my lord. Do you deny that you brought Khaemwase to the Valley of the Kings, as he has testified?"

"I deny it! I deny it!"

"But he says otherwise," Wenatef persisted.

"He lies!"

"And do you deny that you purchased goods from Khaemwase?"

"I didn't know that the man was Khaemwase!" Nuteruhotep cried, his hand at the gold collar of Thutmose III. "If something is for sale, who am I to question its

Diana Wilder

source? Must I ask each man to recount his ancestry? Must I know the provenance of every item I purchase? The ancestry of every slave, the mine from which came the ore that made my necklace?"

"Khaemwase said that you contacted him and offered to let him loot the tombs in the Valley of the Kings. You dealt with Nakht as well."

Nuteruhotep moistened his lips. "Lies! Khaemwase - if it *was* him - he came to me with jewelry and beautiful objects. Who am I to pry into the affairs of others? The objects were magnificent! That is all I know!"

"And yet they, being beautiful, had the names of great kings on them - "

"How do I know that they weren't put there later, to make them seem more valuable?" Nuteruhotep's hand was now clenched on the collar.

"Then if you knew that the objects were grave goods, you would not purchase them?"

"No!"

"And if you knew that they had been stolen, what then?"

"Don't insult me!" snarled Nuteruhotep. "I'll bring a complaint against you before the High Priest - "

"Save your breath," Wenatef said. "You face a higher tribunal at this moment. Or have you forgotten?"

Nuteruhotep whitened and took a deep breath, but he spoke quietly enough. "It is my word against yours."

"You can't lie to these judges," Wenatef pointed out. "And don't forget - when you go before the lesser tribunal - that there is the word of Khaemwase and Seneb, as well."

"Liars!"

"That may be. Can you survive an inquest like that which will surely come? Can you afford to have His Majesty's police go to your dwelling even now and examine its furnishings? And when they question you, as is lawful - what will you say? You are lost already, Nuteruhotep. You

236

can face nothing but condemnation here - but hereafter?"

Nuteruhotep looked down.

Wenatef's voice gentled. "Come," he said. "Tell me of this plot. What made you decide to rob the tombs of the kings? You weren't always an evil man. There is much good in you even now. What turned you? The lust for gold? The passion for collecting beautiful things? What turned you?"

Nuteruhotep seemed to waver. Wenatef sat forward, his hands gripping the arms of the throne, willing the man to turn, to admit his wrongdoing, to admit his repentance, to seek mercy. The air about him seemed almost to throb; he caught a sense of weight shifting, of intense gazes being directed to the man who stood with bowed head before Wenatef, twisting his hands.

Nuteruhotep finally spoke. "There are many who have robbed tombs," he said.

"They must answer for themselves," Wenatef said.

Nuteruhotep did not look up, but his hands suddenly clenched. "It is my word against a known robber and murderer," he said. "I am high in the Temple... I won't suffer for any of this. And you-" He lifted his head with a motion as swift as a striking snake. "You with your madman's talk of tribunals - ! You are nothing! You can do nothing against me! Why, you're a dead man from the moment that I leave this room, for the guard will take you and kill you at my command!"

"On what charge?" Wenatef asked, smiling.

"Blasphemy," Nuteruhotep hissed. "You are a blasphemer and a madman. I can attest to your words against me! "

"I thought for a moment that you weren't lost," Wenatef said. "I was wrong, and I am sorry for that, but the choice was your own... Very well, then, let us play the game your way."

"What do you mean?" Nuteruhotep demanded.

"Just this. You have a point: It is your word against a known robber and murderer. Many who would have spoken against you are dead. But you know that you are guilty, and so do I. You cannot escape judgment in this world or the next, and the judgment will be a terrible one, for the one who will speak against you is mighty indeed in both worlds."

Nuteruhotep's brows drove together. "What do you mean?" he demanded.

"The question is 'who?'" Wenatef corrected. "And the answer is Thutmose the Great. You wear his denunciation about your neck. You're undone, Nuteruhotep, and you have condemned yourself."

"God damn your impudence!" the Steward of Amun cried, his hand at his dagger.

Wenatef did not move. "I am sick from speaking with you," he said. "You're a desperately wicked man. Let us discuss facts instead. The treasures of the dead don't belong to you, whoever else may claim them. You arranged for violent, evil men to come and take them and to kill those who stood in their way. You dealt directly with the head of the robbers without disguising your name, without remorse. You are wearing the necklace of Thutmose III openly at this very moment.

"Knowing yourself to be caught in your crimes, you refuse to speak truly. You have turned from truth and chosen lies: it is my judgment that you deserve death. And death is what you will receive."

The Steward's dagger hissed softly from its sheath as he took two swift steps up the dais. Wenatef heard the rasp of indrawn breath as the dagger slowly arced upward toward his throat.

"And if I go to that death, O Judge," Nuteruhotep said, "Do you think that I will go alone? You say you want truth?

A Killing Among the Dead

You will have it. What do I care for laws formed by those bound by superstition? The wealth is there for the taking, if a man has courage and intelligence!" He bared his teeth in a smile. "But if I am condemned, then I'll take you into the blackness with me."

Wenatef looked silently up along the line of the strong arm to Nuteruhotep's face, and read the determination there. *It is almost at an end,* he thought. *Almost resolved. Almost.*

Words came to him with sudden, irresistible urgency. He spoke them, his gaze never wavering from Nuteruhotep's face.

"And what of Unas?"

He saw the hand tighten on the hilt of the knife as a touch of remorse flickered in the dark eyes.

"I needed a tool," Nuteruhotep replied. "He came to my hand."

"He did not come easily," Wenatef said. "You had to warp him in order to fit him to your grip."

"I did what I had to," Nuteruhotep said. "I didn't mean it to have the effect it did. They were mere exaggerations... Anyone with any sense would have seen it. How could I possibly realize - " The sentence hung incomplete in the air.

" - The terrible harm those lies would do," Wenatef finished.

"I needed to get to the gold," Nuteruhotep said. "He was the way I saw to do it."

"And for the sake of gold a human soul was broken and set on the road to damnation," Wenatef said. "And this was done by one who is a priest."

The condemnation in Wenatef's voice stung Nuteruhotep. "The final choice was his!" he said.

"You could as well tell a man with a millstone round his neck that his is the final choice to sink or swim," Wenatef said. "It was you who set the millstone there. How can you

239

justify it?"

Nuteruhotep could not. Wenatef read it in his suddenly closed expression. The time for pleading was over.

He could feel a stirring about him, a rustling, as though a great wind was blowing beyond and above him. Murmurs rose, whispers that seemed to come from the figures carved on the stones around him, the rustle of wings as the vulture Nekhbet seemed to unfurl her pinions, the sigh of the scales of the cobra Buto, the jangle of sistra, the chant of voices...

Nuteruhotep's eyes widened but his grip did not waver. "Your sorcerer's tricks don't frighten me," he said. "I know more tricks than you can ever learn." His arm seemed to tense...

Wenatef sat back, remembering Nakhtamun's words again. The Blest did not lie. And yet, he would have welcomed death. He was no longer at ease in this, the old dispensation. He knew himself a stranger among a suddenly alien people that clutched at their strange gods and closed their eyes desperately against a truth too splendid for them to see without pain. His return to life among them was as hard and bitter an agony as death had once been.

He smiled and shook his head. "Strike, thief," he said softly. "Strike and see what happens."

CHAPTER XLIII

Nuteruhotep's eyes narrowed dangerously and his hand tightened on the dagger. He opened his mouth to speak -

The heavy cedar doors behind them were flung wide with a crash, booming back against the walls. Archers poured into the room, Medjay warriors with great, curved bows drawn and aimed at Nuteruhotep. Captain Taharka was at their head; Herihor stood behind him, his eyes flashing. Dhutmose stood to the side.

"And now, Steward," said Herihor, his voice as low as the growl of a lion, "We have much to discuss."

** ** **

Nuteruhotep straightened as the archers closed about him. "You have come just in time, Holiness," he said. "This man threatened my life!"

"He is unarmed!" Dhutmose cried. "And *you* have a dagger at his throat!"

Nuteruhotep threw a scornful look at him before turning to Herihor.

Wenatef and sat back in the throne. Matters were out of his hands for the moment, and he could relax and watch developments. To his critical eye, the Steward was quite convincing. But he did not know about the three hidden witnesses.

The thought occurred to Herihor at that moment. He said, "Thutnefer - Petamenophis - Mentemhet - come out."

Nuteruhotep's fist tightened on the haft of the dagger, as

241

the three men came from behind the screen but he made no move to strike. "This man is dangerous, Holiness!" he exclaimed.

"He is quite dangerous," Herihor said. "But not in the way you imply. He turned to the chief scribe. "Thutnefer," he said. "Read what you've written."

The scribe bowed and unrolled the papyrus. He scanned it swiftly before raising his voice to read:

You say you want truth? You will have it. What do I care for laws formed by those bound by superstition? The wealth is there for the taking, if a man has courage and intelligence!"

The room was silent. Thutnefer looked up from the papyrus. "Do you wish to hear more, Holiness?" he asked quietly.

"Can you attest to the way in which the words were spoken?" Herihor asked.

Thutnefer's long-lidded gray eyes lifted to Nuteruhotep's face and lingered for a contemptuous moment before he answered. "I heard the thought behind his words in this and in more dire matters, Holiness. I will swear to it, and so will Petamenophis and Mentemhet. But, My Lord," his cool voice continued, "You would do well to look at the Steward's necklace."

"Your necklace, Steward," Herihor said, nodding to Taharka.

The Captain eased the arrow from his bowstring, set it back in its quiver, and advanced on the Steward, his hand outstretched, his hawk-featured face devoid of emotion.

The Steward recoiled a step.

"The necklace, My Lord," Taharka said.

Nuteruhotep made no move, the knife still gripped in his hand. The archers hung back, afraid to shoot.

Wenatef rose and gently took the dagger from Nuteruhotep and then, as the man whirled, his eyes wide

242

with shock, said, "It is enough. You've condemned yourself. You knew it then and you know it now. Hand over the necklace."

Nuteruhotep slowly unknotted the cord that fastened the heavy collar to its counterpoise, drew the gold from his neck and held it out to Wenatef across his palm. The plates chimed faintly, sweetly - and then clashed as Nuteruhotep gathered them and threw them in Wenatef's face, then turned to leap down the dais, hurling the two nearest archers aside and sending Taharka spinning into the middle of his troop.

The room was filled with shouting and curses. Archers fought to disentangle their bows, to nock arrows. A straight-armed shove sent Herihor sprawling; Nuteruhotep vaulted over him and ran through the high cedar doors and into the hallway.

The soldiers struggled to their feet, swearing.

A scream ripped through the temple hall. Every moment of grief and pain and mortal terror in the existence of mankind seemed to find expression in that one long cry. Silence came crashing back upon them like the recoil of a great wave, leaving the men huddled and shivering.

Wenatef rose and looked around at the white faces around him. No one moved. He descended the dais, picked his way between the archers, and stepped out into the hallway.

Nuteruhotep was flattened on the stone floor. His face was buried in his arms, his breath came in shuddering sobs. Snatches of garbled, half-remembered prayers poured through his clenched teeth.

Wenatef knelt beside him and scanned him for wounds.

The man was mad with terror. He reared up and clutched at Wenatef's hands, gasping pleas for forgiveness.

"I won't hurt you, Steward," Wenatef said, and then paused. He caught the sense of a presence looming just above him, vaster than the spread of the sky, too filled with light to face without pain.

Wenatef bowed to the ground and touched his forehead to the flagstones. "Depart in peace, Lord," he said without daring to raise his face. "By the arm of Your servant You have taken the evildoers, and all is well now."

He felt the presence withdraw, as the sunlight fades when a cloud passes before it. He pushed himself to his knees and then waited beside Nuteruhotep until the priests and the soldiers came to lead him away to his prison.

CHAPTER XLIV

It took two days to sort matters with Herihor's assistance. The guards sent to arrest Khaemwase found him amid the tombs of Abd el Kurna, lying half dead beneath the bright sky. He had died under their questioning, though they had been gentle with him. He had time, though, to thoroughly damn Nuteruhotep and several other influential men in Thebes, Tanis, Bubastis and Per-Ramesse.

Herihor wasn't one to hesitate. Messengers galloped north to Smendes and Pharaoh, with immediate results. The various conspirators were seized and sent to Thebes for questioning within days. Most of them confessed.

Seneb, retrieved from his tomb-prison, had been pale and biddable. Three nights in a tomb had bred a profound and sincere repentance in him, and a willingness to accept whatever punishment might be meted out to him, so long as it would erase his wrongdoing. He confessed to everything, including Roy's murder, before anyone could frame any questions.

Nuteruhotep did not wait for questioning. Whatever he had seen in those moments alone in the hallway at Karnak had turned him completely against his former evildoing and left him desperate to make amends. He confessed to everything and even named some desecrated tombs that Wenatef had not discovered. But more even than this, he had exposed a large, sickening corruption that struck at the heart of Egypt, involving sacrilege and robbery within the very temples of the great gods themselves. His Majesty convened a court of inquiry and the great priesthoods closed in upon themselves, resolving the matter in silence and secrecy.

Wenatef was not comforted. There was one silent, secret matter left unfinished. Unas had never been found. He would have to fight Unas.

He had returned to Deir el Medineh, to a home that had been cleaned and refurbished from top to bottom by a grateful village. He slept on a mattress of finest linen and wore a necklace of the brightest beaten gold, but the days were as stifling and bitter as his newly recovered mortality and the two nights he spent in the town were restless with the raveled ends of feverish dreams.

At last, in the dark watches of the night, he arose from his bed, made his silent way through the dark house, and headed through the deserted streets of the town toward the necropolis.

It was time.

** ** **

Wenatef tucked the mace of Thutmose III into his belt and filled his lungs with the cool night air. The tomb of King Seti I lay along the valley, not far from where he stood. He had returned to Nakhtamun's tomb to fetch the mace. It had been a long trek. He walked slowly along the path through the valley, his mind and heart utterly quiet, almost dreaming in the silver silence of the moonlight. He lifted his face to the night sky and took a shaking breath.

Is this, then, the real reason I was brought to the tombs? he silently asked the host of stars. *Is everything else unimportant?*

The tomb opening was before him, black in the moonlight. Great cedar doors blocked the entrance, but a slanting tunnel cut through the hillside and into the tomb below the first long flight of steps. Another flight lay beyond them, then a stretch of plain hallway, and then a deep pit that ended before a false wall. The robbers had broken the wall down, laying open the antechamber of the tomb.

A steep set of stairs descended to the burial level, reached by another long hallway that opened abruptly to the vaulted sarcophagus chamber. Wenatef had paused during his first visit to gaze in awe at the beautifully carved and painted reliefs of the king celebrating the Litany of the Sun, greeting the gods and goddesses of the pantheon, embracing and worshiping them, eternally elegant and smiling. The workmanship was the finest he had ever seen. His steps had lagged along the hallway that first time, but there was no time for that now.

Wenatef stopped in the entrance. He could see a strange glow of red light and hear the clang and crash of a hammer against stone. He ran down the dark corridor toward the red, flickering light, vaulted the pit and pelted down and down until he stood at the entrance to the burial chamber, and gazed on the destruction there.

Unas had kindled a fire in a carnelian bowl and then set it high on one of the lion-headed beds that crowded into the corner of the chamber. He stood before the sarcophagus, a mallet in one hand and a chisel in the other. By that hot light he was hammering at the sarcophagus and laughing. The lid had somehow been levered from its base and hurled to the floor. The successive nesting coffins had been opened and their lids cast aside.

The body of the king lay on the floor before Unas with a pile of golden objects beside it. The lid of the outermost coffin lay hacked and stripped of its gilding a short distance away, by the yawning edge of a deep pit. The great, dark eyes of the face stared upward at the vaulted, star-flecked ceiling above it.

Unas had not seen Wenatef. His hammer rose and

smashed against the stone. "You are nothing!" he cried, his voice shattering into a thousand echoes against the stone ceiling.

He aimed a blow of his mallet at the name of the king. "You die!" there was another crash of stone. "You die forever!"

Wenatef stepped into the light and advanced on Unas. His feet bare and silent upon the stone floor of the tomb, but Unas looked up. The fraction of a second it took for Unas to see him and compose his face into its habitual mask was enough to turn the wrath in Wenatef's heart to compassion: the man's face was streaked with tears. The sight was piteous, but Wenatef had seen how Merihor had died, had seen the desecration of the bodies of the kings and the wreckage of the tombs. His wrath was tempered with understanding and compassion but he could not indulge in pity.

The crash of the chisel and hammer falling from Unas' nerveless fingers broke the silence. An inrush of air being dragged deep into frightened lungs, and then a scream of sheer terror as Unas cringed away from Wenatef, his fingers fumbling at an amulet that hung around his neck.

Wenatef bent and took the chisel and the hammer. He felt as though the eyes of his flesh and those of his spirit were for a moment disjointed. The tomb itself, for all its grandeur, seemed only a tiny cell in a vast universe, and he and Unas only small lives held within it. All about them were great mountains and wide plains and a river that roared and rippled beyond them like a great serpent while the clouds raced above it, hurled across the sky by a mighty wind.

Unas himself still stood before Wenatef, bent over the sarcophagus, but Wenatef seemed to see two faces. One was the smooth face of a cynical, twisted young man and the other was almost godlike, filled with grief, rage and hatred.

The eyes were wide with terror.

Unas spoke, but his voice was shrill and cracked. "It - it is good that you've come," he said. "The thieves were just here - see what they've done - "

Wenatef advanced a step. "We've passed beyond lies now, Unas," he said. "It is time to deal in truth." He threw the chisel and hammer far from him. "This must end once and for all," he said. "Did you think to revenge yourself on the gods for the lies of one evil man?"

Unas drew a long, shaking breath, and was suddenly calm again, and even smiling. He wiped the tears from his cheeks with the backs of his hands. "You," he said. "I should have known you would be skulking in these tombs, cringing before the paintings of the 'great ones' and mouthing prayers to the empty thrones of empty gods. I thought I had given you your death wound in that tomb. I see it didn't take. But there is still time to do it properly."

"You can't hurt me, Unas," Wenatef said. "You can only cripple and deform yourself."

Unas' mouth stretched in the travesty of a smile. "What does it matter what I do with myself?" he demanded. "There is no one to answer to for the use or misuse of my own soul! There is no law to condemn me, there is no judge to pass sentence!"

"You're speaking lies and you know it," Wenatef said. "Deal in the truth now. You have much to answer for already. Don't make the tally any greater."

Unas began to laugh. "'To answer for'!" he repeated scornfully. "Why should I whimper my reverence to the dried rags of meat that take up wealth and power that belongs to the living?"

"Listen to me, Unas," said Wenatef. "I've seen what I speak of. They are living now, and they hear you! But if they do not - if this life is all - then it still is better to live as you should and die rightly, with nothing in your life to cause shame."

"You sound like a priest!" Unas spat. "I had my fill of priests at Karnak! It is all a sham! There are no 'great ones' and the gods are the puppets of men! I saw the god 'speak' - did you know that? My reverend uncle showed me. We all danced a merry dance at his piping! I had been so filled with - with love - for the god, for the kings who had built that great fortress of stone - but he showed me that I was wrong. There was nothing to deserve my love."

"The actions of one evil man do not discredit the gods, Unas," Wenatef said. "Whatever you saw, wrong though it was, was simply that - wrong and false. And whatever those actions, they weren't those of the gods!

"Nothing we can do in this land of shadows that we call the land of the living can touch the Blessed in the Land of the Blest! It is your own self that you are destroying! You've almost succeeded in making a monster of yourself, Unas. You have a chance to stop before it is too late."

Unas rose to his feet and moved slowly toward Wenatef. "The 'great ones' are nothing but a lie," he said. "And the gods are nothing but a fabrication, and I am their enemy as long as I live."

"By all means be the enemy of lies and fabrications," Wenatef said. "But recognize the truth when you're faced with it!"

Unas motioned to the corpse of the king. "Here is Pharaoh Seti," he said. He drove his foot down upon the brittle flesh, which snapped and splintered beneath his heel, "Do you think this is really hurting me? Or this?" He kicked the mummy again and watched it clatter against the floor of the tomb.

"It certainly isn't hurting him," said Wenatef. "And it is making you look like a fool."

Unas' mouth twisted. "There are only those who live and

those who are dead and gone," he said. "I owe them nothing, living or dead."

"But you owe yourself something," Wenatef said. "And the time has come to pay it." He moved forward.

Unas paled and shrank back. "Get away from me!" he cried. "Leave me alone!"

"I'll leave you, if you really want me to," Wenatef said. "But you'll never have peace while this matter is owing."

Unas backed away. "What you or I want doesn't matter at all!" he said. "If you kill me now, it won't make any difference!"

"That is what Nuteruhotep told you because he wanted you to be his tool," said Wenatef. "You know better."

"I tell you he showed me the statues!" Unas cried. "I saw the tricks!"

Wenatef was backing Unas toward the doorway. "But you don't worship statues, Unas," he said. "How could you forget the time you spent with my father? Didn't you listen to him? You worship the God, not statues. The statues merely serve as symbols of the god you worship. The lowest we'eb priest knows that. Even a superstitious peasant knows it. You stepped into evil and folly for no reason at all."

"I care nothing for the gods or the Great Ones!" Unas repeated.

"Then why do you weep?" Wenatef asked.

Unas gave a cry of pure despair. "Leave me alone!" he screamed. "Don't talk to me! I would rather die than hear another lie!"

"I speak the truth," Wenatef said. "And so did my father. You have heard lies and you have heard truth and you must choose which you'll follow."

Unas seemed to writhe like a flame in a high wind for a moment. "It is too late for me!" he said at last. "I am lost - "

Wenatef felt words coming to him in a cool, soothing

flood, filling his mind with light, rising effortlessly to his lips.

"Listen to me, Unas," he said. "You let yourself become apostate because of the lies of a man who sought your help in robbing tombs. You had no reason to believe such a one, and yet you did, and you did evil knowing it to be evil and rejoicing in the power it gave you. You have seen that you are mistaken. You have the chance to turn back. You can begin again as though nothing had ever gone wrong."

He saw Unas' mouth form words of incredulous denial.

"I tell you it is all true," said Wenatef with the certainty of a prophet. "If you'll only let yourself be turned, you *will* be turned and all will be well once more. I was sent here to offer you that chance. Will you take it?"

Unas stared at Wenatef for the space of time it took to draw a deep, sobbing breath. His hand stretched out almost of its own accord, quivering, eager. Suddenly he wrenched his hand back, turned and bolted from the circle of red light into the darkness beyond.

CHAPTER XLV

Wenatef listened to the uneven footsteps as they blundered up along the stairways and then faded into silence along the upper corridor. "You cannot run away from truth," he shouted after Unas. "Or from mercy! The only way to escape them is to reject them!"

There was no response. He had expected none.

He went to the body of the king, lifted it easily, and set it back into the smallest of the nested coffins. He tossed the hammer and chisel into the pit at the far end of the tomb, and then sat down on the floor and gazed unseeingly ahead of him.

What had he accomplished by facing Unas? He could not say. All he could understand was that he had gone to the man and said what was necessary. The rest lay with the gods. Wenatef rose with a sigh, took the torch from the carnelian bowl, swept one last glance around the chamber, and left.

He passed between the rows of carved and painted gods, and the light of his torch seemed to flash from gold and glint from wide eyes turned toward him. King Seti, flanked by Set and Horus, inclined his head as Wenatef passed. The Prince Ramesses, reading praises of the king from a scroll in his hand, bowed. The goddess Nephthys, her hand upon Seti's shoulder, stretched her other hand toward Wenatef. Falcon-headed Re-Harakhte raised his hand and turned to gaze after him. The blind harpist in the large anteroom stilled the quivering strings of his harp and smiled as Wenatef leapt over the pit beside him and moved out into the night.

The moon was waning now, barely half full, but it shed enough light to make the torch unnecessary. Wenatef tossed it aside and lifted his head in the evening wind. The night air was cool and soothing after the hot closeness of the tomb. The moonlight turned the landscape to silver. Wenatef seemed to hear the great river calling from the east.

He followed the footpath past the ruined temple of Deir el Bahari, lying still and silent under the silver touch of the moon. He paused to gaze up along the terraced stairs to the forest of rubble that had once been colonnades flanking the stairway. The broken stones were peaceful in the moonlight.

He passed on eastward, skirting the temple of Seti I at Gurna, until he stood looking down at the Nile. The river seemed to hum in its banks, a smooth, silver-filled roadway that absorbed the light of the stars and radiated it back at the night sky a thousandfold. Cultivated fields lay east of the great temple, their outlines shining under the moon. The inundation had flooded them and now they lay, a mosaic of still water, inviting him to go to them and bathe away his weariness

He picked his way through the marshes to the catch-basins that edged the river. The banks sloped gently down to the water; he knelt at the edge, dipped his hands, and brought them to his face.

The air was cool; the water still held the warmth of the sun. He unfastened the waist strap of his kilt and set the garment aside with the mace of Thutmose III beside it, then slipped into the river. Ripples fanned out from him as he swam noiselessly on his back and gazed up at the stars. He could almost imagine himself in the Land of the West once more, far from greed and fear.

Dark shapes were approaching him in the water: the

crocodiles, led by the huge patriarch who had been his companion once before. Their eyes glowed in the reflected light of the stars as they moved slowly toward him. He smiled at them: they almost seemed like friends now.

He ducked his head backward under the water, slicking his hair back from his forehead, then rose and climbed to the bank. The eastern sky was growing light: soon it would be dawn, but the land still lay under silent darkness. Across the Nile, the great bulk of Karnak, glowing with lamplight, sent a shimmering reflection on the water. Wenatef let his eyes rest on the reflection of the light, and lost himself in the silence and the beauty.

He did not know how many minutes passed before he realized that he was not alone, but suddenly the peace of the night had faded and he could sense the hot, suffocating presence of fear.

"I could kill you now," a voice said behind him. "I have your mace, and I've killed before."

Wenatef stiffened, then made himself relax. "Have you made your choice?" he asked.

The huge patriarch was moving toward him, the ripples to either side of its great head silver in the starlight. Wenatef watched it approach, caught by the sudden glitter in the beast's eyes, the intentness of its movements.

"Aren't you afraid of me?" asked Unas.

"What is there to fear?" Wenatef asked.

Sudden harsh, tearing sobs were the only response.

Seeking almost desperately to hurl himself into the abyss of the God's love... That was what Hapuseneb had told Wenatef all those years ago. And now Wenatef could see that his father had been right. He gazed across at Karnak; the smaller crocodiles were lying motionless in the water before him.

The sobs quieted a little, and Unas spoke after a time. "I

could feel it at times, like strands of cobweb drifting across my face. The madness. And then I was trapped in it, bound by it - I even rejoiced in it for the strength it gave me through others' fear... To turn away from that - to fight free.." He drew a shaking breath and was still.

"You can do it," Wenatef said. "The choice is yours."

The crocodiles were at the river bank now. The patriarch heaved itself up out of the water and lifted its narrow head, streaming with glittering water, toward Wenatef. Its glowing eyes fixed on Wenatef as it raised itself and moved slowly up the bank.

Wenatef turned from him to look at Unas. The man was standing behind him, his face a mask of anguish, his hands clenched around the mace.

"The gods are real, Unas," said Wenatef. "I've seen them: they have touched me. Nothing Nuteruhotep said or did could change them. You can see them, yourself if you will only let yourself turn and look."

With those words he turned - straight into the dripping, tooth-fringed jaws of the huge crocodile. The great beast had come silently up while he was speaking to Unas. Whatever spell of peace had been laid on it while Wenatef was in the tomb had been broken when he returned to the living.

There was no room to flee; Wenatef steeled himself for the slash of those teeth in his flesh.

Unas' hands gripped his shoulder and hurled him aside just as the great jaws crashed shut above him. The next moment he saw a blur of motion and felt the bite of stones and dust against his half-shut eyes as two bodies thudded together and thrashed against the ground.

He scrambled backward to see Unas, locked in a struggle with the crocodile, raise the mace of Thutmose III and bring it crashing down on the monster's skull with the sound of an axe biting into wood. The mace raised and fell again, and the crocodile, now mortally wounded, raked its claws down Unas' body as it tried to turn and flee.

The struggles ceased abruptly.

All this had happened in the space of time it had taken Wenatef to get to his feet and cast about for a weapon. His fingers closed about a stone; he threw it aside and went to his knees beside Unas.

The man was sprawled face-forward on the ground, his breath coming in ragged gasps. His left leg was wet and red. The crocodile was stretched out beside him on the bank like a great, misshapen log. The skull had been crushed.

Wenatef gently turned Unas, and then sat back on his heels, shaking his head. One of the beast's claws had caught him high on the inner thigh, where it met the groin, and severed the artery there.

There was nothing to do; even as Wenatef realized this, Unas' eyes fixed on his, brightened, and then faded.

Wenatef looked over at Unas again, then across at Karnak. Unas had made his choice and was at peace. He would be buried as soon as possible. It only remained to go back to the village.

CHAPTER XLVI

Wenatef found himself in a strange position. The leaders of the Priesthood of Amun showed him almost the reverence accorded a god. The Theban and Necropolis Guards both treated him as a great hero, and although Herihor had not spoken with him since the capture of Nuteruhotep, Prince Sekhemkhet himself had twice summoned him and offered him positions of highest rank as a prince of Thebes.

Wenatef had bowed to Sekhemkhet and courteously refused the honor. How could he explain that he must leave Egypt forever?

He made arrangements for Unas' burial through the Theban embalmer who had directed his parents' entombment. He had learned that Unas had no living kin, aside from Nuteruhotep, and he had been young enough to ignore the need for a tomb. Looking back, Wenatef doubted that that young man would have halted his mad career to construct one at any rate. Not before he turned. There was room for Unas in his parents' tomb. Hapuseneb and Neitneferti would never object to sharing it with one who had saved their son and his own soul at the cost of his life.

No one mentioned Thutiy during this time, and Wenatef did not speak of him, either, after going before the two foremen and solemnly swearing that Thutiy had no part in the present tomb robberies. He offered to put his name on a document attesting to this, and though the offer was declined, Khons and Harmose seemed somehow eased. He saw the old man once or twice in the following week. He seemed frail and exhausted by grief. Apart from directing a smile and a bow to him, Wenatef did not seek him out, nor did Thutiy attempt to speak with Wenatef.

** ** **

Life settled back into the easy routine it had had before Merihor's death and Wenatef's capture, although the villagers themselves seemed a little afraid of him. The children surrounded him as before, though, begging to help with his horses or just to sit in the sun with him and listen to stories of Nubia and Memphis and his meeting with His Majesty two years before, when he had been awarded the Gold of Honor. They would touch the pendant, which had been returned to him by Dhutmose, and smile up at him with awe.

The inundation showed no signs of turning yet, and Wenatef had given his word to remain with the village until then. And so he ordered the guarding of the tomb of His Majesty, directed the patrolling of the entire Necropolis area, and doubled the watch along the heights.

** ** **

Within two weeks of the arrests came the news that the leaders of Nubia, emboldened by the weakening rule of His Majesty, had flared again into open revolt. Messengers raced into Thebes from Elephantine, Buhen and Napata, and the border forts of Semna and Kumneh. The Army of Upper Egypt was called up and readied for action under Herihor's command.

Wenatef made no comment, but he went each morning to the lookout point beside the Nile and scanned the river, seeking a sign that the flood had turned.

** ** **

Herihor sent for him two days after the news of the revolt reached Thebes. "I think matters with the village are settled now," Herihor said, motioning to a serving girl who stepped forward to fill Wenatef's cup with fine wine and then retreat with discreetly lowered eyes. Those demure eyes flashed at beneath her lashes. Wenatef smiled and raised the cup slightly to her.

Herihor nodded in dismissal and the girl left, lingering at the doorway to catch Wenatef's eye and smile slowly, with lowered lashes. The invitation was clear and very tempting. Wenatef returned the smile and watched her leave, the smile widening as he caught Herihor's amused expression.

"You're a hero in Thebes," Herihor said.

Wenatef sipped his wine. "You are very kind," he replied.

Herihor's strong hand motioned deprecatingly. "Not at all," he said. His light eyes fastened for a moment on Wenatef and then narrowed in a smile. "You single-handedly foiled the most sacrilegious plot since the attempted murder of Ramesses III. Alone against many, mighty foes, you kept your head and won. You're a man to honor in this time of unrest, a man to rely on for leadership in the armies and, after, in the governing of cities."

Wenatef set his cup on the table before him and raised his eyes to Herihor's face. He knew what was coming.

Herihor's expression was eager but somehow hesitant, and his voice was almost pleading. "I will lead my armies into Nubia, to crush this revolt for all time. I want you at my right hand. You would be a general commanding a division. The gods favor you and I admire you. I admit it. What do you say? Will you come to Nubia and fight beside me?"

Even as his heart leapt at the thought of battle, Wenatef could hear Nakhtamun's voice. 'None may tarry in the Land of Egypt, nor may you, my son, when your task is ended'. There was his answer, and he had to give it truly. He lifted his head and said, "Holiness, Egypt is the home I have fought for time and again. But I must leave. I promised to defend Deir el Medineh until the turn of the flood, but then I must leave this land forever. I can't stay, not even to fight beside you, no matter how much I might want to."

This was far from what Herihor had expected. Vertical lines appeared between his brows, but he smiled and said, "What sort of talk is this? You're leaving Egypt? By whose command? His Majesty's? I'll send a message to him and ask that he release you."

"This comes from someone mightier than His Majesty or yourself," Wenatef said. "Let's not speak of this any further."

"But I want to speak of it!" Herihor cried. "If you're sworn to leave Egypt, then do so by all means! Nubia isn't closed to you! You'll come with me to Nubia! What more is there to say?"

Wenatef's eyes narrowed and rested on Herihor long enough to make the High Priest shift his position. "I can't come, Holiness," he said softly, "I wish that I could! Please: don't press me."

Herihor sighed and lowered his eyes. "Isn't there anything I can say to change your mind?" he asked.

"Nothing," Wenatef answered. "It isn't my choice. There may be life for me in other lands, but not here, where I no longer belong. If I were to stay in Egypt, I would die finally within the year."

Herihor's frown had changed slightly. It faded after a moment and he gazed at Wenatef with sudden understanding. "Where will you go, then?" he asked.

It was Wenatef's turn to look away. "If only I knew," he said.

Herihor was silent for a moment. "The priests here tell me," he said at last, "that a man can have no comfort in this world once he has walked with the gods. I have heard such a fate called blessed, but it seems a dreadful blessing and a lonely fate." His deep, harsh voice became almost gentle. "But I can give you this comfort," he said. "You're a soldier,

261

as I am.   You're used to giving commands to your subordinates and obeying the commands of your masters. A good commander never leaves his men without guidance. Be patient."

CHAPTER XLVII

Wenatef returned to Deir el Medineh late that afternoon. He went slowly, almost dreamily, for the restlessness within him had quieted. He now knew where his path lay, and there was no need to peer uneasily into the future and wonder.

He had met a trader on his way back from Karnak, a man who sold big, beautiful horses that came, he said, from high hills covered with trees that would dwarf even the cedars of Byblos. He had told Wenatef about those hills and the strange, cold white dust that covered them in winter, drifting like feathers from the white skies above them.

He had spoken of swords and arrows forged from the hard metal that he called iron, weapons and implements of the metal that were more plentiful than the rocks in the hillsides. He had told of folk who rode on the backs of horses such as he was selling. He had told of his people, pale-haired, pale-eyed folk as tall and straight as himself, the women with hair that fell like golden silk to their hips, the men bearded and powerful. It was a new land, the man had said, settled within the memory of the ancients, and life was harsh and clean and vigorous, not like the luxury and laziness found in the land of Egypt.

The trader had seen the sudden bright interest in Wenatef's eyes, and had understood some of his weariness and longing. He had smiled at Wenatef and said, "Come with me. See my land. They would welcome you there."

"When do you leave?" Wenatef had asked.

263

The man had squinted into the sun and counted on his fingers. "I stay here perhaps the space of a moon," he had said at last. "From Thebes I go to Per-Ramesse to pay my respects to Pharaoh and bring a gift of horses. I would have gone to him first, but I wanted to put his horses into the best possible condition before I present them, since they're a gift from the king of Babylon. There are others there who want my horses. Two weeks in Per-Ramesse with His Majesty's Master of Horses, then some other commissions... And then the prince Smendes of Tanis requires several of my horses - the white one there is for him - so I'll be in Tanis for a time as well before I sail for home. Two moons total? Maybe three? Will you come? I can wait for you."

"I will," Wenatef had said. "I would like to see those hills and that powder. I have matters to settle here, but they'll be finished within the week... Yes, trader, I'll go with you. What is your name?"

"Thraximander," the man had answered, holding out his hand.

Wenatef clasped it, then nodded, mounted his chariot, and turned his horses back toward the river and Deir el Medineh.

**   **   **

He went slowly down the main street and scanned the many houses that were suddenly empty. Almost a third of the villagers had gone to live in Thebes. They would remain in the city and be summoned each week to their work in His Majesty's tomb. The rest of the villagers would move to the precincts of Medinet Habu. They were awaiting the construction of mud-brick houses, which were being erected under the watchful eye of Butehamun, Dhutmose's son.

Those villagers were waiting for Wenatef, and he heard shouted congratulations on his being chosen by Herihor.

Dhutmose and Duwah were waiting for him by his house.

"You have received a flattering offer," Dhutmose said

with an attempt at a smile. "I congratulate you."

"And so has he received one," Duwah said.

"Is that so?" asked Wenatef.

"Herihor himself has assigned him to a division of the army as Chief Scribe," said Duwah. "Our warrior scribe will be a warrior indeed!"

Wenatef saw that Dhutmose looked thoughtful. "Isn't it good news, then?" he asked gently.

Dhutmose lowered his head. "I am told it is an honor," he said. "And if that is so, then I..." He could not finish the sentence. Suddenly he seemed old and almost frail. "I had thought to live out my days here among my family," he said. "I...don't think I will return."

"Nonsense!" Duwah said bracingly. "You'll have another scar and get another wife - "

Wenatef silenced him with a look.

Dhutmose tried to smile again, but his eyes were bleak when he looked up at Wenatef. "I must go and tell Baketamun," he said.

He left.

Wenatef watched him walk away. He shook his head after a moment and turned to find Duwah looking him over.

Duwah's eyes were suddenly sharp and frowning, and he followed Wenatef into his house. "You aren't going to go with him," he said. It was a statement, not a question.

Wenatef tried to smile. "You've always been one for guessing my thoughts, Duwah," he said.

"Your thoughts are usually easy to read," Duwah said, locating Wenatef's store of wine and pouring some. "I have never lost the knack. I - I hope I won't lose it, wherever you go... Wenatef, what will you do?"

"What I said I'd do before," Wenatef said. "I'll go to other lands. There is a place I have heard of where they have a thing called snow... Have you heard of it?"

Duwah made an impatient motion with one hand. "Fairy tales," he said, and then he softened. "But if you must see it, you must see it. Wenatef, won't I ever see you again?"

Wenatef smiled and shook his head. "No," he said. "Never again in Egypt"

Duwah made a sound in his throat like a strangled sob. He pushed himself from his chair and hurried to Wenatef, gripping his shoulders hard before pulling him into a rough, almost painful embrace. "Damn it, Weni!" he said. "We were boys together! We were like brothers!"

Wenatef returned the embrace. "Boys grow up," he said. "Brothers set up their own households. But the friendship remains, no matter where they go. You know that. You'll always be my friend, and we won't be separated except by distance...and even that won't be forever."

Duwah released him and looked away. He wiped at his eyes with the back of his hand. "You speak like..." he began, and then stopped. "Wenatef, what did you see during your time in that tomb?"

Wenatef shook his head with a slight smile, and touched Duwah's shoulder for a moment. "Don't fear death, Duwah," he said. "I won't be leaving just yet at any rate. The Nile hasn't turned, and I still have some matters to settle."

Duwah looked up. He showed signs of emotion but his voice was flat as he said, "Thutiy."

"Thutiy," Wenatef agreed.

"Why don't you just turn that old robber over to Herihor and have done with him?" Duwah demanded.

"Because he is old," Wenatef replied. "And because, whatever you may think, Thutiy is not a robber. I must speak with him soon."

Duwah lowered his head. "It is in your hands," he said. "But Wenatef - you won't leave without telling me, will you?"

Wenatef smiled at him; the smile wavered. "How could I

do that?' he asked. "You're all the family that I have left in this life."

** ** **

After Duwah had gone, Wenatef sat down and thought for a long time. There was much to say and little time in which to say it. This last loose end was the most difficult to tie fast and the one closest to his own peace of mind. He finally sighed and brought out a square of new, white papyrus and the writing kit that his father had given him upon his departure for Nubia. He had written many messages with it, and the cakes of pigment were almost used up, but there was enough for one last message.

He spat on the black cake and selected a brush. He chewed its end to make certain that the fibers were well separated, rubbed it against the pigment, and then wrote:

Master Thutiy:

I will soon be departing from the land of Egypt, and I will not return in this life. I wish to speak with you before I leave, and I hope that I will be able to visit you tomorrow at dusk, as I have done before

Wenatef, Guardian of the Tomb

He stepped outside for a moment, called to a passing boy and arranged for the delivery of the message in return for a sweetmeat. And then he sat down with his back to the wall of his house and looked up at the sky. One more day and all would be settled...

Diana Wilder

CHAPTER XLVIII

Very few of the people of Deir el Medineh knew all the facts of the tomb-robbings, though word of some sort had filtered through the community. They had heard of the corpses found by His Majesty's tomb, and they knew that two of them had been Thutiy's sons, and that involvement with something disgraceful had led to their deaths, but that was the sum of the common knowledge.

Whispers spread: great disturbance in Thebes. The Captains of the Village had been about more than usual. Groups of soldiers from the Necropolis Police and the Karnak Temple Guard had also come through the village, but its memory was long and this sort of commotion had often been the herald of the commissioning of a new tomb, whether of a great noble, like Herihor, perhaps, or a member of the royal family. But then had come the attack of the raiders and the announcement that Deir el Medineh was to be disbanded and its people moved to other places.

The village buzzed with talk and speculation, and much of that speculation centered on Thutiy. His years and the long respect in which they had held him could not protect him once they had decided that he was, in some way, the author of all their misfortunes. He became the target of petty persecution.

Wenatef approached Thutiy's house and paused to frown at a group of children who, like their parents, had caught some hint of the displeasure directed at the old embalmer. They were engaged in writing impolite phrases on the wall

A Killing Among the Dead

of his house with red paint. Their writings were no credit to the scribe who taught them. Wenatef shooed them off.

"What are you doing? Master Thutiy is an old man and deserves better of you! How would you like it if someone did that to your grandfather? Shame on you! Now begone! And don't do any more writing until you can spell better!"

He watched them run off and then looked up toward the terrace. It was hidden from his view by the wall of the house, but he knew that Thutiy was there. He took a deep breath and entered the embalming studio.

It was dark. He could dimly make out the shapes of the large embalming tubs. Four of them. One for Merihor, one for Nebo, one for Ipy. Who was the fourth for? Had there been a death that he did not know about? He frowned down at the tub and then turned his back on it. He was not one to paw through natron in order to gape at the faces of the dead. He ascended the steps to the terrace.

Thutiy was there. His small galaxy of oil lamps were clustered about him, waiting to be lit at dusk. He was motionless, gazing out toward the hillside. Two open jugs of wine sat beside him, and there was an empty chair, too. He turned his head once and looked at Wenatef. He seemed to smile, though the smile was quickly gone and may have been a trick of the shifting light of sunset.

"Come, sit down," Thutiy said. "I have been expecting you. Wine?"

"Please," Wenatef said, and watched him pour a cup from one of the jugs and hand it to him. Thutiy filled another cup for himself from the other jug, which bore an inscription in red ink. He frowned at the two jugs, then looked down at Thutiy, who had raised his own cup to his lips and was sipping noisily from it. He sat after a moment, lifted his cup and drained it.

Thutiy suddenly smiled at him and reached across the

low table to clasp his hand for a moment before sitting back and gazing toward the west. "I was glad to receive your note," he said. "I had thought...that you wouldn't wish to speak to me."

"Why? Because the townsfolk are like grains of sand before a wind? They're fools! I meant to speak with you sooner. I'm sorry I kept you waiting so long...Nakht."

Thutiy did not react to the name. He reached for the uninscribed jug and poured more wine into Wenatef's cup, and then looked up at him. "I knew you would find out the truth," he said. "Did you expect me to deny it? 'Nakht' is the name my grandfather used when he entered the first tomb and took small goods to buy food for the villagers."

"I noticed the earlier robberies," Wenatef said. "And I noticed, as well, the accuracy of the later robberies. Give me the map, Thutiy."

Thutiy smiled across at him and said, "And is it the Guardian of the Tomb who speaks, or Wenatef, my friend, who could have been my son?"

"It is the Guardian who speaks for the moment," Wenatef answered.

Thutiy shrugged and reached down beside his chair. After a moment he handed Wenatef a large roll of papyrus.

Wenatef unrolled it and scanned the contents. It was, as he had suspected, a very detailed and precise map of the Valley with the dimensions of the tombs given and their orientation to various landmarks carefully noted. Additions had been made to it, the newer ink showing darker against the yellowed papyrus. He rolled the map up again and set it on the brazier, watching silently as it writhed and twisted in the flames until it was nothing but a pile of glowing ashes and a lingering, sweet scent. He looked up at Thutiy through the smoke.

The old man had refilled his cup from the inscribed jar, then set the jar down and sat back. The sky was still pale toward the western horizon, but the first tentative stars could be seen near the zenith of the sky. He touched a dry stick to the small brazier beside him and carefully lit each oil lamp, then blew out the little flame and sat back again. His expression was wry.

"The map was among the effects of a priest of Osiris who died in the summer heat of Thebes," he said, "My family embalmed him. This was at the end of King Merneptah's reign, at the start of the unrest and the terrible years. My grandfather found the map and he would have returned it, but the civil wars came too quickly and Thebes was in turmoil. Those were terrible times, and the foreman, Neferhotep, was murdered in the streets of the town. There was famine and fighting within the village and many people robbed the lesser tombs in order to obtain treasures that they could trade for food. My family did the same, and they used the treasures they found to help feed the townsfolk. Once the map had been used, once the tombs robbed, there was no turning back - "

"They could have burned the map," Wenatef pointed out.

"Could they?" Thutiy asked. "I wonder what you would do if little Aahmose were starving and your only alternatives were to rob tombs or to let her starve. Do you have an answer?"

"There is always an alternative to doing evil," Wenatef said. His voice gentled. "But you once said that there are reasons and reasons for doing a thing, and while something may be wrong in itself, the reason for doing it is as important as the deed. I disagreed at the time, but I have changed my mind. The right reason for doing an evil thing can make the evil as nothing. I don't dispute it. But how did Ipy and Nebo become involved in these robberies?"

"Greed," Thutiy answered. "Nebo was an acolyte at Karnak with Unas. And to think my family had viewed that

271

as >rising' in the world! He shared Unas' disillusionment, though he didn't go mad. When Nuteruhotep contacted Khaemwase about robbing the tombs, he used Unas as a go-between. Unas spoke to Nebo, who spoke to Ipy. Unas was an evil man, and I wanted no part of any plot of his making. They found the map - my fault for not burning it before they did - and after they realized that I wouldn't help them, they did their own digging."

Wenatef nodded. "Just as I thought," he said.

Thutiy drained his cup and poured more wine. His eyes were very bright, but he spoke quietly. "You were magnificent," he said. "Magnificent and terrible as the Great Ones themselves... Unas, Khaemwase, Nuteruhotep - they stood no chance against one such as you, fearless and honest, armed with the might of the West..." He smiled and closed his eyes and leaned his head back against the wall behind him. "It did my heart good," he said.

Wenatef frowned at him and then reached for the inscribed jug.

Thutiy opened his eyes and said, "No. The other one is yours." He sat up, smiling a little at Wenatef's suddenly understanding expression, and said, "So... Why didn't you turn me in to Herihor once you had captured the others? Surely one as honest and unbending as yourself wouldn't have balked - " He broke off and considered. "No," he amended. "You would have balked. It would have hurt you, I think - but you didn't do it. Why not?"

Wenatef eyed the inscribed jug and then frowned at Thutiy's slightly dreamy expression. "I didn't turn you in," he said quietly, but with growing intensity, "because I knew, Thutiy, that you have never in your life robbed any tomb. You, too, were the Guardian of the Tombs, you, too, were fighting the evil, as I was, old and alone though you were. It must have been terrible, with your son and grandson and all Khaemwase's horde against you."

A Killing Among the Dead

He set his wine aside and knelt beside Thutiy's chair, taking the old man's dry, hot hand between his and gripping it. "I did not turn you in because I knew that it was you who stood between me and my captors when I lay unconscious in that stable, you who put layers of cloth about my wrists to spare me pain, you who left light and water and a knife of iron in that tomb. How could you think I didn't know? I loved you, Thutiy. I love you still. You might have been my father. You don't need to die. Tell me the poison you used. I'm sure there's an antidote."

Thutiy laid his fingertip across Wenatef's lips and silenced him. "Hush," he said. "It's too late, and I have no wish to be moved to Medinet Habu, to live my life out amid a huddle of mud huts... Smile for me Wenatef," he said. "I'm not worth the tears of a hero."

He closed his eyes again. "It was a splendid fight... Do you know - " his voice was becoming a little slow and thick. "I had a son like you. Did you know? He died young. You are so like him, so uncompromising in matters of good and evil... When I learned that the others wanted to kill you, I forbade it. They feared me. I had convinced them that you knew nothing of this plot, and when you staggered up to the door of my house that night, your wrists bloody, half-dead of exhaustion, I saw everything falling apart. I hid you, commanded Nebo and Ipy to say nothing, and then tried to convince you to leave Egypt, though I didn't think that I could. When you refused to go, I had one hope left to me, and that was to allow you to be captured and then come to you in secret and try to talk some sense into you. I couldn't have you remain, for it would have meant death for Nebo and Ipy, who were wavering. But I was too late. You had escaped."

"You didn't think, then, that I had been killed by Unas or by the lions?"

"Do you think I'm a fool?" Thutiy demanded. "I have been among these tombs for generations. I saw the blood, but I also found your tunnel, and I saw, as well, how far you had dug, and how fast. I knew the strength that you had behind you. What could I do after that but warn Nebo and Ipy to keep out of it? They wouldn't listen. I had to watch them go on to their ends..."

He opened his eyes and smiled one last time at Wenatef. "No, leave be," he said, laying his hand on Wenatef's shoulder. It lifted to his hair after a moment. "I can live no longer. The old guard always retires when the new guard takes his post. I would be an embarrassment, and I am too old now to change. And I am tired... The gods will forgive me this one lapse. Go now, Wenatef, and don't weep for me." His eyes closed and he laid his head back and sighed. "Don't weep for me..." he murmured again, the sound trailing off into silence.

But Wenatef disobeyed him. He gathered Thutiy in his arms and held him until he had stopped breathing and his heart was still. And then he sat a while longer within the constellation of Thutiy's little lamps, gazing up at the stars that mirrored them.

CHAPTER XLIX

Wenatef returned to Nakhtamun's tomb for the last time that night, creeping in through the tunnel and into the bleak burial chamber. Everything had been moved and the tomb swept clear of debris, though he could see here and there the glint of gold flakes chipped from the stripped furnishings. The seated statue was still in place, and the sarcophagus lay in the far corner of the room, empty of its coffins and the body of Nakhtamun. The pieces of its lid were still undisturbed on the ground beyond it. The beautifully painted bas-reliefs on the wall seemed strangely bright against the emptiness of the tomb, and the bloodstain large and dark in the middle of the room.

The strangeness almost frightened Wenatef, but it was worse in the village. He could not return just then, not with Thutiy newly dead, not with the death lying so heavy and painful on his heart.

Not worth the tears of a hero. Wenatef could hear Thutiy saying the words again. A hero. He had done what was necessary, what was right, as had Thutiy. Who was the hero, then?

He raised his hands to his face and wiped at his tears with shaking fingers. He was exhausted and heartsore, longing for sleep. He lay down with his head on the feet of the statue and, for the first time since his childhood, cried himself to sleep.

He slept very lightly, awaking several times during the

275

night to rear upright and gaze around the tomb, which was dimly lit by two tiny lamps, before settling back down and closing his eyes again. It was the strain of the past weeks, he knew, combined with the sudden grief of Thutiy's death. It would pass in time. But that knowledge did not make the strain and the grief any easier to bear.

He saw Nakhtamun once more during a wakeful episode.

He had just settled his head against the statue's feet and taken one last quick glance around, when he saw that the light from the two lamps now appeared insignificant, as though there were a greater source of light beyond them. The outlines of the burial chamber, too, were altering.

Wenatef had once watched a Master Outline Scribe correcting the sketch of an apprentice, drawn on the wall of a tomb. The apprentice's sketch had been done in red ink, and the master's corrections had been drawn over it in black. But instead of making the apprentice's tentative lines more firm, the master, conceiving an even grander plan, and had disregarded them completely. The pale red lines had outlined a smaller conception while the bold black strokes expressed something larger.

So it was with the burial chamber. Its lines were now indistinct, and Wenatef could see a great palace beyond them, blazing with sunlight and thronging with bright, joyous people. Warriors carried bows and swords, scribes bore their palettes and rolls of papyrus, and he saw peasants there, too, browned and sturdy with work-worn hands, laughing and making merry with the rest. There were people of the Tjehenu, people from Byblos and Kush, and far lands that bred tall, pale-haired people. There was no difference in status between the lords and the peasants. All walks of life now walked together without shame or pride.

One of the nobles turned toward Wenatef and approached him, smiling. Nakhtamun.

Wenatef tried to sit up, but he found that he could not

move. Nakhtamun paused at the wall of the burial chamber and turned to make a comment over his shoulder at the throng. Wenatef could not hear what was said, but Nakhtamun's smile had deepened when he turned again and stepped within the chamber, passing through the limestone wall and the brightly painted carvings as though they had been hangings of gauze.

He was dressed as a courtier in a long, pleated, belted tunic. For the first time since Wenatef had dreamed of him, he wore the cobra diadem of a king. Gold bracelets circled his arms and wrists and he wore two cylindrical gold necklaces, military decorations of the highest order. The sunlight of the West flashed from the gold to shower sparks through the chamber.

Nakhtamun went to Wenatef and knelt beside him, and it seemed to Wenatef that he was reading his expression, understanding the grief that had gripped him all that night.

He finally spoke. *Answer some questions for me, Wenatef, my son, ponder the answers in your heart and take comfort from them. First: which is more precious, wealth or the health and safety of a human soul? Second: which is more important, the act or the reason behind that act? And third: if you're a wise father and you know that your children have learned of the presence of a trove of sweetmeats or treats that they greatly desire, and you know, further, that the knowledge of this trove of sweetmeats has progressed from the stealing of a sweet or two to all kinds of wickedness, what do you do?*

Wenatef gazed up into Nakhtamun's face. Finally he replied, "A human soul is the most precious thing on this earth, King."

Continue, said Nakhtamun.

"As for the second question, the reason is more important than the act, so that..." He had to pause and draw breath, but the answer was choking him with gladness, " - so that a thief, if he steals for a good reason, is not as much to blame as one who steals from greed and lust."

Nakhtamun inclined his head. Light seemed to scatter throughout the tomb from the motion.

"And finally," Wenatef said, "I would punish the children and remove the sweetmeats."

You have answered well, said Nakhtamun. *And now one last question: If you, as the father, are far from the children but you have learned of their wickedness and wish to stop it, to whom do you entrust the mission? A slave? Or a valued friend?*

"I…" Wenatef fell silent.

Nakhtamun touched Wenatef's shoulder, and once again the touch seemed more solid and more real than anything in Wenatef's world. *You have done all that was necessary,* he said. *You dealt justice and brought mercy. You halted the wickedness for now and saved the one who needed to be saved. You did all this at a hard cost to yourself, and it was all well done. You have truly earned the Gold of Honor, good and trusted friend. And you shall have it, my Wenatef.*

He touched the necklace at his own throat and suddenly smiled. *You shall have it to carry with you into the lands of snow and horses where life is new and strong and free of decay and hidden evil.*

Nakhtamun raised his hands to his throat and unknotted the cord of the necklace. He held it up for Wenatef to see and then bent and placed it in Wenatef's hand, and closed his fingers about the warm, heavy gold. *It is yours, he said. I give it to you with my blessing.*

He rose and went to the edge of the burial chamber, and it seemed that one foot was in the palace and one still in the chamber.

Never doubt it, he said. *And don't doubt us as your time upon this earth passes, for we are here and you will be with us one day. The span of mortal life, even the longest, is very brief. 'Fair will the welcome that awaits him who has reached the Lands of the West...'*

He turned back to the tomb one last time and went to the sarcophagus, to lift the massive pieces of the lid and set them in place once more. And then the palace seemed to fade from Wenatef's vision and all that remained for the fraction of a second was Nakhtamun's face, and then that, too, vanished.

CHAPTER L

Wenatef sat up, his hand to his forehead. The dream was fading even as he tried to remember. This time he knew it would be the last. He felt a touch of sadness, but it was a gentle melancholy and even somehow comforting.

His hand was cramped. He must have rolled over on it at some point during the night. He looked down at it and drew a shaking breath. A necklace of honor was clenched in his hand, a necklace that was the mate to Nakhtamun's. It had not been a dream. He straightened his stiff fingers and then placed the necklace in the pouch at his belt.

He turned his eyes to the crack in the wall. Blue sky shone through it; he had slept very late. He got to his feet and brushed the dust from his kilt, and then turned slowly to take one last look at the statue and the sarcophagus. What he saw made the breath halt in his throat and his heart leap like a gazelle.

Neatly reassembled like the pieces of a child's puzzle, the sarcophagus lid lay atop its base.

** ** **

He went to the sarcophagus and touched the pieces of the lid. "I believe," he said. "I do believe..."

He smiled at the statue one last time and then brought his fist to his heart in salute and left that room. He crawled through his tunnel and into the sunlight and wind of a magnificent day. Clouds raced overhead, and he tossed his head in the wind and laughed again with the sudden sensation of complete freedom.

He had won. He had won! They had won, and all was well!

He sighed, still smiling, and turned to cover the hole of the tunnel entrance with stones. With luck no one would discover it until Egypt was no more and the writings of the sages could no longer be understood. The rocks seemed almost light, as though he had retained some of the strength of the West. Before much time had passed, the entryway was completely blocked by large rocks and scree, and Wenatef was dusting his hands on his kilt and casting one last glance at the hillside. He froze as the notes of a trumpet sounded and echoed through the hills, fading along the ridges and returning, deeper and brighter, full of rejoicing and thanksgiving. Louder and louder they came until Wenatef seemed to be drowning in a sea of clear, wine-sweet notes, caught in the joy.

Wenatef laughed again, his voice joining the trumpet call, the signal sent forth from the great temples of Karnak and Luxor, passed on from Aswan down the Nile from village to village and temple to temple, heralding the change of the season and the fulfillment of Wenatef's promise to the village. The Nile had turned.

LIST OF CHARACTERS

Aahmose ....Child at Deir el Medineh

Akh .... 'Bright spirit'

Akhu ....Plural of Akh: 'The Blessed'

Amenhotep I ....Pharaoh of Egypt; patron of Deir el Medineh and the necropolis

Amenhotep............High Priest of Amun, defeated by Herihor

Amun ....One of the chief gods of Egypt, special patron of Thebes

Anpu ....Worker at the tomb of Ramesses XI

Anubis...................One of the chief gods of Egypt, patron of burials

Baketamun ....Dhutmose's daughter

Deir el Medineh ....City of artisans near the Theban necropolis

Duammerset..........Daughter of the Foreman Khons of Deir el Medinet

Duwah...................Architect constructing the tomb

Eater of Shades .....Egyptian deity who disposes of those judged to be unjust

Dhutmose..............Chief Scribe of Deir el Medineh

Great Ones ....Another term for the Akhu

Hapuseneb ....Wenatef's father; high-ranking priest at Karnak

Harmose................Co-Foreman of Deir el Medineh

Hemshire...............Dhutmose's second wife

Herihor..................High Priest of Amun at Karnak

Horus ....A chief god of Egypt

A Killing Among the Dead

Ipuky .... Tomb robber

Ipy .... Thutiy's son, Nebo's father

Ka .... The soul

Karnak .... The great temple of Amun in Thebes

Khaemwase .... A criminal from northern Egypt

Kheft .... Evil spirit

Khons .... Co-foreman of Deir el Medineh

Khentiy .... Guardsman in the Necropolis Police

Medinet Habu .... Fortress-temple of Ramesses III

Mekiwetef .... Tomb Guardsman under Wenatef's command

Mentemhet .... Priest at Karnak

Merihor .... Guardsman under Wenatef's command

Montu .... Egyptian god of war

Nakht .... Nickname for a local hero of Deir el Medineh

Nakhtamun .... Son of Seti I, co-regent with his father, buried in the Valley of the Kings

Nakhtmin .... Sculptor in Thebes

Nebo .... Ipy's son; Thutiy's grandson

Neitneferti .... Wenatef's mother

Nuteruhotep .... Steward of the Temple of Amun

Paynedjem .... Wenatef's charioteer

Pennut .... Guardsman of the Tomb under Wenatef

Petamenophis .... Priest at Karnak

Ramesses XI .... Pharaoh of Egypt

Ramses .... Seti's son, second in command of Wenatef's guard

Roy .... Platoon Commander of Necropolis Police

Sakhmet .... Egyptian goddess of war and vengeance

Sekhemkhet .... Vizier and Prince

Semna .... Fortress in Nubia

Seneb ....Officer in the Necropolis Police
Sennedjem ....Guardsman of the Tomb under Wenatef's command
Seti ....Former captain of the guard for Deir el Medineh. Father of Ramses
Seti I.....................Pharaoh of Egypt, buried in the Valley of the Kings
Si-Iset...................Captain of the Necropolis Police
Smendes................See Nesubanebdedet
Sobek ....A major god of Egypt, generally depicted as a crocodile
Swift.....................Wenatef's horse
Taharka ....Captain of the Karnak Temple Guard
Tamit....................Merihor's wife
Thoth....................One of the chief gods of Egypt, patron of scribes
Thraximander........Thracian dealer in horses
Thutiy...................Embalmer in Deir el Medineh
Thutmose III ....Pharaoh of Egypt, buried in the Valley of the Kings
Thutnefer ....Priest and Chief Scribe of Amun at Karnak
Tjah......................Guardsman in the Necropolis Police
Tjehenu ....Libyan tribe
Tjekker.................Tribe of enemies of Egypt
Unas.....................Nephew of Nuteruhotep; guardsman in the Necropolis Police
Wenatef................General of Ramesses XI's personal guard; assigned to guard Pharaoh's tomb under construction

AFTERWORD

Researching and writing *A Killing Among the Dead* has been a joy from beginning to end. Because this is historical fiction, however, I think it is necessary to point out those parts of the story in which I strayed from the strictly factual into the conjectural and even the imaginary. These are many, but anyone who has done even a very little research on the end of the XXth dynasty of Egypt will understand the rather sketchy nature of the available information and will be tolerant of any inaccuracies. I have not tried to set forth any new theories on controversial material, and any genuine Egyptologist reading this story will see at a glance that it is the work of a layman and an amateur.

The scandal of the royal tomb-robberies spanned several reigns, beginning with that of Ramesses IX. For the sake of the plot I condensed events covering several decades into a period of about two years. I set the action of this story in the middle of the reign of Ramesses XI for reasons of my own. In fact, while the relocation of the village of Deir el Medineh did take place around the time frame of this story, the actual moving of the bodies and treasure of the kings probably did not take place until after the death of Herihor, the first priest-king of the XXIst dynasty.

Nakhtamun is my own invention. Some students of the period believe that Ramesses II had an elder brother who died during the lifetime of their father, Seti I. This is not improbable: Seti was a fighting king and an eldest son might have fallen while helping to reconquer lost territory in Palestine. Ramesses himself appears to have lost one or more crown princes in this fashion, including Amunhorkhepechef, one of the main characters of my book, *Pharaoh's Son*. I have chosen to use this speculation in *A Killing Among the Dead*, but I cannot emphasize too strongly that it is purely conjecture.

Wenatef, Duwah, Unas, Thutiy, and Ramses never lived outside this story, and while the names of most of the key villagers from Deir el Medineh (Dhutmose, Khons, Harmose, Butehamun) are historical, their personalities arise solely from my plot. The rest of the characters, except for Ramesses XI and Herihor, are my own inventions.

Most experts agree that Deir el Medineh's involvement with the tomb-robberies was surprisingly limited, comprising only a handful of individuals, with the greatest part of the corruption being on the part of the Necropolis Police and the great mortuary temples at Gurna.

I have tried to show some disillusionment with the gods because the time in question was one of hardship and waning royal influence, and the discovery that a line of god-kings had feet of clay would inevitably be reflected in the common view of the gods. The god Amun was the object of genuine personal piety among private persons, as several surviving stelae attest, but he was also the focus of a great state religion that was the most powerful force in the land at that time. There were other, lesser, gods and goddesses, revered to a greater or lesser degree depending on the individual worshiper.

The Land of the West, as depicted in A Killing Among the Dead, reflects my own thoughts, and not necessarily my understanding of the orthodox Egyptian view of the afterlife. Those who wish to learn more about Egyptian religious practices (or, rather, our interpretation of them) should consult other books on the subject.

I have tried to be accurate about distance and geographical features. Those who have actually visited Egypt will be able to see if I have gone wrong in my interpretation of maps and photographs. My description of the tunnels of the thieves leading through rock and into the tombs is generally inaccurate. Thieves did not have that sort of time and patience. Most illicit entries appear to have been made through the doorways which had already been hacked through the limestone of the Theban hills.

I have followed my own inclinations with place and personal names. Ramses the archer and Ramesses the king have the same name. I have altered the spelling to avoid confusion. When referring to reigning kings I have used their throne names (Men-Kheper-Re) and their personal names (Thutmose and Seti) almost interchangeably. I suspect that the average Egyptian would have used the throne name, but we are accustomed to using the personal names.

I have used historical place names where possible (Thebes instead of Luxor) and modern names where practical (Deir el Medineh and Abd el Kurnah). I have stayed away from the purely Egyptian names such as Mennefer for Memphis or Waset for Thebes, since the average reader, myself included, would find them difficult to keep sorted.

The spelling of Egyptian names is a subject of considerable debate. Is it Nofretete or Nefertiti? Senusert, Usertsen, or Senwosret? Is it Ramessu or Ramses or Ramesses? Sethos, Sety, Sutekhi, Sethi, or Seti? I spelled the names the way I liked them, and I apologize if anyone is troubled or annoyed by those spellings. Those problems aside, I hope *A Killing Among the Dead* is as enjoyable to read as it was to write.

ABOUT THE AUTHOR

Diana Wilder grew up in a military family that traveled throughout the United States and spent generations in the orient. The constant travel honed her love for people-watching and gave her plenty of material for stories, whether set in the present or in the distant past. She has published three novels set in ancient Egypt and one set in the American civil war. Currently, she is working on a fourth novel in her Egyptian cycle and another civil war story. In between these, she is polishing a novel in two parts set in France of the 1830's and two non-magical fantasy novels.

When she is not writing, Diana is showing cats, working in graphic design and trying to knit.

2088408R00157

Printed in Great Britain
by Amazon.co.uk, Ltd.,
Marston Gate.